A Monkee On My Shoulder

Jerri Keele

Cover design by Jerri Keele

DEDICATION

This book is dedicated to
The Davy Jones Equine Memorial Foundation
and to David Thomas Jones,
the boy with the stars in his eyes and love in his heart,
who this girl first fell in love with in 1966.

All proceeds from this book benefit
The Davy Jones Equine Memorial Foundation.

ACKNOWLEDGMENTS

I send my sincere thanks and appreciation to the following individuals and groups for their support and guidance:

Brian Keele

Colleen Gruver

Andrea Gilbey

Ginny Fleming

Jody Proetta

The Jones Girls (Talia, Sarah, Jessica and Annabel)

All of my supporters at NaNoWriMo

All of my supporters on Facebook

THE MONKEES® is the federally registered trademark of Rhino Entertainment Company. There is no affiliation, endorsement or connection between Rhino Entertainment Company and this book or its author.

"I'd Do Anything" (from the Broadway play Oliver! written by Lionel Bart) (Chapter 11)
Lyrics by Lionel Bart

"Daydream Believer" (Chapter 14, 25, 28)
Lyrics by John Stewart

"Consider Yourself" (from the Broadway play Oliver! written by Lionel Bart) (Chapter 22)
Lyrics by Lionel Bart

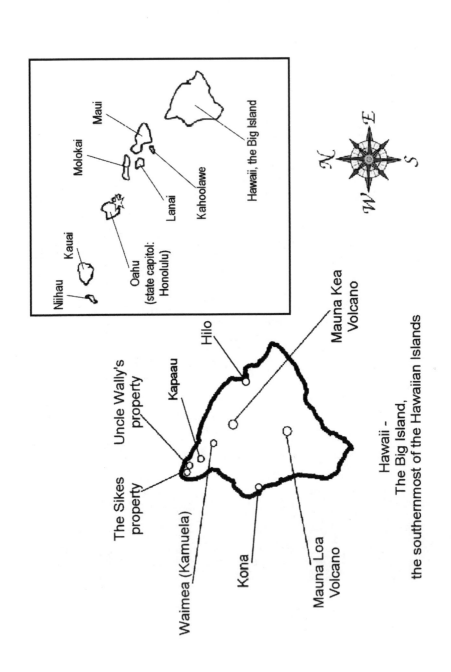

Niihau

Kauai

Oahu
(state capitol:
Honolulu)

Molokai

Lanai

Kahoolawe

Maui

Hawaii, the Big Island

N
E
S
W

The Sikes
property

Uncle Wally's
property

Kapaau

Hilo

Mauna Kea
Volcano

Waimea (Kamuela)

Kona

Mauna Loa
Volcano

Hawaii -
The Big Island,
the southernmost of the Hawaiian Islands

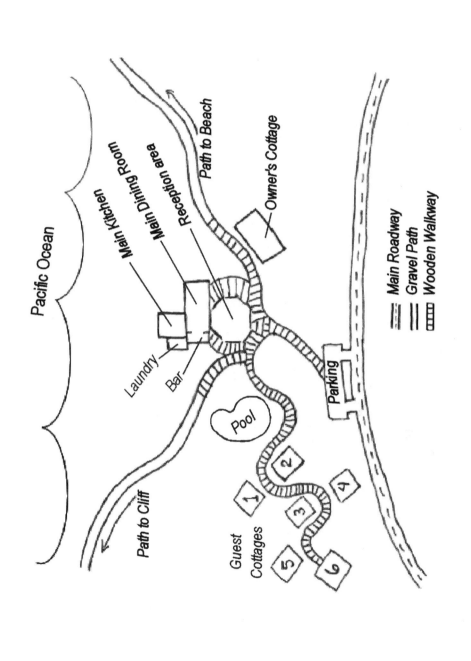

Pacific Ocean

Main Kitchen

Main Dining Room

Reception area

Path to Beach

Owner's Cottage

Laundry

Bar

Pool

Path to Cliff

Parking

Guest Cottages

1 2 3 4 5 6

Main Roadway
Gravel Path
Wooden Walkway

ONE

Leaving Los Angeles

Donuts in an empty field. *Wait, what?*

I woke up at that moment craving donuts. *Not on the diet. Grab a granola bar instead. I mean, it's almost like donuts, right? RIGHT?* No one answered me. Not even The Pest. Where was he anyway?

My bedroom appeared to be empty, so I figured it was safe enough to get up and begin my day. No intrusions, no hovering entities, no prying eyes. Yet part of me did wonder where The Pest was. Had he finally found someone else to annoy, perhaps? Oh, that lucky person! And then I wondered if I would actually miss him.

These conflicting thoughts plagued me as I performed my minimal morning duties on my minimally average looks. Shower, check. Brush teeth, check. Comb through shoulder-length dark blond but very wet hair, check. The slight wave in my hair would spring back as it air-dried. I dusted my face with some Bare Minerals and swiped a bit of plain gel on my eyelashes to accentuate my blue eyes. I considered those my best feature.

Having laid out clothes the night before, I was able to dress quickly in the only items that I had not packed away, my favorite scoop-necked Nike tee-shirt in a lovely powder blue, a thigh-length faded denim skirt that buttoned all the way up the front, and dark blue espadrille wedgies. Small hoop earrings and my mother's sapphire studs filled the holes in my ear lobes and helix, which completed the ensemble designed for comfort during the very long day ahead.

I took a last look in the mirror. These were my final hours in Los Angeles, in California, the state in which I had been born and raised. The Golden State had served me well, for I was a fit and healthy 27 year old. My weight rarely fluctuated from 115 pounds, which was considered average for my 5'5" height. That's me, remarkably… average.

Rolling up the borrowed blanket that I'd slept on, I left it for its owner, the manager of the building in which I'd spent these last years. I wandered through my tiny apartment, now devoid of all furniture and personal belongings, most of which had been donated to the local

1

shelter and thrift store. My wadded up night shirt was in my hand, so I stuffed it into one of the two suitcases stacked by the front door.

The place looked huge in its naked state. Not that I was a hoarder or anything, but I had indeed accumulated my share of "things." It had been such a cathartic moment several days earlier when I said goodbye to the mountain of boxes. All that was left were some simple summery items of clothing, my books, music, and of course Chester. Chester was currently perched on the very top of the open door of the bathroom, disdain in his bright green eyes. His orange stripes clashed with the pale pink paint in the bathroom.

"I know, Bud; you're not happy." I patted my shoulder and he jumped onto it ever so lightly to rub his furry face against my ear. "I promise you'll be even less thrilled in a couple of hours."

His first flight had been a few months ago, just a test run from Los Angeles to San Francisco to see how he tolerated the altitude and confinement in the place he hated most: his pet carrier. Although he wasn't a happy camper during the hour-long flight, he tolerated it well, tucked between my feet under the seat in front of me. The flights today, however, would be a far longer total of about seven hours, with stopovers in San Francisco and Honolulu before our final destination of Hilo. I dreaded it as much as he would, had he known the day's plans. I pulled him off my shoulder and held him to my chest, all 16 pounds of smooth orange fur, and gave him head kisses and slow-blinks.

"Come on, Chester. In you go." I firmly persuaded him into the small, softly padded carrier and zipped the flap. "Think of today as a true adventure, an aero-safari!" He looked far too unimpressed.

Still no sign of The Pest. I nodded my head with a slight smirk. This was good. A knock on the door caused me to peek out the window to see that the shuttle had arrived. I opened the door and smiled.

"Just those two bags. I'll take the cat." I pointed to the small pile of luggage, a sad symbol of what was left of my life, except for Chester – he was the high point.

As the shuttle slowly made its way to Los Angeles International Airport, I held Chester's carrier in my lap and reflected on what my life had been, and more importantly, what it had become.

2

Growing Up and Sideways

My name is Macca. Yes, you read that correctly. Blame my parents for the moniker; they were huge fans of The Beatles. My father was a John Lennon fan, while my mother's heart was with Paul McCartney. At the age of eighteen, Dad had legally changed his name, taking on the weighty Jude Kharma Liberty. My mother and father had told me their story countless times, and I never tired of hearing of their unusual beginnings.

Donning love beads, frayed bell-bottomed jeans, sandals, and a Nehru jacket, Jude had left Anaheim, California, his parents, and his older brother Wally, and taken up with a group of like-minded individuals to the north in Berkeley, California. He grew his light brown hair long, nearly obscuring his bright green eyes with the mop. Living meagerly in a communal compound, he searched for his own truths to believe while imbibing a multitude of mind-expanding substances.

It was there that he met 16-year-old Willow Bodhi, the daughter of a newly arrived family to the commune. It was the autumn of 1966, and while most kids rebelled against their conservative parents, Willow rebelled against her hippie father and mother. She wanted more in her life than communal living. In fact, she'd happily continued to attend public school and maintained a circle of local school friends, not minding the long walk from their compound on the outskirts of the city.

Jude had loved Willow from the moment he'd laid eyes on her dressed in a flowing white gauzy skirt and a tie-dyed tee-shirt. Her long, straight, and very blond hair hung down past her waist from a part in the middle of her head. She used ribbons, flowers, and feathers to tie it off her face at times. Her pale blue eyes were soft, and her lips were full and pink from the strawberry she'd been munching and was still holding in her hand. She blushed, the rose in her cheeks matching the fruit that was staining her hands and lips.   But while Jude was shy, Willow was not. She boldly walked up to him and kissed his lips, then fed him some of the strawberries she'd just picked from the large

3

container they kept protected in the garden. She then skipped back to the garden to continue her gathering chores, for she was one of those on the duty list for cooking that day, but it had already happened – Willow had stolen Jude's heart.

The only problem was that Willow's heart was elsewhere, for she was completely in love with Paul McCartney of The Beatles and Davy Jones of The Monkees. Willow's passion for Davy Jones was fully shared by her best friend Annie Thompson, and the two girls would watch The Monkees TV show together every Monday night at Annie's home. To show her appreciation to Annie's parents, Willow would always bring along a small basket of produce gathered from the communal vegetable garden whenever she made the mile-long trek to the Thompson's home in the heart of town, and afterward she would thank them before beginning her long walk home. After a few weeks, Jude began meeting her partway in order to escort her safely home. He didn't care that all she talked about was Davy this and Davy that, for it was simply musical to hear her voice. She would even sing some of the songs to him. "Daydream Believer" was her favorite.

The pair fell in love but never married, claiming a piece of paper in no way determined the validity of their love. Also, Willow never stopped loving Paul McCartney and Davy Jones, while Jude never stopped admiring John Lennon. Since children hadn't yet come to them, they focused their attention on the music and followed the lives and tours of their musical idols instead.

Middle-aged pregnancies were not common in the 1980s, so when I was born twenty-two years into their love-filled union, I was quite the surprise, and it was obvious what to name me – at least it was to them. It was a choice of Lennon or Macca. Or both. Yes, I am Macca Lennon Daydream Liberty.

I apparently attended a Paul McCartney concert and a Monkees reunion concert before the age of two. Had John Lennon not lost his life well before his time, I'm sure I would have attended his performances as well.

My parents passed away suddenly when I was ten, my mother from an undetected heart irregularity, and my father from what I can only consider to have been extreme grief. His older brother and sister-in-law, Wally and Fran, had taken me in as their own child.

My parents and I had loved each other fiercely, but I remember that as the years passed, the memories of my mother and father began to fade. I often had dreams of one or both of them, but always upon waking couldn't quite pull the threads of the fabric of the dreams together to form a complete memory. In my teenage years, I was depressed and distraught over the loss of these precious bits of my history. Aunt Fran and Uncle Wally were so patient with me, and it was only their love and the sharing of their own memories of my parents that eased the pain. By the age of eighteen, I'd about given up most of my childhood memories. There were brief recollections, similar to that feeling of déjà vu that often flashed in my mind. Amazingly enough, songs from The Beatles and The Monkees that my parents had loved and taught me to sing along with remained solidly on the tip of my tongue.

Aunt Fran passed during my early college years, most likely exhausted from chasing me around in her later years. On my graduation day, Uncle Wally had presented me with the keys to his cherry 1966 Mustang classic in silver blue.

"I've had the most lovely opportunity drop into my lap, little Chickadee." He'd used his personal nickname for me as I gaped at the Mustang fob and accompanying keys lying so innocently in my hands. If only they'd known then, those keys would have jumped out of my palm and run like hell.

"W-w-what do you mean?"

"An old army buddy of mine recently passed away, and he left me his home in Hawaii."

My eyes shot up from the magnificent, unbelievable, and absolutely fantastic keys in my hands and bore into his, the sudden shock chilling me. "What?" I remember thinking I couldn't have heard him right.

"He had no family left," Uncle Wally continued, "so he left me his home and a small business on the Big Island. I won't need the old 'stang any more. It's the bicycle life for me!"

"So, you're leaving?" I felt a combination of panic and loss.

"I fly out this Tuesday. Drive me to the airport, Chickadee?"

I recall hugging him in stunned silence, trying to hold back the tears. My last bit of family would be half an ocean away.

On that Tuesday, I drove Uncle Wally to LAX, waved goodbye tearfully, and headed back home in his baby, his 'stang. He'd maintained that beauty so perfectly all those decades, and I totaled it within the month. Miserable with guilt, I couldn't bring myself to tell him.

I kept myself busy, beginning a new life utilizing the business degree I'd obtained. It was two years after graduating that I realized how incredibly boring "business" can be. I jumped from position to position, job to job, never quite finding my niche. I also jumped from date to date, boyfriend to boyfriend. I mean, how do you top the love story that your parents had set before you? I was perfectly happy to sit at home at night with Chester on my lap, a good book at hand, or banging out a story on my laptop. The books were never classics, but they were fun to read, and the stories I wrote never went anywhere, but I enjoyed creating them.

It had been just six months ago that I'd gotten that dreadful phone call, quite late at night. Uncle Wally had been run off the road while riding his bicycle. They were unable to locate anything more than the bike, a Nike running shoe, and a baseball cap.

Numb and speechless I sat for more than an hour before looking up flight information from LAX to Hawaii, but the phone rang again just a few hours later. His body had been found down an embankment. The coroner would be performing an autopsy, but preliminary findings were that he'd been struck by a vehicle. The driver had fled the scene and was still unaccounted for. I thanked the officer and hung up the phone, my mind enveloped in some internal fog.

Uncle Wally had always been an avid cycler. I attributed his good health to the practice. So, it was with absolute cruel irony that he'd met his death on two wheels.

Selfishly, I asked myself why my loved ones were always leaving me. Sure, everyone is entitled to a moment of pure lapse of empathy, but I knew my parents would have found it nearly inexcusable.

THREE

Enter The Pest

Upon hearing of Uncle Wally's untimely passing, I did what any educated, organized, and motivated person would do: I sat in my pajamas for five days straight. I called my crappy job every day and said I was sick. I didn't shower, I barely ate, and I drank tea. Lots of tea. By that fifth day, I could barely stand the smell of myself. Even Chester had abandoned me and hidden in the other room.

"Oi! What y'doin' there?"

I heard the voice as though he was sitting right next to me. I jumped off the sofa and whirled around, looking for a person to attach to the words that had been spoken, but I was all alone.

"Who's there?" I demanded, picking up Uncle Wally's baseball bat that I kept at the front door.

"Don't worry, luv. It's just me," and the air shimmered a bit, right next to that spot on the sofa where I'd been sitting. I frowned and cocked my head to the side, watching out of one eye as the shimmer began to settle and take on a form – a human form! What the hell?

He was short and rather old, with grey hair, dark brown eyes that twinkled, and gnarled hands. I reached out and hesitantly put my hand out to touch his shoulder, but it went right through. I gasped and jumped back.

"Oh, sorry then, luv – forgot yer new to this scene." He gave a little purposeful shudder and another shimmer, and the image before me changed. The grey hair turned long, a dark and silky brown; the eyes still twinkled, and the years fell away. His skin appeared smooth and unlined, his deep tan offset by shiny white teeth. He was dressed in dark bell-bottomed pants, white dress boots, and a red velvet shirt with eight buttons on a front panel, rather like the cavalry. Seeing the love beads around his neck clicked something in my memory. Ohmygod. I felt my eyebrows arch up almost to my hairline.

"I know you… sort of. But… aren't you… you know… gone?" I didn't know how else to say it, but he had indeed passed away on February 29, 2012 – a Wednesday. I remember it well because I had mourned for him on behalf of my mother.

"Last I looked, yeah, I am. But I keep meself busy." He turned on a rather lop-sided and impish grin.

Davy Jones, in full 1960s Monkees garb, sat on my sofa. Mine. In my living room. Again, mine. I closed my eyes and shook my head. When I opened them again, I expected the hallucination would be gone. He looked exactly like all the magazine clippings my mother had saved and which were safely stashed away in one of the boxes I'd packed. His shiny hair was cut round about his face, and his full and soft looking lips curved in a smile. He was a whopping 5'3" tall and about 115 pounds if he was lucky. And soaking wet. And wearing heavy clothing such as… right now. And he was cute. Handsome. Face it – he was gorgeous. I blinked a few times.

"Still here." He chuckled deep in his throat.

I dropped the bat and slapped my hands over my eyes, shaking my head.

"No, no, no," I moaned. "This can't be. This just seems… wrong. I mean, wrong on so many levels! Firstly, if I'm going to start seeing ghosts, why couldn't it be my parents?"

"O! Yer mum sends her love. She and yer dad are… well… busy, if you know what I mean. They're always busy." He waggled his eyebrows.

I let my hands drop to my sides. This wasn't happening.

"Darlin'," his voice was slightly gravelly as he extended his arm towards me. "Come sit beside me a bit and let me tell you a tale."

The hair on the back of my neck stood to attention as I moved to sit beside him. I reached out again to touch his shoulder and this time I could feel the velvet of his shirt and pulled my hand back sharply.

"BOO!" He yelled and dissolved into fits of laughter. I glared at him and sat back, my arms crossed. "It's quite all right, you know," he continued after he was able to control his giggles. "I won't bite… at least, not very hard." There was that twinkle in his eyes that made me want to feel at ease, but let's face it – this was a ghost! Sitting in my living room!

"So, are you the back-up spirit because my parents are… um… busy?" I knew what that euphemism meant; my parents had been "busy" quite often when they were alive.

He seemed to give it a few moments' thought before nodding. "You could say that."

I admit that I wanted to put my hands over my ears and sing "la-la-la-la-la-la-la-la" at the top of my lungs. I mean... does anyone *ever* want to hear anything remotely sexual about their parents? YUCK!

But on the other hand, what on earth was Davy Jones – formerly of The Monkees, once upon a time winning jockey, theater star, Tony award nominee – doing in MY living room? I mean... really?

"So let me get this straight. I'm suffering yet another crisis, and you show up because Jude and Willow are busy having sex again? Or still?"

"Something like that, yeah. Disappointed?"

"A little, yes."

He clutched his velvet-covered chest, "Oh! I'm hurt; I'm stabbed; you've kilt me... again!" He collapsed across the sofa and I held my breath a moment until he opened one eye and grinned. "Did I scare you?"

I brushed him away. "Please. You cannot kill a ghost. That's what you are, right?"

"Oh, that just sounds so boring. I'm a spectre. A spirit. A phantom." He seemed to take on more energy and sat upright again. "I'm an apparition looking for a purpose. That would look good on my resume, yes? If I needed one, that is." He considered this for another moment before adding, "Funny thing. I never needed a resume."

"Lucky you."

He rested his chin on my shoulder; I could actually feel the pressure, but I could also see the impish glee in his face out of the corner of my eye. I was starting to feel very unlucky myself.

"So, Davy, how does this work? I call upon you..."

"What, now I'm The Great Oz? You saw how that ended for him!"

"Okay then, I call your name and you'll appear and give me advice?"

"Ha ha ha, if only 'twere that simple, my darrrrrlin'. No, I shall be your ever-present companion, buddy, cohort, friend..."

"Have you been studying a thesaurus or something?"

9

"I've had a little time on my hands."

"Wait a minute!" This new reality was just dawning on me. "You'll be with me at ALL times?!"

"Yes! All times! Good times, bad times, boring times – please keep those to a minimum, I beg you – and sleeping times, waking times, eating times… which reminds me… I haven't eaten in years. What've you got?" He bounced up from the sofa and headed to my fridge. Peering inside, he muttered into the appliance, "Cheese – good; bread – good; milk, good; carrots, celery, spinach – all good. But where is the beer?"

"I have wine…" why was I answering him? He was like a pesky little brother, or what I thought a pesky little brother would be like, never having had one of my own.

"That will do, then!" He stood up straight, closing the refrigerator door, a slice of Cheddar cheese in his hand. "Well?"

"Well, what?"

"The wine!" He began opening and closing cupboards, presumably in search of a glass.

"Since when are ghosts able to open and close things?"

"It's a learning thing. Like I said, I've been busy."

Call me crazy, but I actually sighed, retrieved two wine glasses from the cupboard, and poured us both a very generous amount of Cabernet. I needed it. He munched his cheese and sipped his wine. I just drank. I hadn't had any wine since before the dreaded phone call, so I could feel the effects rather quickly as my head began to lighten.

Davy thrust his half-eaten piece of cheese in my face. "You should eat."

"Thank you, but I'll get my own." I pulled crackers from the pantry, more cheese from the refrigerator, and set it all upon the kitchen table. I wearily dropped into a chair while Davy bounded around the room. Where *did* he get all this energy? And could he share some, please? "You really are a pest, aren't you?"

He ignored my question and continued to nose inside all my cupboards, drawers, and cozy hideaway spots. "So, when do you think you'll want to shower again? You're a bit," he turned to me and wrinkled his nose, "ripe."

10

I pulled my cheap fleece robe more tightly around my body and ran a hand through my oily hair. "I hadn't been expecting guests," I muttered, "or I would have put out the Wedgwood."

"Cheeky. I quite like that about you."

I rolled my eyes and marched past him, heading toward my bathroom. I felt his presence behind me and whipped around. "You're not going in there with me."

He looked crushed. "Why not?"

"Because it's private. P-r-i-v-a-t-e Private."

He put his hands up, surrendering, or so it seemed. I locked the bathroom door behind me, just in case it might help. Showering was quick for me anyway, but today I made it even quicker, constantly looking over my shoulder and peeking around the shower curtain. Although my robe was rather rank, I pulled it on just to slip through my bedroom door. Dropping the robe into the laundry basket, I turned to grab fresh clothing.

"Very nice," The Pest grinned.

I gasped and grabbed up my discarded robe. "I *told* you, it's private!"

"You said that about the loo. You said nothing about this room." That impish grin was back, but this time it was irritating. I blamed it on the embarrassment.

"Get out! Get out NOW!"

He showed the universal sign of surrender again, but I couldn't help thinking it was just an act. I saw misery in my future, not to mention a definite cramping of my already suffering love life.

Finally alone, I dressed quickly. I could already see that his presence was going to cause me to break speed records in personal hygiene and wardrobe. I ran a comb through my wet hair and left the safety of my bedroom. Dressed in comfy jeans and a loose sweater, I was prepared to confront him yet again, but when I rounded the corner of the hall, I saw him sitting on the sofa, Chester firmly planted on his lap. Davy stroked the giant orange boy, whose purrs I could hear all the way across the room. I tried to hide a smile, but it was impossible. Davy looked like a little boy, taking great pleasure in the fellow imp of the feline variety sitting blissfully on his lap.

"Traitor." I tried to appear serious when I spat the word at Chester on my way to the kitchen to retrieve my wine. Chester's response was to slowly blink his eyes at me and then squeeze them closed contentedly.

Davy patted the sofa beside him, and I dropped wearily into the seat. "So, let's discuss the elephant in the room," he spoke quietly. "Have you ever wondered where that term came from? It's rather absurd, don't you think?"

I smiled and nodded, picking at the seam of the sofa cushion.

"So," he continued, watching me closely, "your parents passed away when you were young. I can identify with that. And now your Uncle Wally has passed in a tragic accident. That I can't identify with, but... I think it's why I'm really here."

"You mean... you don't actually know why you're here?"

"Not really. I mean, there isn't a manual or anything. We just do what we have to do..."

I nodded again, wishing a great ghostly plague upon my parents for not being here, but sending a total stranger in their places.

"I'm not really a stranger, Macca, and a ghostly version of the plague would be rather pointless, don't ya think?"

I jerked my head up to peer at him. *Now he reads minds?* I held my tongue though. This entire day was bizarre, so what was one more bizarre occurrence, right? I needn't have worried about my silence though, for he went on. He did like to talk.

"So, you're facing another major life change. What are you going to do?"

I looked at him, peered at the cat, and examined the peeling paint on the wall. And then it dawned on me. "Do? Am I supposed to do something? I'm all alone now except for Chester." I reached over and gave the orange guy's cheek a little skritch.

"Well, you have me too."

I snorted – a combination of manic giggle and derision. "I've already heard from Uncle Wally's attorney, and the details will be sent to me next week. For now, I only have to get up each morning, breathe, and exist."

"Although that sounds simple enough, I know it isn't."

12

I peered at him from under my lashes, still guarded. "Thank you."

"You're welcome." He stretched his arms across the back of the sofa. "So, I guess I'll just hang out and see what Uncle Wally's will says."

"No, no, no, you can go. I'll be fine."

"I'm sorry, but I can't do that. I was sent here to help you."

"Help me? I don't need help."

"Someone thinks you do."

"What kind of someone?" I was wondering if this was going to be the answer to The Big Mystery of Life.

"The guy who sits with a checklist and sends us here and there and everywhere. He rather looks like Bob Hope." He grinned, his eyes twinkling, and I could tell he was toying with me.

My shoulders slumped. So much for answers. "Look, I'm a big girl, and frankly, this just isn't going to work. I'm a private person and I need my space."

"But I don't take up much space, see?" he indicated his small stature, and while this was endearing, I was now truly convinced he was a pest – a cute and very dearly departed pest, but a pest nonetheless.

"Look," I shook my head resignedly, rising to my feet, "I'm tired. I don't even know why I got dressed. I need to sleep. How about we discuss this tomorrow?" I was hoping he wouldn't be here then.

"That sounds fair enough."

"By the way..." My eyes narrowed as I formed one last question for him. "Do ghosts sleep?"

He chuckled. "Believe me; there will be plenty of time for sleep."

I shrugged, suddenly too bone-tired to think about his response. "Goodnight then."

"Goodnight, darlin'!"

I locked my bedroom door for some odd emotional reason, then stripped down to a tee-shirt and climbed into my bed. Mine. All mine. I had a dream that night, of running along the beach with my mother. I seemed to be around nine or ten years old. She held my hand and we were laughing. "I must meet him," she kept calling to me excitedly, pulling me along. Just as we came upon a huge crowd I awoke,

13

confused. I was trying to decide if it was a dream, or one of many recollections from my childhood that I had suppressed in the wake of my parents' passing.

FOUR

Was It Just My Imagination?

I woke up feeling fuzzy, like gauze had been draped across the world. No matter how much I rubbed my eyes, the sleep wouldn't go away entirely. Eye crust. Yuck. Glancing at the clock made me jump out of bed with a start. It was 11:11 am and I hadn't fed Chester! How on earth – *what* on earth could have caused me to sleep this late?

I grabbed at the clothes I'd recklessly discarded on the floor the night before and dressed quickly. Reaching for the handle of my bedroom door made me wonder what had possessed me to lock it. It was then that I remembered and froze. Davy Jones. What the hell was going on? Had it been just a dream, albeit a very vivid one? I quietly turned the lock and opened the door a crack, hoping for… what? What exactly was I hoping for? *Stoppit, Mac. You're being silly.*

Chester met me in the hallway and I picked him up for a nuzzle. "I'm so sorry, Mr. Chester," taking him into the bathroom with me and locking that door as well. I quickly performed the perfunctory morning duties, being chided by Chester the entire time. He was impatient for his morning meal. Picking him up and snuggling him close, I wandered toward the kitchen, making a point not to look into the living room as I passed.

Fresh water for Chester and his usual small serving of kitty crackers were in order before I could put on a pot of tea for myself. After my first sip, I felt a brightening in my muddled brain. I left Chester to crunch his crackers and slipped quietly to the door. Peeking around the frame, I peered inside the living room. There, floating just a few inches above the sofa, was the softly transparent horizontal form of The Pest, seemingly fast asleep. I turned back into the hallway quickly and closed my eyes, my head resting back against the wall. Cursing quietly under my breath, I quickly took another peek. Yep, that was him all right. Why wasn't I more freaked out though? Shaking my head, I took a deep breath and straightened as I stepped into the room.

"Good morning," I spoke more confidently than I felt.

He seemed to wake with a start. "Oh! Sorry luv. Must have dozed off."

"You're floating."

He looked at the sofa below him. "Oh, so I am. So sorry about that. Must have misjudged the height of it."

"Huh?"

"It was just a guess as to where the blasted thing really was. Missed it by *that* much." He did a perfect imitation of Maxwell Smart and I had to smile. As he woke further, his transparency became less, and he seemed much more solid again.

"How do you *do* all that?" I waved my hand at his form. I do admit that I was fascinated by this.

"Practice. Practice, practice, practice, until I get it right. I promise to have the sleeping nailed and on cue soon enough."

I felt my brow furrow, and I took another sip of tea. "So, you plan on staying long then?"

He sat up, stretching. "I promised I'd be here until you get it right."

"Get *what* right?" This was making me nervous. I felt one brow arch. The only things I'd done right so far in my life were to graduate college and rescue Chester.

He remained silent while our eyes locked. His drifted away before mine as they dropped to gaze at the cup of tea in my hands. "I'd love a cuppa. Milk and sugar, please."

I hesitated for a moment as I realized he was either avoiding the answer or didn't know it himself. Finally, I rolled off the door frame and hooked my thumb toward the kitchen.

"Oh, I see." He smirked as he floated down to the sofa he'd been hovering above and then rose to his feet and sort of drifted to the other room. "This is a serve yourself joint. I get it now."

I huffed a sigh into my tea while I sipped, careful not to suck it up and choke myself to death. I wasn't quite ready to join Mr. Jones in the afterlife.

"And I appreciate that. I'd hate to fail at helping you."

I'd forgotten that he could hear my thoughts. Crap. Before offering my help, I listened for a beat as he slammed a few more cupboard doors that he hadn't already abused the previous night while looking for glasses. He was definitely a slammer.

"Sugar?" He slammed another door.

I calmly opened the correct cabinet door and handed him the small sugar jar, then quietly closed the door again. Lead by example, right?

"You didn't put any in your own tea," he quizzed me, a frown knitting his brows together – as if they could be any closer.

"No, just milk."

He made a face and stirred half the jar of sugar into his own cup.

I sat at the small kitchen table, and he soon joined me. As he brought the steaming mug to his lips, I wondered and marveled yet again about the science of this, or more accurately, the lack thereof.

"What are we doing today?" he asked me when he'd set his cup down.

"We?"

"The royal we, I suppose. I know what I'm doing. What are *you* doing?" He grinned at me.

"I haven't a clue, actually. I'm a bit lost right now." I felt the tears burning behind my eyes. "I miss Uncle Wally."

His eyes softened and he reached out to pat the back of my hand. I averted my eyes and blinked them dry. It was going to be another long day.

FIVE

Ch-Ch-Changes
(Imagine That, Wrong Group)

Restlessness haunted me as I lay in bed hopelessly awaiting sleep that wouldn't come and hadn't come easily in the two weeks since Uncle Wally's passing. I drifted through each day unable to focus, feeling totally alone and abandoned. Chester and The Pest had become good buddies, but both were very watchful of me. I needed some space though so I spent a lot of time huddled in my bedroom.

At the end of the third week, the package arrived from Mr. Baldwin, Uncle Wally's attorney. Surprisingly, it was quite bulky. I plopped down on the sofa and pulled my legs up, sitting in a sort of half-lotus position. Limber, I am not. The Pest was sitting beside me suddenly. He just appeared. I am not sure from where he came and didn't want to take the time to question him. He leaned over my shoulder and read silently with me.

Uncle Wally, or more properly known as Walter Robert Collins, had set up a trust that left me his entire estate, consisting of a small resort of sorts on the northern coast of Hawaii, the Big Island, including a cottage adjacent to the property. My hands began to shake. Holy crap! This was bigger than I'd thought. He'd never mentioned any details in the few telephone conversations we'd had over the last couple of years.

I flipped through the other pages and saw financials on the inn. He'd been running in the red for the last two years. I heard a low whistle over my shoulder as The Pest caught up with me in reading the documents. He pulled back a little and faced me.

"You're a landowner, luv!"

All I could do was shake my head and shuffle through the stack of documents. And I'd thought I'd felt lost before! What the hell was I going to do with an inn? And... an inn that was in financial trouble? My degree in business administration was all on paper, and I'd had very little practice in actually administering anything throughout the string of unfulfilling jobs I'd held over the past few years.

18

I read the cover letter once again. There was also a small life insurance policy Uncle Wally had taken out, with me as the beneficiary. The death certificate had been issued and a wire transfer was pending. I briefly wondered how the attorney had made that happen so quickly until I saw the last names of both the insurance company representative and the attorney himself. Related. Small island. I had a vision of many relationships colliding in their little world of business.

Mr. Baldwin was suggesting airlines to Honolulu, then onto Hilo, and a particular rental car agency, and giving me instructions about bringing Chester with me. There would be a lot of paperwork, vet visits, and finally, a pet inspection at Honolulu, but we were putting the feline on the fast track for immediate release from quarantine at the Honolulu airport. The timing for vaccinations and documentation had to be precise, but Mr. Baldwin was putting forth all efforts so that we would not be separated. Poor Chester.

The Pest had been reading over my shoulder, but I felt him suddenly perk up. "Oh! Road trip!" His glee was childlike and, again, endearing. "We used to travel the country in a bus, performing on tour. It'll be fun! But promise me – no bus?"

I rubbed my forehead and pondered my next move. Sighing deeply, I leaned back and caught Davy's gaze. "Ever been to Hawaii?"

"Yes!" He nearly bounced in excitement and it was rather contagious. "You'll love Hawaii! Warm breezes, soft sand, and green all around you! Not like this concrete wasteland of a city they call L.A." He paused and studied me. "Don't tell me you've never been to Hawaii? With an uncle running an inn there? My goodness gracious me." He shook his head. "We must change that, you know. I just don't see L.A. as your type of city." He rubbed his palms together, ready to dig into this new project of his: Me.

"I'm not so sure. Maybe it would be better to just have Mr. Baldwin list the property and get it sold."

"Are you really happy here?" His eyes narrowed, waiting for my response. He already knew the truth. What sense was there in lying?

"My life sucked before Uncle Wally died. Now... it's just... suckier."

19

"If you want to change your life," Davy patted my hand, "you have to change the way you look at it. I read that in a book somewhere. I've never forgotten it."

SIX

Back to the Present
or Flying High and Hating It

Why must airports be so inefficient? I sat in the terminal at LAX for an interminably long time. Delays, changes, restructures of schedules. Poor Chester – in the carrier he didn't really like – was a trooper. I did take a moment to feed him a few more of his crackers. Sitting on the floor of the ladies room, far away from the main door, I poked my hand into his carrier to give him a skritch and a few of his yummies.

"Why," I asked him, "are there doggie facilities in the airport, but nothing for kitties? Hmm? Seems we need some equal rights, don't you think?" He continued munching his little bit of kibble, ignoring me as usual.

I still felt terribly guilty over Chester's imprisonment. He finished his snack and then turned his back on me, crouching down in the far corner of his carrier. *Take that, Human*, he seemed to say. I sighed, gave him a slow blink, and closed the carrier. For extra privacy and protection, I draped my light sweatshirt over the mesh of his prison. "Sorry, big guy."

When at last it seemed we were to board the plane, I crouched in a little corner of the ladies' restroom and let Chester use the little mini litter box I'd created. He wasn't happy about having to "perform" at will, but he did so. I figured I could sneak another litter box trip in the airplane lavatory mid-flight as well, but for now we were covered. I was exhausted.

I was nervous on the first leg of our journey, but thankfully it was a short one, under an hour. Chester meowed loudly as we deplaned, and my fellow passengers chuckled. "Sorry, Bud."

I slept the first part of the longer flight, as did my trooper Chester. It was only when the passenger sitting beside me decided to take a walk that The Pest appeared.

"Long flight, yeah?" He was far too cheerful.

I groaned and looked away. "Go away. Go harass some flight attendants," I grumbled.

"Been there. Done that. Bored now." He seemed to be bouncing.

I squinted and peered at him from the corner of my eye. "Have you been hitting up the First Class beverage cart?"

"How'd ya know?" He bounced.

I realized people were looking my way. I'm certain they were wondering who the crazy woman was talking to, so I made a big show of leaning down and talking to Chester who was sound asleep in his carrier.

"Davy," I whispered frantically, "go away! People are staring!"

He looked around and waved, knowing full well that they could not see him. I stifled a giggle, but shooed him out of my seatmate's spot. He scurried off after a particularly young and attractive flight attendant.

I snickered behind my hand and made an exaggerated show of opening the file I'd made for my Uncle Wally's documents, to study them further. It was quite satisfying to see The Pest pestering someone other than me.

SEVEN

Hello Big Island!
North Kohala, Here We Come

We landed at last in Hilo. As soon as we stepped off the plane, the humidity hit me like the wall of soggy air that it was. I felt my hair take on a new life of its own. Imagine those magic washcloths that are the size of a coin until immersed in water, then PFFFFT, HUGE! Yep, that was my hair. I felt like an upended (unused) toilet brush.

I had arranged for a small rental car, but by the time I checked in, all that was left was a "special deal" for a micro-mini Smart Car. Oh well, I was all for helping the environment, and it was only me, Chester, a couple of bags... and The Pest. The Pest could fit anywhere, after all. And because they admitted to messing up my reservation, the rental deal they gave me for sixty days was an excellent savings.

With my map in hand and my GPS programmed, we set out on our adventure. And I do mean adventure. Driving in Hawaii is ... a unique experience. Unless you're on the main highways of the more frequently traveled islands, the roads can be small and full of potholes. Potholes? In a Smart Car? You feel every single one, and there are times when you wonder if the little car is going to fall into one and never get out. I wouldn't have been surprised if a head-on collision with a kamikaze bug could have rolled this little scooter over, leaving us stranded like a tortoise on its back, wheels spinning like little flailing tortoise-legs. I briefly wondered if I had a few granola bars stashed in my bags. Chester and I could live off of one for a day or so. Not pleasantly, mind you, but just in case.

I tried to keep my mind on the GPS directions and the annoying voice emanating from the blasted machine, but there was another voice that was quickly becoming just as annoying.

"You're bloody crazy. You know that? You're trying to get us all killed. One of those potholes could swallow us up and we'd never be seen or heard from again! Watch it! Ohmygod! To the right, to the right! This isn't bloody England you're driving in!"

23

"There are more potholes on the right!"

"Oh bloody hell. We're all doomed!"

I had to smile just a teeny bit at his words. He was the only safe one. "Just enjoy the scenery!"

He was silent for a very short minute. "It's rather amazing, don't you think?" he ruminated as he peered out the car window. "Some trees spend hundreds of years growing just so I can blow my nose... or write a letter."

I smiled but kept my eyes on the bumpy road ahead. He continued. "People grow trees, cut them down, make paper out of them, and then write on the paper, 'Save the trees.'" He chuckled.

"You should take your show on the road. Soon."

"But you'd miss me. Admit it. I know Chester would." Chester was just waking up and giving Davy slow blinks. Traitor.

I pulled the car/scooter/whatever-you-want-to-call-it into a grocery store parking lot in Kamuela, which appeared to be the halfway point between Hilo and our destination. "Stay here with Chester, please?" I nearly begged as I unfolded myself out of the car-scooter-skateboard-skate formerly known as a Smart Car. "Do you want anything?"

"Beer."

"No beer. We're driving."

"Crisps then. And a Bubble-Up."

"What is a Bubble-Up?"

"Alright, a 7-Up then. And definitely crisps. Something interesting. I'm bored."

I sighed and walked toward the storefront, grateful to have a few moments of peace. It was like traveling with a toddler at times. My first stop was the small pet supply store beside the grocery. Wow, prices were sky-high. I guess it was the shipping costs, but it was almost enough to make me run back to the car-scooter-skateboard-skate and return to Hilo to hop a flight back home. And then I realized... I had no home yet. My new home was our destination. The thought was both frightening and exciting at the same time.

I bought the new items for Chester, not having wanted to pay an extra bag fee on the flights. Litter box, litter, Blue Buffalo cat food, two bowls, a soft bed, and a small scratching post.

24

At the grocery store, I used the facilities first, and then picked up a couple of apples, some grapes – oooh! – a mango, and a pineapple. Heading to the drinks and snacks area, I found the 7-Up and some plain sparking water for me. Crisps – I had heard that term before and knew he meant chips. I picked up a bag of sour cream and onion chips, some corn chips, and some pretzels for myself. Sticker shock awaited me at the checkout, but I sucked it up and paid for our items, then headed back to the car-scooter-skateboard-skate.

I could see Davy chatting with Chester, and I had to smile. He really wasn't so bad. I just wasn't used to having constant human company. I was beginning to see what dear Willow had seen in him, and it brought back warm memories of her laughter. I shook off the melancholy and loaded the larger items into the small back area, then refolded myself into the car-scooter-skateboard-skate.

"'Ello luv. Did ya find e'erything?"

"Yes, but I'll need to take a mortgage out on the inn to pay for groceries." I passed the bags across to his side of the car-scooter-skateboard-skate and he peeked inside. Little exclamations of delight echoed out of the plastic bags as he nosed around. We popped the tops of our drink cans, and he ripped open the corn chips.

"Party time!" He popped a chip into his mouth and grinned. I sent him a warm smile and saw that lovely twinkle in his eye. "That's my girl. Gotta make the best of it, right?!"

"Right," I answered firmly, but I know my voice didn't hold the same conviction that his had conveyed. I started up the car-scooter-skateboard-skate, and Ms. GPS raised her infuriating voice again.

Davy looked at me, an evil smirk on his face. "She is a grating bugger, isn't she? Auntie Agony."

I had to laugh. "Auntie Agony? How perfect is that?"

He leaned towards the GPS. "Where d'we go from here, Auntie Agony?"

"Turn left," she responded, and we busted up laughing. Chester was not amused, having a severe case of feline jet lag. Or something. He kept turning in his carrier, seeming to be looking for a more comfortable position for some serious sleeps. I'm certain our laughter was keeping him up, and the look on his face would have given Grumpy Cat a run for her money.

25

EIGHT

Well, Here's Another Fine Mess You've Gotten Me Into, Stanley (aka Uncle Wally)

While it seemed an eternity since we'd left Los Angeles, it had been merely half a day or so. But when I finally pulled the car-scooter-skateboard-skate into the small parking lot at the address Mr. Baldwin's documents had provided, I thought I had made a wrong turn. It looked more like a "turnaround" – a small spot that would fit perhaps five or six cars – and terribly overgrown with tropical plants. I stuck my head out the window, expecting Tarzan to swing by at any moment.

I angled the car-scooter-skateboard-skate into a space by a lush hedge closest to the road. Ours was the only car.

"Well, this is a fine adventure," Davy marveled, a bit more quietly than his usual banter. He was peering up at the tall greenery as well. Suddenly he leaned back, beat his chest, and gave a most impressive imitation of a Tarzan call. I nearly wet my pants bending over in laughter. He shrugged then, his face lit by that standard impish grin of his. "When in Rome, right?"

I clutched the file in my hand, the papers firmly captured inside with prongs. If they hadn't been, my shaking might truly have had them scattered to the breezes. "C'mon Chester; we're home." I lifted his carrier out of the back of the car-scooter-skateboard-skate and locked up.

Mraaaooooowwww. He wasn't too happy. I wasn't enthralled myself. Even Davy seemed to have lost a bit of his enthusiasm. I squinted into the darkened shadows at the edges of the growth and found a small set of wooden steps descending... well.... somewhere.

Behind me, Davy broke out in song – at the top of his lungs I might add – ever the entertainer. "Another pleasant valley Sunday...."

I chuckled as I held the rickety stair rail and watched my footing. We were totally surrounded by foliage by this time. It was rather like walking into the Bat Tunnel. Davy abruptly stopped his singing and began to hum the Batman theme. About thirty steps down, the foliage

26

began to open up, bringing us to a clearing. A weathered wooden arch declared that we had arrived at Haole Hale.

"What the ...?" Davy's thick brows wrinkled together.

"What?"

"Hale means house, and Haole means white man, I think. White Man's House." Behind me, he stood on the second step and grinned down into my face. "Imagine the Hilton being named 'Old Rich Guy's House.'"

I looked back at the sign and wrinkled my nose. So far, this wasn't giving me any warm fuzzies in the security department. Had I made a huge mistake in leaving it all behind? *Wait*, I admonished myself. *What "all" had I actually left?* Point taken.

We pushed on, carefully avoiding brushing against the rickety sign for fear it would topple over on us. Another huge growth of tropical bushes parted, and a structure stood before us. *Whew*. No tents. I'd begun to worry. The white paint was flaking, and the windows had seen better days – and no recent soap, for that matter – but it was a small octagonal building with glassless storm-shuttered windows on seven of the eight sides and surrounded by a deck. The short steps up to the deck looked wobbly. I tested each one with my foot before putting weight down.

Suddenly, a middle-aged man in casual but neat clothing rounded the corner and stood smiling before us. His hair was sandy blond with flecks of grey at the sides, and his polo shirt barely contained a bit of a gut.

"Miss Liberty, I presume?" His voice was quiet and gentle but warm.

"Mr. Baldwin?" Alexander Baldwin looked nothing like Alec Baldwin, by the way. He was of medium height – perhaps 5'9"– and had a tanned yet weathered face. He nodded emphatically and beckoned me to the open door.

The building appeared to be a reception lobby. There were two small love seats flanking the doorway and a rather tacky bamboo covered front desk. To the right was a dark kitchen counter top with an ancient coffee pot, which unfortunately stood cold and empty; I could have used the caffeine jolt. To the left of that was a small windowed room that appeared to be a gift shop, filled with kitschy tourist items.

"Welcome to Wally's Wonderland! He never did get the sign changed, but that's what he called the establishment."

Really? Establishment was even a far fetched idea. It was a hovel. I only hoped the guest rooms held more promise.

A sudden flutter of feathers caught my eye, along with an accompanying screech. *Wally's Wonder, Wally's Wonder*, the creature squawked. A parrot sat on a perch just outside on the deck, an open cage behind him. He was a lovely grey, like velvet, with bright red tail feathers. Chester hissed in his carrier.

"Shh," I admonished the cat.

Here kitty, kitty...

"Oh, that's Winston! He's an African Grey Parrot. Say hello to Miss Liberty, Winston!"

Hello pretty chickie. Pretty bird.

Behind me, I heard Davy chuckle. "The bird is making a move on the bird."

I glanced back at him quickly, squinting, puzzled at his words, but I bit my tongue to keep from asking in front of Mr. Baldwin.

"Bird. Y'know. Chick, skirt, babe, fox..." He went on... and on. I suppressed a grin and turned back to the bird.

"Hello there, Winston. You're quite a handsome fella." I wanted to stroke his feathers but was hesitant. "Does he bite?"

"Winston?" Mr. Baldwin seemed appalled at the idea. "Oh, no. Winston is a very well mannered resident. He does like to socialize with the staff and guests though. From what your uncle told me, they all seem to love him."

I put my fingers up to his beak and he nuzzled them gently. I slowly stroked his breast feathers. They were so soft. I could see why he was loved. What a fun and gentle creature!

The Irish are odd; refuse to be English. Irish are odd. Irish are odd.

"Lookit that! Winston knows Winston... Churchill." Davy chuckled.

I like pigs. Dogs look up. Cats look down. Pigs are equals. Equals. And birds. Pretty bird.

28

All of us chuckled, but only some of us could hear all of us. Wait. What?

Mr. Baldwin spoke up, "I believe that's who he was named after. Your uncle's wife was a fan of Churchill and taught him many of the great man's famous quotes." Mr. Baldwin stopped speaking suddenly and looked into my eyes. "I'm sure you're quite tired after your trip. Perhaps I can show you around and then take you to your uncle's cottage?"

"That would be perfect, Mr. Baldwin. Thank you." I figured I must look like crap if even a total stranger could see I was tired. I held Chester's carrier close and followed the attorney past the parrot. "Goodbye Winston!"

So long, farewell, I'll see you in the morning, he sang to the tune of the *Sound of Music* song. I heard Davy chuckle behind us.

On the other side of the octagonal building and deck were another set of dilapidated steps and a wood-slatted trail to six bungalows connected by wooden walkways. "These are the rooms – numbered one through six."

With the wood slatted trails set with rope handrails, the complex had the feel of an expansive treehouse on the bluffs overlooking the Pacific Ocean.

"Are there any guests staying here at the moment?" I asked, looking at the nicely lettered number signs on each bungalow – obviously Uncle Wally's personal touch.

"No, the last guest left a few days after your Uncle's passing, and from what I've been told, new guests won't arrive until Wednesday."

Hmm...three days away. No wonder the inn is in the red, I thought. *This place needs to be packed, and in order to do that, it needs some scrubbing and a coat of paint – or perhaps stain might be better, to further give it that feeling of a treehouse.*

Still following Mr. Baldwin, we circled around the back of the sixth bungalow to a nice pool area. It was smallish but cozy and inviting, if not just a little overgrown. That was an easy fix.

Looping back, we came upon another building behind the reception area. Decorated in shabby 60s tiki fashion, it was the main dining area, with a fairly large commercial kitchen and a small bar.

Already, ideas were forming in my mind, but I needed to work out the financial details first.

Back through the reception building, on the far side of the property, was a separate bungalow.

"This is the residence. We've left Mr. Collins' belongings inside for you to manage. I hope that's all right by you?"

"Of course, and I do appreciate that" I tried to smile, but the feeling of loss tugged at the corners of my mouth.

Moving inside, I saw a very plainly decorated area, but with the most fantastic view of lush greenery and the ocean beyond. A large expanse of windows wrapped around two sides of the residence, giving the benefit of the view from the living room, dinette area, kitchenette, and one of two bedrooms. My breath caught in my chest. It was then I heard the rustle of feathers and saw Winston land upon the back of a chair.

We do not covet anything from any nation except their respect. I grinned at his Churchill quote until he continued. *R-E-S-P-E-C-T! Find out what it means to me! R-E-S-P-E-C-T!*

"All right, Aretha, thank you." I briefly stroked the top of his head. Turning to Mr. Baldwin, I asked about the bird's ability to fly out of his cage as he pleased. "Weren't they worried that Winston would fly away?"

"Winston? Oh, no, miss. Winston has lived here most all of his life. Dr. Josh, our local veterinarian, believes him to be around 21 years of age."

"Old enough to share a little lemonade at the bar with me," Davy chuckled behind me and I tried to hide my smile.

"All he requires," Mr. Baldwin continued, "is that you cover his cage at night, uncover him in the morning and open his door, and keep his food and water dishes filled." Gesturing back toward the reception building, "His food is kept below the coffeemaker." He smiled then, almost as if he was relieved he'd reached the end of his directions. "And that's about it. I hope I haven't left anything out. But please do give us a call if you have any questions."

"I assume you have more paperwork for me though, right, Mr. Baldwin?"

30

"Yes, but we can take care of that another time, in my office in town – on Tuesday, perhaps – 11am?"

Although I was chomping at the bit to get into this project, I was also very tired and not just a little bit overwhelmed. I was grateful for the two-day delay.

"I would appreciate that. Thank you very much. For now though, are the few employees' salaries taken care of?"

"Yes. Mr. Collins may have been having financial difficulties, but he always made certain to have a fund for salaries set aside – two months' worth at all times."

I briefly wondered how he'd managed that, having had a brief view of those financials, but I smiled when I realized it was just like Uncle Wally to be sure that others' needs were taken care of first. Mr. Baldwin smiled as well.

"Your uncle was a very kind man. Everyone loved him. I'm so very sorry for your loss."

"Thank you." The room got suddenly still and extremely quiet. I gave Winston a gentle prod.

Uncle Wally loves Macca... rawwwk on.

I realized I was smiling through tears then. I shook Mr. Baldwin's hand and he graciously left me on my own, keeping the bungalow door open to allow Winston his freedom. I waited until I was quite certain we were alone before speaking to Davy.

"Wow," I pulled a paper towel off the roll in the kitchen and wiped my eyes and nose.

"Overwhelming?" Davy's voice was soft and gentle.

"Just a little bit, yes." I straightened my shoulders and took a deep breath. "I'll go unload the car. I'm sure Chester is more than ready to stretch his legs." I left Davy and Chester together, while Winston flew ahead of me and landed on the perch outside his cage.

It took three trips to drag everything inside. At the end of a short hallway, I dumped the luggage in Uncle Wally's bedroom. MY bedroom. Getting used to that was going to take a while. The room held a queen-sized bed, which surprised me a bit, as Uncle Wally had always been a king-sized kind of guy.

The bathroom stood next to the master bedroom and was surprisingly roomy for such a small cottage, with a perfect little alcove behind the door. I was beginning to truly appreciate certain aspects of older construction as I set up Chester's litter box. There was even room to keep a few of his supplies behind the door. Being a tidy little giant of a cat, I had no problems sharing the bathroom with him. In fact, I was fairly certain that, in his eyes, I fell far below his standards for cleanliness.

Between the bathroom and the living room was a small guest room, nicely furnished with two twin beds. The short hallway connected all of these rooms to the living room.

I found a sunny spot in the living room for the new cat bed and a corner area for the scratching post. It was wonderful that the sofa was angled to take full advantage of the view outside and off the balcony. I pictured Uncle Wally sitting with a glass of chardonnay, watching the sun set over the trees and on the ocean view horizon.

In the kitchenette area, I peeked into cupboards and drawers. It was well stocked; Aunt Fran had trained Uncle Wally well. I found an extra placemat and put it on the floor, filling one new bowl with water, and the other with a few pieces of Chester's kibble.

"Chester! You're home! Welcome to your NEW home!" I unzipped his carrier and held him close for a moment. He was anxious to get down though, squirming in my arms. "Ingrate!" I let him leap to the floor and watched as he cautiously checked out his new but clearly outdated digs. "Wow, Davy," I grinned at him lounging on the olive green and orange rattan sofa. "You should feel right at home, here. It's like a bad 60s trip flashback!"

He was smiling, his arms along the back of the cushions. "Ahhh, those were some good days. And bad days, too. But enough about me. How are you holding up?"

"I'm... hanging in there," I nodded as if I was trying to convince myself. "The setting for this place is truly gorgeous, with all the tropical growth surrounding us, and the nice beach just a medium walk away. No wonder there are financial difficulties in keeping this place thriving though. I'll bet the property taxes and upkeep expenses are huge!"

"It's also quite a bit off the beaten track, don'tcha think?"

I sighed and nodded. How on earth would I be able to make this a viable business again – if it ever had been? I made a mental note to research the area more, once I was in town on Tuesday.

Deep in thought, I only half-watched Chester roam around. He'd found his food and water, and was now checking out the birds in the trees outside the living room window. I made yet another mental note to be certain Winston would be safe from this small but mighty feline hunter. My head ached from all the mental notes I kept making. Oh, to be able to borrow Professor Dumbledore's Pensieve to store them in!

"Listen, I'm going to take a bath and then a short nap. No peeking, okay? You stay here – or in the other bedroom – or even the kitchen," I was trying to cover all the bases. "Or, take a walk!"

"I got your message," he chuckled. "Have a good bath… and rest."

The Shape of Things to Come
(Whaddya Know, *Still* the Wrong Group)

After a hot soak and a short nap, I did feel quite refreshed. Pulling some comfortable blue shorts and a yellow tee-shirt out of one of my bags, I dressed and turned to other tasks at hand. I collected Uncle Wally's clothing in a corner to look at later, and then unpacked my luggage. Despite missing my uncle deeply, I was beginning to have that "nesting in a new home" feeling. It was both comforting and scary as hell.

I sat on the bed and looked out the window at the darkening sky. I was completely lost as to what time it was, having gained three hours from Los Angeles yet having traveled for much of the day. A glance at the clock told me it was almost time for dinner. I wandered out to the living room, but there was no sign of Davy. Chester, however, had finished his kibble, used his litter box (good boy!) and was snoozing in his new bed. I smiled at the sleeping pile of fur, grateful for having such an easy-going companion. I made yet another mental note to buy him some catnip mice, as his one lone mouse that I'd brought in my suitcase seemed to have been beaten within an inch of its life and left in the corner by the television. I wondered if Chester had taken out his travel anxieties on the poor sewn creature.

Outside the cottage, the rest of the property was also quite peaceful. I hadn't seen any employees yet, so I assumed they would arrive sometime before the next guests.

Wandering, I found my way again to the main kitchen facility and poked into the cupboards and shelves. There was one whole shelf dedicated to canned Spam. I had to laugh at that.

"It's a Hawaiian food staple," I heard that now familiar British accent behind me. I turned to see Davy leaning his elbows against the worktable that ran down the center of the small commercial kitchen.

"I guess I'd heard of that, but it struck me as funny. There's enough Spam to last a year or more, isn't there?"

34

"Probably not. Think about it. If it's served at breakfast, lunch, and dinner, to six or more guests, that's at least one can per meal."

"Wow." The cache of Spam was probably only about a month's worth then. "Wow," I repeated myself. I had so much to learn – Hawaiian culture, how to run an inn, and how to run a business for real and not just in a textbook. Shaking myself out of my reverie, I peered into the refrigeration unit. I was surprised to find it nicely stocked. "Hungry?"

"I could eat."

"Tell me again how that works?"

"I told you – practice. Lots of it." It was then that I realized his presence was comforting. "But I'll let you cook... Haven't yet mastered that yet, but I'm close."

I grinned nervously as visions of grease fires danced in my head. I pulled out an open chilled bottle of chardonnay and poured two glasses. All I needed now was some bread and cheese along with an apple and some raisins. Two grilled cheese sandwiches and an apple and raisin salad later, we sat back and sipped our wine.

"Oh, I could SO easily get drunk right about now," I laughed. We clinked glasses. Grabbing the bottle, we headed back to the cottage, stopping at Winston's cage and covering him up for the night.

Chester met us at the door, and I put just a few more crackers in his dish. It would be a slow readjustment to his usual two meals a day. For now, I just wanted him happy and comfortable. Looking about the living room, I saw a low-lying cabinet with sliding doors in front. Hmmm...could it be? Sliding the doors back and forth, I uncovered a fairly new television set. "Ha! Uncle Wally camouflaged his modern electronics." I also found a cd player, and a dvd player as well. All the comforts of home. Wait. This *was* home. The entire situation was still so surreal.

I refreshed our glasses and then thought of something to check out that hadn't even dawned on me before. Uncle Wally loved wine and was quite probably responsible for my love of the stuff. I hurried to the kitchenette.

"Oh my god!"

"What?!!" Davy came running to join me.

"Look!"

A built-in wine cooler sat under the counter beside the refrigerator.

"Whoaaaaa." We both stood in awe. I crouched and peered inside. There was chardonnay and pinot grigio and a lovely Soave Bolla – an inexpensive wine that he'd taught me to love. "My hero." And we let the wine we'd already consumed allow us a moment of raucous laughter.

"Wait," Davy suddenly interrupted our merriment. "Come with me!" He grabbed my hand and I marveled at how it felt so warm and alive. How *did* he do that? He dragged me to the guest room and slid the closet door open. There, stacked about four feet high and three feet wide were boxes. The writing on the boxes indicated… a lovely treasure inside. I nearly squealed in delight as I tore open the top box.

"Wine!" The labels indicated several vineyards, including one that was probably local.

"Oh, Uncle Wally," Davy smiled angelically at the ceiling. "I hardly knew ya, but yet I know ya now. Thank you." He grinned at me then. "Now, if there be beer in your bedroom closet, my wishes have come true."

"You sound like Captain Jack Sparrow searching for his rum."

He crossed his arms and flashed a look of indignance my way, *"The problem is not the problem. The problem is your attitude about the problem. Do you understand?"*

He'd executed a perfect Cap'n Jack and I bowed to his talent. "I promise we will find beer on this island. Somewhere."

He gave a curt nod and blinked his eyes. "Very well. It's good that we have our priorities straight then, innit."

I couldn't hold it in any longer and burst out laughing. We were soon chuckling together as we went back to our bottle of wine in the living room.

TEN

Wandering and Wondering

It was still a quarter past too early as I sat at the small dinette table the next morning, my hands cupping a steaming mug of tea. Hungover? Yes indeed. A small plate of nearly burnt toast sat at my left. I'd thought it would be a good idea to put something bland in my stomach, but my eyes were saying "Do NOT put that to your lips!" And my head hurt too. Wine hangovers are the worst. They're rough, they're invasive, they're downright abusive, and every time I have one, I swear off the wine. Will I never learn? Apparently not.

Chester was crunching his kibble, and I winced with each chomp of his jaws. So I sucked down my cup of tea, poured another, and sucked that down as well. I managed to nibble on most of the toast before staggering to the shower. Hot water always seemed to do the trick, and this time was no different.

One look in the mirror though and all feelings of refreshment were dashed. My toilet brush hair now resembled a porcupine whose quills had been stuck in an electric socket. I smoothed it back and tucked it into a scrunchie; now it looked like a powder puff instead. I gave up for the time being because I was actually feeling almost halfway human otherwise.

I dressed in a loose cotton shift and flip flops. I was determined to explore the property, taking notes on the pad of paper I carried with me.

The reception area was the first stop, and I uncovered Winston's cage and bid him good morning. His response was very loud squawking.

"Use your words, bird!" I unlatched his door but he seemed slow to exit, so I left him to his own speed and turned to look inside the octagonal hut. I noted that the décor needed updating. Also, the coffee and tea area could use a little freshening up. It needed to be inviting and not make visitors dread the day ahead. Even the enticing aroma of Bennie's delicious Kona would draw people inside more if the area was more inviting to the eye.

The gift shop was too crowded in my opinion, with far too many homemade signs scattered about. The sign that especially caught my eye was by the door. "Shoplifters Will Be Prostituted." I wondered if this was an accidental error or the result of some inexplicable bit of junior high school humor on the part of the employee in charge. Either way, it had to go. Also, a little kitsch was good for tourism, but too much clutter was enough to drive even the most spendy tourist away.

The reception desk looked neat and tidy, with a computer system to control the bookings. I'd have to learn more about that later. As for now, I didn't have access.

In the adjoining building were the commercial kitchen we'd used the night before and the dining room and bar areas. The bar needed to have a bit more separation from the diners so that it didn't appear to be a giant wedding reception with open bar. I wondered how costly it would be to put up a partition. I made more notes.

I had no notes for the kitchen but desperately wanted to discuss the groceries with the chef, and more importantly make sure we actually *had* a chef.

The pool area was nice, especially at this hour. I sat on one of the reclining lounges and took it all in. The pool seemed large enough, definitely clean enough, and only a little bit of wear on the inner paint and tile. The lack of a bar made me wonder though, until I realized that the inside bar really wasn't that far away. Perhaps there was even a chance of reorganizing the bar and dining room to move the former closer to the pool. I made a note that it was something to consider and to discuss.

And then it dawned on me – who was I going to discuss all this with? Uncle Wally? I felt completely alone once again. I could only hope that there was a sort of assistant manager or something who would show up for work on Wednesday when the first new guest was due to arrive. I continued my "tour."

The rooms themselves were decorated in basic motel style. It wasn't really that inviting, but I put that note at the bottom of my list. I also wondered if the communal dining room size corresponded correctly with the number of guests, and if we accepted diners who were not actually booked. I guess it all depended too upon how tasty our food was and how favorable the service. Again, I'd have to wait a couple of days to get some of these answers, but at least now I felt a bit more prepared.

It was nearing noon, and I decided to walk along some of the many paths and trails that connected around the property. Several times I simply stopped to listen to the wind and the creatures in the rustling leaves. It truly was beautiful, and I could now appreciate what Uncle Wally had loved.

Stay on the path. Stay on the trail. Winston joined me, perching on a handrail.

"Good morning Winston. How are you this fine morning?"

Winston is a pretty bird. Winston is.

I couldn't help myself; I'd fallen in love with this amazing creature. I could tell that there were some actual thought processes behind his words at times. Never underestimate the intelligence of other living beings. Uncle Wally and Aunt Fran had told me this many times.

A thought popped into my mind and I patted my shoulder, just as I did for Chester at times. Would he respond? My question was answered almost immediately with a flutter of grey wings as Winston gently alighted upon my shoulder and then adeptly tucked his wings against his body. "Hello there, good boy!"

Like Chester often did, he rubbed his beak along my hair.

"The bird whisperer," I heard Davy say. He'd found me and had been watching with keen interest; I could see it in his youthful features. I couldn't help but chuckle.

"He's quite the character – and extremely smart!"

Davy moved closer and bobbed his head at Winston, who returned the gesture. I gasped.

"He can see you, then?"

"Yes. He's quite happy on your shoulder. That's what he just told me."

"So you speak 'bird' now too?"

"No. We just speak the common language of all compassionate beings: love."

My heart swelled. I wished then that I had known this man during his living years, but I could see why my mother had adored him, even if it had been from afar.

"Polly wants a cracker," Davy broke the mood with humor and chuckled at his own stale joke.

ELEVEN

Putting Pen to Paper and the Inn Is Mine

Tuesday dawned bright and clear as usual. Listening to Davy singing a medley of old songs and Auntie Agony giving me mechanical directions in her extremely irritating voice, I drove the car-scooter-skateboard-skate into town. Mr. Baldwin's office was easy to find in a modest cinder block building set back from the road, next to a strip mall of sorts.

Davy was serenading me in the parking lot with a medley from his Broadway days, dancing around as we walked from the car-scooter-skateboard-skate, even rolling an imaginary hat off his head and down his arm. "I'd do anything for you dear, anything..."

It was quite amusing to hear him sing both the male and female parts of the song.

"Would you climb a hill?" He continued dancing. "Anything!" He stuck his thumbs in imaginary coat lapels. "Even fight my Bill? Wot, fisticuffs?"

I found myself trying to stifle chuckles in case someone was watching, especially at his mock outrage at the idea of using his fists.

"You know," I tried to say the words without moving my lips, "one day they are going to commit me to the state mental institution."

"It's all right, luv. I'll visit yer." He jumped up and clicked his heels, then did a little spin and a deep bow, tipping that imaginary top hat down to his fingertips again.

Pushing the door open to the small law office, I heard a little bell tinkle above me. An elderly lady sat at a small and cluttered desk. Miss Prinze, her rusted and tarnished nameplate stated.

"Ms. Liberty, I presume?"

"Why, yes, thank you!" I held my hand out to shake hers and she seemed surprised, but she recovered quickly and limply grasped my hand in a manner that I always found amusing in older women who were unfamiliar with the standard firm handshakes expected in the modern business world.

"I'll just let Mr. Baldwin know you're here," and she pivoted to knock on one of the doors behind her.

41

I took the time to glance around. The office seemed to have shared the same decorator as the inn. Did everyone live in a time warp in Hawaii?

Mr. Baldwin did not keep me waiting even a minute and greeted me warmly with a firm handshake as he had when we first met. It almost felt as if we were old friends already, and perhaps that was because he was my last link to Uncle Wally.

As we entered his office, Miss Prinze offered me a drink, but I declined. Once we were alone and seated, Mr. Baldwin leaned forward on his desk and clasped his hands. "I hope you got some rest?"

"I'm settling in quite nicely now, and I took some time to tour the property in more depth. I'm assuming employees will show up today or tomorrow at the latest since our next guest arrives tomorrow?"

"Oh, yes. I have a list of the six employees and a schedule here for you, including their names, duties, phone numbers, and addresses, all of it. Bennie should be the first employee on-site tomorrow morning."

Behind me, Davy began to sing, "*B-B-B-Bennie and the Jetsssssss*…. Oops, whaddya know, wrong singer…"

I bit my lower lip to keep from laughing and tried to block him out.

"Bennie oversees the other employees, in an unofficial capacity, that is. Your uncle had mentioned making him an assistant manager, but time just slipped away …" he trailed off and I worked hard to swallow the lump in my throat. The roller coaster emotions were exhausting.

Softly, in the far corner of the office, I heard Davy singing about the Jetssssss again.

I bit my tongue to keep from saying his catchline, but he saved the day by saying it himself. "Whaddya know again… STILL the wrong singer."

I knew what he was trying to do, and he was succeeding – helping to lighten a mood that could have easily gone dark. I smiled at him in his corner and he threw me an exaggerated wink, getting jaw and crinkly nose action into it. Mr. Baldwin glanced over his shoulder, trying to figure out what I was smiling at.

Recovering quickly, I pointed to a photo on the wall. "I was just admiring that picture. Very nicely done."

"Thank you." He didn't seem completely convinced, but turned back to the papers stacked in front of him.

It took the better part of an hour for all the documents to be signed, with Miss Prinze, the resident Notary Public, witnessing and stamping where required. I was pleased to see many of the documents I'd been wondering about and could hardly wait to get into a more detailed review once we were home again.

"Now," he leaned back and eyed me carefully, "I must tell you that there has been an offer to purchase Wally's Wonderland."

"Oh, really?" I frowned. This was a new wrinkle.

"The owner of the adjacent property has offered a hefty sum, if you're interested." He pushed a piece of paper toward me.

Davy dashed... erm... floated quickly to my chair, leaning over my shoulder to look. "He must be joking!" he shouted, making me jump a little. The figure was indeed... interesting.

"Is the property really worth that much?"

Mr. Baldwin considered for a moment. "Probably only to this individual. Mr. Sikes owns several parcels around Wally's Wonderland, but none as prime as yours. He was steadfastly pursuing your uncle, trying to convince him to sell."

This was big news. Did I want to sell? "I'll keep it in mind, but at this moment, I really don't want to consider selling."

"I didn't think you would," Mr. Baldwin smiled warmly.

"And I thank you for your time, Mr. Baldwin."

I stood up as we finished, and he extended his hand once again. "Please call me Alex, and I hope you'll remember that you can telephone me if you ever have any questions or concerns. Although I was his attorney, I considered your uncle a dear friend as well."

"Thank you. I appreciate that, Mr. Ba... Alex. And please, call me Macca."

I saw his eyes mist over a little. "Your uncle spoke of you often."

"It was terribly remiss of me not to find time to visit him. One of many regrets, I'm afraid."

"He understood, Macca. He truly did." I released Alex's handshake then and felt Davy beside me touching my elbow – my little emotional bodyguard from the 60s.

I said my goodbyes to Alex and to Miss Prinze as we took our leave. In the parking lot, Davy whooped in amazement. "Did you SEE that figure? Wow, the horse feed that could buy…" he was mumbling on the way back to the car-scooter-skateboard-skate.

I really looked forward to being able to return this vehicle – if you could call it that – for something more comfortable. I'd have to study Uncle Wally's finances first though and set up a budget. I was terrible at budgets, but I set my jaw, figuratively speaking, and was determined to make this a viable and profitable business.

I let Davy do all the talking – and singing – on the way home. I had much to think about and had to admit to myself that the size of that offer for the property was not only overwhelming but disconcerting as well. Something didn't feel right.

"Tuppence for your thoughts, luv."

"Mr. Sikes."

"Oh, *him*. I tell you, never, ever, ever, EVER trust someone named Sikes. I'll bet his first name is Bill."

I frowned, not understanding his reference for a moment, until it dawned on me that Bill Sikes was a rather villainous character in *Oliver!* I chuckled. Davy broke into song again. He was easily distracted.

TWELVE

We are Reopened for Business

I was really excited to greet my first guest, so I awoke early, showered, and dressed in a cotton skirt and lightweight shirt. Quickly learning the ropes with my humidity-hating hair, I wrangled it into a pony tail while it was still wet, then braided the tail itself. Take THAT, porcupine-head!

I had a quick snack before I went to the reception area where I uncovered Winston's cage and greeted him with an air kiss. He squawked and bobbed his head, alighting on my shoulder and nuzzling my hair with his beak. He fluttered off to his perch while I went inside to face my new unchosen profession as innkeeper. Just as I was marveling at the heavenly scent of freshly brewed coffee, I heard footsteps approach.

"Hello, Miss?" A youthful voice behind me made me turn to see a fit young man striding across the small lobby, his hand extended to shake mine. "I am Bennie. You were expecting me, I hope?"

I grasped his hand warmly, "Yes, Bennie. It's so very nice to meet you! I'm Macca."

He shyly smiled and ducked his head in greeting. His skin was tanned and he looked to be a mixture of both Asian and Latin background. The smile on his lips showed in his dark and friendly eyes as well.

He took some time to show me what tasks he usually tended to while he was there, including the bookings and the guest ledgers that were kept locked up. He showed me which keys on Uncle Wally's ring would open cupboards, closets, and doors. We discussed many of the details of the daily operation of the inn. It was then I interrupted him.

"I'd love a cup of coffee before our guests arrive. Did you make some?"

"Yes, ma'am. I always make the Kona in the mornings."

We poured two cups, and I stirred a little cream into mine, while I noticed Bennie drank his black.

"Oh," I swooned. "This is the best coffee I've ever tasted!"

45

He ducked his head again and grinned. "Thank you, ma'am."

"Please call me Macca, okay?" I smiled as I saw him loosen up a bit.

"Yes ma'am... I mean... yes, Miss Macca."

Hi there. I'm a pretty bird. I smiled hearing Winston greeting someone just outside, hopefully our first guests, followed by laughter as the arriving couple reacted to Winston.

I stepped aside and watched Bennie work. He was warm and friendly, and I recognized what Uncle Wally had seen in him. Bennie was someone I felt the need to watch and evaluate. Perhaps Uncle Wally's intention to promote him was something to pursue. As I watched him chat with the guests, I was quite glad that Davy wasn't hanging around singing about the Jetssss.

It was only after Bennie had finished checking our guests in that I greeted them and introduced myself. They seemed like a nice young couple. This was their first trip to the Big Island. As Bennie hefted their luggage and showed them to their room, I peeked at the guest ledger. Mr. and Mrs. Allen. I felt a little thrill go through my core. My first guests. They were in the furthest cottage, No. 6.

When Bennie returned, smiling, I jumped up and down, squealing with delight. He chuckled and put my thoughts into the exact same words. "Your first guests!"

"Yes! It feels so good!" We took just a moment to laugh together until it was back to business. A young Asian woman with dark silky chin-length hair and sad eyes arrived and Bennie introduced her as Mingzhu, the maid for the inn, but everyone just called her Ming. She was very slender and appeared to be in her late thirties, and I would guess she was just barely five feet tall. We chatted for just a few moments until she said she had some duties to attend to. She wandered out the back door with her bucket of cleaning supplies as another employee arrived and was introduced to me as Sam. He handled the small guest shop and the bar. He fit all the clichés about your average surfer dude from his sun-bleached shoulder-length hair, to his suntanned skin and manner of speech. He was perhaps 5'10"– lean and muscular.

Louis dashed in next and there were more introductions. He looked to be in his early twenties, with sunburned cheeks and nose.

Louis maintained the pool area and the grounds – which didn't look like a large job since it was mostly lush native tropical growth.

The cook and the server arrived together several minutes later. Bennie had clued me in that Kalei and Lani had been married for just a few years and were native Hawaiian. Kalei was a considerably large man with a broad face and deep brown eyes framed by crinkly smile lines at the corners. His hair was long and dark but pulled back neatly in a thin ponytail and secured by a cord of some sort. His wife Lani was quite small and shared her husband's same soft and friendly features. Her long brown hair reached to her waist but was neatly tucked into a single French braid. I admit that I was just a tad jealous of her silky hair, but what caught my attention the most were the loving looks the two shared frequently with each other.

I was feeling an odd mixture of exhilaration and exhaustion, and it was only 1:00 in the afternoon. When I saw Sam unlock the little shop, I decided now was a good time to discuss the sign, among other things.

"Hi again, Sam. Tell me a bit about your duties here in the shop, please?"

"I keep the shelves clean and stocked, Miss."

"Who handles the sales?"

"I do, if I'm nearby. Sometimes Bennie makes the sales. It depends on where we all happen to be." This made sense, since it was such a small operation. I nodded and listened to him as he showed me around the six foot by six foot room. I decided to leave the subject of reorganizing the merchandise for another time.

"Very good," I started with a positive. "I only have one thing I'd like to change." I pulled down the sign, Shoplifters Will Be Prostituted.

"You don't want to warn people?" He looked puzzled. It was then that I realized he truly didn't understand the misuse of the word.

Smiling, I patted him on the back. "I don't think it's necessary in such a small establishment, do you?"

He returned my smile and nodded. "Okay, Miss." He turned back to the shelves he was dusting, and I found Bennie wiping down the reception counter.

"I'll be in my cottage if you need anything, Bennie."

47

"Okay, Miss Macca," he smiled.

Davy was sitting on the sofa watching television with Chester on his lap. I flopped down beside him. "It's official. I own an inn and I have six employees." I groaned. "I think I'm a little overwhelmed."

"Oh, pshaw," he laughed at me.

It was midway through the afternoon when I decided to take a stroll around the property again. The atmosphere was different, charged, if you will. I heard laughter and then splashing from the pool area. There seemed to be at least six guests now, so I headed for the front desk to peek at our check-ins. Bennie was on the phone so I turned the ledger around. Cottages two, three, and six were now occupied. In fact, there were nine guests, including the couple I'd seen first, and two small groups of traveling companions in cottages two and three. It was nice to see that Uncle Wally's attracted more than just couples. Each cottage held two full bedrooms, making it just as comfortable for families and roommates. I smiled and nodded, pleased so far.

Bennie hung up the phone, where he'd been booking another reservation for later in the month. "We're back in business!" He was grinning as well. It seems the weeks of shutdown out of respect for Uncle Wally's passing hadn't hurt the clientele. I thanked Bennie and wandered to the kitchen.

"Hello Kalei," I smiled at the big man. I had to crane my neck to meet his eyes. "How is business looking in here?"

"There will be six for dinner so far, Miss Macca," he smiled, showing shiny white teeth, "and it's still early." He seemed eager to encourage me. I'm sure the employees were concerned that I might sell the inn and walk away. I thanked Kalei and went back to the front desk, deciding to call a casual meeting. I wasn't big on meetings, but gathering the six dedicated staff members together for a few brief words seemed appropriate. Bennie said he could pull everyone together around 4:00, and I thanked him. We could meet in the large kitchen, for there we would have privacy from the guests.

Davy accompanied me to the meeting, despite my objections, as he was curious to see the team or "motley crew" as he jokingly referred to them. They were already gathered there when I arrived, and looking quite worried as well.

48

"Hello, Team Wally. And that's how I think of you." I smiled and gave each one a brief moment of eye contact. "I just wanted to thank you for hanging in there these past few weeks and for taking care of my uncle's inn after his passing. I miss him terribly, and I'm sure you do as well, but I wanted to assure you all that I intend to use all my energy to keep this business together, to improve it to a point where we're making a nice profit, and to do it all in honor of my uncle, Walter Collins. I hope you'll stay on board and work as hard under my guidance as you did with him."

I could see smiles begin to light up their faces, obvious relief in the air as I continued. "Although I do have business knowledge, I don't have hotel experience, so I hope you'll let me know when you see something you think we could be doing in a better manner."

They were silent, but I could see eyes narrowing as thought processes shifted into gear. An idea came to me, then. "Also, I'll be putting a suggestion box behind the front desk, and I hope you'll feel free to write a note if you think of something. Or, if you'd prefer, just let me know and we can arrange a time to talk."

I looked around at their smiling faces, and my heart soared. I wasn't without family after all. I just had to open up to these strangers and let them become a new type of family to me. We all had two things in common: the inn and our love for Uncle Wally. I clasped my hands together and grinned. "And now, let's get back to making our guests have such a memorable experience that they'll re-book, and then they'll go home and tell their friends all about us."

I put my hand out in front of me and motioned for them to join me. They eagerly piled their hands on top of mine and I said emphatically, but quietly enough to not carry out toward the common areas, "Go Team Wally!" There were happy smiles on their faces. Ming ran back to the laundry, Kalei and Lani returned to their prep work on the other side of the kitchen, while Sam and Louis slowly wandered away, chatting about ideas for the inn. Bennie remained behind for a moment, smiling.

"I sensed everyone was a little worried," I spoke softly.

"I think so, yes. Not any more though." He looked contentedly at our surroundings for a moment before continuing. "We have felt like this is a home of sorts, and Wally was our family. It was... a great loss." He struggled to keep his voice in control. "And now, I have work to do. Mahalo."

He cleared his throat, ducked his head, and hurried to the front desk. I turned to Davy, grinning like a fool in the corner, hovering just a few inches above the floor. How did he *do*... all that he did. I chuckled to myself.

"Well done, you." He put an arm around me as we walked back to the cottage. "Now what?"

I waited until we were inside before answering. "It's very simple. I need to make a suggestion box."

He rolled his eyes. "That's all you brought away from that meeting?"

Laughing, I poked through the closet until I found a nice sized box. "No, but that's the immediate chore." I cut a hole in the top and covered it with photocopier paper that sat next to Uncle Wally's printer. I froze. Printer? Where was the computer? I spun around and poked in cupboards, drawers, and under the bed. Nothing.

"What's troubling you, luv?" Davy had been studying me. I'd felt his eyes on me, but had ignored him up until then.

"Uncle Wally has a printer," I vaguely motioned to it on the desk, "but I can't seem to find any trace of a computer. Why have a printer without a computer?"

Davy's expression confirmed it was a puzzle. He wandered around the premises, poking here and there while I finished making the box. Using a felt tip pen, I hand-lettered SUGGESTION BOX across the front. "I'll be right back," I called to my ghostly companion and headed back to the front desk. Bennie smiled happily as he checked in yet more guests – a middle-aged couple and their teen-aged daughter. My eyebrows arched in appreciation and he gave me a sly "thumbs-up." I placed the homemade box under the counter and greeted our new guests.

When Bennie returned from taking the guests to their cottage, I thanked him. "Hey, Bennie, did Uncle Wally have a computer?"

"Yeah, an old laptop. He was always complaining that it didn't work right, but I think it was mostly user error," he grinned sheepishly.

50

I thought for a moment before asking my next question, careful not to let it sound like I was accusing anyone. "Do you know what happened to it?"

He frowned, clearly bewildered. "No, Miss Macca. It's not in his cottage?"

"No. The printer is there, but I looked all over for the laptop and there's no sign of it anywhere in the cottage."

Without hesitation, he used his keys to unlock a storage room that hid between the front desk and the gift shop area. He pulled on an old overhead chain and a bare light bulb illuminated the closet, for that was all it really was. Bennie looked on each shelf as I peered over his shoulder. All I saw were basic supplies and a few files with papers stuffed haphazardly inside.

"I don't see it." He seemed a little concerned. He locked up the room again and made sure I remembered which key on my own ring would open it if I needed. He then hurried back to the desktop computer at the front desk. "I'm changing our password, just in case," he spoke distractedly, typing quickly on the keyboard. "Have you asked Mr. Baldwin about the laptop? Perhaps he has it in his office?"

This didn't sound practical, but I said I'd call him anyway. "Are all the bank accounts available on this computer?" I indicated the screen he was peering at. "Yes, but only Mr. Wally had passwords for that. Did Mr. Baldwin give them to you?"

"No," I said, my finger tapping my chin as I thought about it. "The only access I have is to go to the bank and do my business there. Excuse me," I said hurriedly and trotted back toward the cottage.

"I'll give you this new password and show you how to use it later," he called after me and I thanked him over my shoulder. In my bedroom, I dug into the pockets of the clothing I'd worn yesterday and found Alex's business card. Dialing the number, my heart thrummed.

"Hello Alex." I had been holding my breath and it came out in a whoosh. "It's Macca. Listen, do you by chance have possession of my Uncle Wally's laptop?"

"Laptop? I wasn't aware he had a laptop, I'm sorry! Are you sure he had one?"

51

"Yes, Bennie just confirmed it and we've looked everywhere. The printer is here, but no laptop. Also, did Uncle Wally provide you with passwords for his online banking accounts?"

I heard the worry in his voice. "No! Oh dear. He never even told me he accessed his accounts online!" I heard papers rustling on his end. "I'm going to call the bank and I'll call you right back."

I dug my own laptop out of the bedroom closet and set it aside. When I met with Bennie later, I'd be sure to figure out how to get access to the business records from my own system as well. It was important to have more than one back-up.

My phone rang, the ringtone playing "Daydream Believer." I shook my head and rolled my eyes at Davy, who had the good sense to look properly guilty. "Hello?"

"The bank manager, Dan Yoshikawa, says there hasn't been any improper activity on the accounts," Alex began without preamble, "but to be safe, he's frozen all online accounts. You'll need to meet with him to get online access granted again. And in light of your uncle's... manner of death, I'm alerting the police as well. They may wish to speak with you. Detective Green may call you."

"Very well. Thank you so much. I'll make arrangements to meet with Mr. Yoshikawa."

I ended the call and tossed my phone on the sofa beside Davy. "Fix it."

"What? You don't care for that song?" His eyes twinkled and my mood softened.

It was just at that moment that I had a realization, an epiphany, if you will. I was the luckiest female in the world. Maybe even the universe. Yes, I'd lost my parents at an early age and yes, my beloved aunt and uncle followed along too soon for my liking. But my mother, epic Davy Jones fan of all time, in my opinion of course, had sent me an angel. In fact, I knew that thousands and perhaps millions of women young and old would have given nearly anything to be in my shoes, even if just for a few hours. Despite the business struggles sure to be ahead of me, I had been lucky enough to have this beloved specter in my life for weeks now.

"Never mind." I actually loved the song, having enjoyed the many times my mother had played it over and over again until I could sing it right alongside her, but sometimes those happy memories turned a bit melancholy. I resolved then that this was a new beginning. I was going to focus only on the joyfulness of the song and the happy memories of my parents. Missing laptop or not, life was going to get easier. I was determined.

THIRTEEN

Those Aren't Laps He's Swimming in That Pool

Waking in this paradise was bliss. Little did I know that my newly found happiness was soon to become a complete nightmare.

I left Specter-Davy snoozing about a foot above the sofa, wondering why he didn't prefer the extra bedroom, but not giving it much more thought than that. Nodding a hello to Bennie at the front desk, I filled my cup with his Kona blend. I couldn't figure out why his coffee tasted about a million times better than the coffee I made, even when we were using the same beans, the same grinder, and the same water. Mentally shrugging it off, I sipped the black gold, letting the steam wake me up and the caffeine rejuvenate me.

"Everyone seems to have the early-get-ups today," Bennie chuckled. "Most of the guests have left for the day already. I've already had inquiries about Mauna Kea, horseback riding in the Waimea area, shopping, fishing, and food in Kona."

"Happy tourists, happy guests, right?" I smiled over my coffee cup.

"This is quite true." He turned back to whatever task he'd been working at but turned back to me momentarily. "Would this be a good time to go over the software program and the records we discussed yesterday?"

"Sounds like a great idea! I'll get my laptop."

We spent about an hour and a half getting our software installed, syncing my laptop to the inn's records, and putting passwords in place. I picked it up pretty easily, having plenty of experience with many business programs over the years. I felt pretty secure in the set-up and in Bennie's mastery of it.

At one point, while he was showing me the file system for the records, I pulled my errant hair out of its bondage band to rub my aching head. Bennie stopped mid-sentence and stared at the mop on my head. I caught his eye and felt the blush rising up from my neck.

"Bad, isn't it?" I pulled a face of disgust.

"It's... not meant to do that?" He was trying so hard to be kind.

"No. In Los Angeles it was a mild-mannered mop of hair. Now it's a Medusa of Hawaiian snakes. I don't know what to do!"

He grinned suddenly and dashed back to the kitchen, returning with a jar of organic coconut oil, in solid form of course.

"Miss Macca, I promise you, if you melt some of this, massage it into your hair, leave it on for half an hour, then rinse, you'll be happier."

"Really?" I'd never heard of using coconut oil in my hair. I'd led such a sheltered life. "Thank you! I'll try it!"

I put the laptop safely back in the cottage along with my new (hopefully) best friend the coconut oil. I decided to wander around and catch moments to say hello to my Team Wally members one by one.

Ming's maid cart stood outside cottage number six with the door propped open. I saw her bending over the queen-sized bed, smoothing the comforter.

"Good morning, Ming!" I called to her and she flashed a happy and relaxed grin my way.

"Aloha, Miss Macca." She joined me at the cart, as I'd not wanted to intrude on the Allen's privacy in their room by traipsing through it. "How are you today?"

"I'm doing really well, settling in, and loving this place. How about you?"

"I'm very happy you're staying. Much relief." She did indeed have a bit of an accent, but she was still extremely easy to understand, and her demure nature was quite endearing. I gave her a gentle pat on her shoulder and we parted.

As I turned toward the pool area, a dark shadow in the normally bright blue pool water caught my eye. I stood rooted to my spot as it floated and turned as the water rippled with the breeze. Someone was floating in the pool, but Bennie had said all the guests had left. My brain seemed to be functioning through a million layers of disbelief as I found the courage to inch closer. My brain was still in disconnect until I saw he was face down. A scream tried to bubble from my throat, but I'd never screamed in my entire life and so the sound didn't seem to know how to actually escape my lips.

55

Rushing forward, I dropped my paper coffee cup somewhere and jumped into the water. The body seemed to float just beyond my grasp, but I kept trying to reach for it. I thrashed about and heard loud voices poolside yelling my name. I finally reached the wrist of the man and pulled him toward the shallow end. Bennie, Kalei, Lani, and Ming had apparently heard me splashing about and helped me pull him out of the water. Kalei turned him over to begin CPR, and we all gasped. It was Louis, and from the looks of him, CPR wasn't going to help. Bennie checked Louis' pulse then pulled Kalei away and made us all back off.

"Call 911!" I shouted. Lani pulled out her cell phone, put a finger in her open ear, and turned away from all the activity, presumably to block out our noise.

But it had suddenly become very quiet as we all stood looking at our dead friend and employee. His eyes were bulging and there was a deep red mark around his neck. Ming brought me a towel and I stood shivering between her and Bennie. I saw Davy materialize on the other side of the pool, his eyes searching my face, most likely assessing my level of freak-out. I gave a short nod his way, and he moved closer to examine poor Louis.

The police arrived about three hours later, but in reality it had only been five minutes. We were immediately split up and put in separate areas for reasons only they truly knew for sure. Now is when I needed human contact, but I assumed it was to keep us from discussing any of this until they could get our statements. I'd watched enough *Law & Order* and *CSI* to know that much at the very least. I was lucky though because Davy stayed at my side, pulling the towel closer now and then and making comforting noises. I finally looked into his eyes and began to cry. I'd never seen a murdered person before. I'd seen my share of death, sure, but it was mostly in sterile surroundings, with doctors, nurses, and the like.

"It's all right, luv; it's not your fault," he cooed, brushing my wet hair out of my face at times. Oh, how I longed for my cup of coffee. And my bed. But I didn't even know where my cup was at this point. I found myself gazing longingly toward the path to my cottage.

An average-height, average-build, average-aged, and very average man walked quite silently my way. His average face showed

56

no emotion. He dragged a chair to me, turned it around and straddled it, a small notepad in one hand and a pen in the other.

"I'm Detective Green."

"Hi," I responded meekly. "I'm ..."

"I know who you are. So tell me about today, Miss Liberty," he began, and I saw Davy straighten up as if he were six feet tall and not five feet three inches. In heels. Davy stood behind the detective, bending to look over his shoulder at what had been written in the note pad. I saw many emotions flit across his face, like flipping the channels on a television. He raised his head and looked at me, shaking his head and making signs as though warning me to be careful. I frowned in confusion as the detective decided what he wanted me to say.

Davy shimmered, disappeared, and reappeared beside me. How *did* he *do* that? "Only," he whispered in my ear, "ONLY give him the direct answers he's looking for. Do not embellish, okay?" I moved my thumb as if to show a thumbs up, but just enough for him to see, and not the detective.

"What do you want to know? I found Louis in the pool."

"Why were you walking around the grounds so early this morning?"

My hackles were raised over such a question. "Because, Detective Green," I straightened my posture, "I own this establishment."

"How did you come to be the only one to find the body?"

"I don't know. I can only assume it was because everyone else was busy doing their jobs, and the guests were off doing what tourists do, but perhaps you should ask all of them."

He scribbled something in his book and Davy shimmered behind him and then reappeared beside me. "He wrote: Not a suspect, but bad attitude." I bristled but Davy put his hand on my arm. "Relax, Babe. He's just egging you on." I let out an impatient sigh.

"What, Miss Liberty?" Detective Green looked up from his stupid notebook. "Do you have someplace else you'd rather be?"

"No. Do you?"

He pulled his head back sharply and looked at me with only one eye, his head tilted slightly away. Davy snickered and shimmered

57

again to stand behind the detective. I tried to keep my face completely straight and my expression bland as he casually knocked the notebook out of Detective Green's hand. It skittered across the floor, taking the detective by surprise. He simply sat and stared at it for a moment before stooping to retrieve the errant object. I looked elsewhere, anywhere – out the window, at the ceiling, at the floor. I caught another movement though and saw Davy flip the pen out of the detective's hand. It too went flying, landing about three feet away. Again, I was careful to show that my attention was elsewhere.

"Very well then." Detective Green tried to recover his composure as he bent to retrieve the pen. "Thank you for your time." He stood and straightened his posture. "Oh, by the way, I was informed that your uncle's laptop is missing? Has that turned up?"

"No. Does your office have it as evidence or something?" I raised an eyebrow.

"No; it's not inventoried. Perhaps…" he took strength again, merely from his mightier-than-me position, "Perhaps you found that Louis took it and that's why he ended up in the pool?"

I did a double take. Was this guy for real? I heard Davy growl deep in his throat, but I answered calmly. "No, sir, it hasn't shown up and I would never suspect any of our employees. Am I free to go?"

He stood looking at me for a few beats before answering, "Just don't leave the island."

What a creep! "I have no intention of leaving. I live here."

He regarded me suspiciously anyway and then headed out the door. I counted to ten, then I counted to twenty, and then I blew out a huge breath of very frustrated air.

FOURTEEN

Witness Protection Program for Parrots

I waited until Davy and I were safely behind closed doors in the cottage before I exploded in anger. "The nerve of that guy! What an ass!" I paced the living room, waving my arms like a wild woman. Then I whirled and suddenly looked at Davy as he stood with his arms crossed and leaning ever so calmly against the door frame, grinning. "And YOU! You were brilliant! Ohmygosh, I could kiss you!" And with that I gave him a little peck on the cheek. "Promise me you will do that to that detective again. And again. And yet again!"

Davy laughed, dropped his arms to his sides and flopped onto the sofa. "I'll admit it was quite fun."

I stopped what I was doing for a moment as I tried to recall something. "Oh my…"

"What?"

"Have you seen Winston?" I realized he hadn't been on his perch today.

"No, I was too busy restraining myself from tripping that detective so that he fell on his face."

I dashed out the door and trotted to the main building. No Winston. A quick search of the premises confirmed there was no bird, no Winston. My heart sank. And then I heard it – a flutter of feathers, a flapping of wings. I didn't know where he was, but I patted my shoulder and looked to the skies. He swooped gracefully from the top of the Haole Hale sign near the parking area. "Hello, my sweet boy, pretty bird," I told him and nuzzled his chest with my cheek. I took him with me back to the cottage and closed Chester in the bedroom, apologizing.

Here kitty, kitty. I won't bite.

I sat on the sofa with Davy, and Winston perched on the coffee table before us. "I don't know why, but I just worried that something had happened to him, you know?"

"I know. It's that big heart of yours." Davy squeezed my hand. *Mahalo.*

I chuckled. "You're welcome, Winston."

59

Victory at all costs, victory in spite of all terror.

"He's quoting Churchill again," Davy said and we chuckled. Then we looked at each other, wide-eyed.

"Winston," I leaned forward, "did you see Louis today?"

Louis Louis Lou-EYE. He sang the old nonsensical song. He bobbed his head a few times, clearly agitated. *Angel and the Bad Man.* He recited a John Wayne movie title. *Louis met the bad man. Batman. Nana-nana-nana-nana Batman.*

Davy and I stared at each other, shocked. Winston had been there this morning! I knew then that we had to keep him safe. Ruthless people do crazy things, and poor Winston was an innocent.

Winston stayed with Davy while I retrieved the large bird cage and separate perch. We would bring him in with us each evening. I would let Bennie, but no one else, know of my suspicions about the too-smart-for-his-own-good parrot.

Returning to the cottage with Winston's supplies, I found Davy teaching the bird to sing "Daydream Believer." I had to laugh.

"What?" he asked so innocently. "It's my signature song," and he stuck his tongue out at me.

Sleepy Jean Sleepy Jean

"You're almost there, little mate. We'll just keep practicing."

Wings of a bluebird. Wings.

I chuckled and my stomach growled. Realizing I was famished, I whipped up a quick meal for the two of us. Later, sitting on the sofa with the television turned to some bland program playing softly in the background, Davy took my hand in his, intertwining our fingers. "I'm worried," he stated so simply, so quietly. His deep brown eyes met mine. "I'm worried for your safety. I can only do so much you know."

"I know. But just having you here is so comforting. You are the only one I can truly trust besides Chester and Winston." He smiled and glanced over at the orange cat, who was none too happy to be sharing his new home with a bird. Chester crawled into his bed, but I knew he was listening for Winston, for his ear was cocked and he twisted it now and then to follow the sound of squawks and rustling feathers.

FIFTEEN

Normal?
I Have Completely Lost Track of
What is Deemed Normal!

As I wandered about the inn the next day checking on my remaining Team Wally members, there were mutterings by various individuals about "trying to get back to normal," but I'd lost sight of "normal" long ago.

I made sure Kalei and Lani were prepared for meals that day. When I encountered a guest, I expressed my sincere apologies for having their holiday upset by such a sad occurrence and the ensuing legalities. Not a one of them complained though. Easy for them; they weren't around when it had started. However, I was quite relieved when the police were able to rule out any guest involvement. Still, everyone was questioned. I shuddered, hoping they'd been treated more politely than I had been.

Heading back to the front desk, I noticed that Sam had a new sign posted on the gift shop – "Shoplifters will be thrown into Mauna Loa. Survivors will be prosecuted." Oh no! I picked up the hand lettered cardboard and smiled at him.

"I learned the right word, Miss Macca!" He seemed so proud of himself. "And I add a little humor. It's okay?"

I touched his shoulder and smiled wider. "Maybe with all that happened yesterday, it's not the right kind of humor. Do you agree?"

His smile instantly turned sad. "Oh, Miss Macca, I didn't even think of it that way! I'm so sorry!" He took the sign and tossed it into the waste bucket. I patted his shoulder, thanked him, and left him smiling.

Ming was putting fresh water and food in Winston's cage, while the nosy little bird supervised from his outside perch.

Don't scrimp, don't scrimp, don't scrimp on the seed!

"Shhh," she admonished him lovingly and stroked his feathers. "Pretty bird."

61

Verrrrry pretty bird. Very. She chuckled and turned toward her cart, catching sight of me watching her. "Good morning, Miss Macca," she said softly, retrieving her sense of decorum in light of Louis' passing.

"It's okay to smile. Louis would have smiled at him, don't you think?"

She relaxed her demeanor a bit and nodded. "I miss him though."

"I understand, sweetie. I'm terribly sorry I never got the chance to really know him."

"We didn't know him very well, but here at work he was our friend. He was very private." She gathered herself again before adding, "I must get back to work now. Mahalo."

She pushed the heavy cart down the walkway and I approached Winston for more feather strokes. He made sweet little chortle noises and rubbed my fingers with his beak.

There was crime scene tape around the pool area still, but the technicians were working to clear it so that we were able to get back to business. The water had been drained and a crew was scrubbing the pool surface. It would be refilled and warmed again by morning. I hoped. Most of the guests had opted to visit the beach while others went sightseeing.

Toward lunchtime I wandered back to the cottage. Davy was bent over a magazine and didn't even seem to hear me enter. Or so I thought. Suddenly he jumped up, making me give a little yelp as he startled me.

"Oh, sorry, luv." He grinned but shoved the magazine at me. "Look! I found this article about Sikes!"

"Sikes? Really?" It was a brief piece, but it had two photos of his inn. It was much more modern than ours and boasted fine dining as well. In the article he claimed he was planning a small expansion since business was booming. Booming? I wondered what that felt like.

"So," I joked with Davy, "is his name Bill, like you suggested?"

He rolled his eyes. "No, it's Gilbert. But I think we can see now why he wants to buy your inn. He wants to expand his property!"

"Well, let him expand in the other direction."

62

Davy nodded, considering my words and sat back down to stroke Chester and further study the magazine article.

My glance fell upon the coconut oil Bennie had given me. I snatched it off the counter and scooped some into a measuring cup. It only took a few seconds in the microwave to melt it. Grabbing a towel, I leaned over the kitchen sink and began to work the gooey stuff into my hair. I covered my head in plastic wrap and used the towel as a turban, then sat on the couch to watch television. Thirty minutes later, I rinsed out the oil, did a quick shampoo and condition, then combed out. The result was pure silk, but the true test would be the drying process. I parked myself out on the deck with a book and let the tropical breezes do their job. An hour later I had a slight sunburn and a growling stomach, but my hair looked fantastic – and felt that way too! *Bennie might get a raise for this*, I thought to myself, *or at least a good hug.*

I fixed a small salad of frisee and leafy lettuces with a poached egg on top for Davy and myself. "This is interesting." He smiled as he joined me at the tiny table and poked at the egg so that the yolk oozed down and created a dressing of sorts. "It's good too," he proclaimed in between bites.

"Thank you! My Aunt Fran taught me this trick."

"Your hair looks good again too," he said between bites.

"Thank you! Bennie is my new hero."

"I see," he teased. "I've been replaced." He sniffed and ate more salad.

"You could never be replaced. At least not right away." I winked and he kicked me under the table.

SIXTEEN

Learning the Ropes

Bennie, Kalei, and Lani had been teaching me a bit of the local language, and I was practicing every chance I had.

"I ku ka makemake e hele mai." – it wasn't as beautiful as when they said it – "hele no me ka malo `elo `e." Translated loosely, it was: *Hospitality: If the wish to come arises, walk firmly.* My new motto.

As the week went on, we welcomed more guests and bade farewell to others. I awoke each morning with that wonderful feeling of anticipation, enjoying the idea of meeting new guests at what I was quickly beginning to think of as my home. My Team Wally were proving still that they worked smoothly together. They faced difficult questions and tasks with the ease of wise elders. Equally important to me, they were fast becoming my family.

I wandered to the front desk one morning and began greeting my new "family" and encouraging them for the day. As I passed the small gift shop, I noticed Sam working inside. I backtracked and greeted him, believing that perhaps now would be the time to rearrange the overly crowded shelves. The tiny room, packed with multiples of multiples of the same tourist fare was surely a nightmare for any claustrophobic shopper.

"Sam," my own smile was returned by his eager one, "perhaps we could put some of the merchandise back in the storage closet and make this room look bigger and more inviting. What do you think?"

He looked alarmed at first. "We can't sell them if they are hidden, Miss Macca."

"Think of it this way," I led him to the worst offending shelf and plucked half the items off, cradling them in my hands. "If there is reduced clutter for the eye to see, the mind might be less overwhelmed."

I could see him thinking on that, chewing on his knuckle. I'm not sure he was convinced, but he nodded emphatically. "We can try!"

"Let's start now!" I rummaged around in the supply closet and came up with some boxes and packing material. "I'll help you with the first few shelves, okay? If we keep only a few of each item on display, you can quickly replace them as needed."

Together we tackled the project for the better part of an hour. As we stepped back to look, he grinned. "Yes, Miss Macca! Looks much better! Mahalo!" Nodding his head, he eagerly tackled another shelf, and I turned to scan the other areas of the small shop.

There was a peg board filled with small cellophane packages of macadamia nuts. A few of the nuts seemed to have escaped their packaging and were on the floor. Sam had put up a sign that said, "Warning: Loose nuts on floor." I bit the inside of my cheek to keep from laughing, and snatched the sign down.

"Sam, here's one more suggestion for you. Instead of putting up a sign like this, how about we just keep the floor tidy?"

He smiled again and nodded. "I will take care of it, Miss Macca, yes!"

"I'll clean these up right now for you," I said and swept up the few nuts that I could find before leaving him to his chores.

At Bennie's suggestion I had hired a young local man to fill Louis' empty position. Alberto was a very likeable man, perhaps in his early thirties. He was of average height and build, and seemed happiest when he was tending to plant life. A native plant enthusiast, he seemed to have an incredible amount of energy. Bennie took him under his wing and showed him the ropes. I came across Alberto by the pool. He was crouched by a particularly lush growth of ferns and palms, pulling out brown leaves and dead sections of the plants. I turned in a slow circle to view the lovely tropical setting. He had pruned a lot of the vegetation back and it was such a remarkable improvement.

He sat back on his heels to look up at me, shading his eyes with his dirty hands. "You like?"

"I love it, Alberto! You're an artist of plant life!"

He grinned and ducked his head shyly, turning back to his work. Kalei had set up a chilled urn of refreshing iced tea nearby and I grabbed a glass of the sweet but minty goodness. He had a way with mangoes and mint with tea, indeed! I casually grabbed a second glass along with a straw and headed back to the cottage.

Davy was sitting in the sun on the wraparound deck and I handed him the glass. He took a sip and his smile widened. "Whoa... That's delicious!"

"Kalei performs magic yet again."

He took the long white wrapper from the straw and knotted it in four evenly spaced spots so that it looked rather like a short string of paper beads, and then he set it aside. I sat beside him on the chaise and we sipped in silence, admiring the view for a few minutes before I headed back to the front desk. We were expecting another guest this afternoon and I thought I'd spiff up the coffee area. Ming had enough to do with all the rooms and the laundry.

Bennie stood at the computer entering data of some sort. His efficiency was something I was coming to rely on, and now I wanted to reward him along with the other employees.

Davy and I had been formulating a plan to give each employee a day off once per week, the same day each week, so they could actually make personal plans. As it was now, they alternated days off only based on the guest activity, and the practice was haphazard and uncertain at times. I figured I could cover a day each of jobs for Bennie, Ming, Alberto, and Sam, then pick one day a week where the dining area would be closed so that Lani and Kalei could have a day off together like a married couple should have.

I met with Bennie, Lani, and Kalei, and we decided that Wednesdays were probably the best day to close the restaurant as that was the least likely day for arriving guests to check in and departing guests to check out, so that would be Bennie's day. We randomly chose Monday for Sam, Tuesday for Alberto, and Thursday for Ming. I could handle four days a week of duties rather easily. Or so I hoped. We decided to give it a try beginning Monday. Their bright faces showed me that it was the right decision to make. I truly felt like I was being guided – and not only by Davy.

In the evenings I studied hotel management by enrolling in an online course given by an extension of my alma mater. It wasn't necessarily cheap, but I was sure it would be worth the tuition. Some of the information was quite surprising and made me open my mind to apply new ideas to Uncle Wally's Wonderland. Ugh, I really hated that name. But Haole Hale wasn't much better. I would have to give that some thought as well.

SEVENTEEN

Waiwai Ho'opuka
Translation: We're Making a Profit!

After the first month, I was able to access the financial software safely thanks to Mr. Yoshikawa at the bank. I took great joy in watching the numbers rise, and we were slowly creeping out of the red. Our webpage had been updated and expanded with more photos, and I had suspended the print ads in travel magazines to save on costs. So many more people used the internet to search for holiday locations, and I'd decided the money was better spent there. Also, I'd increased our deductibles on our insurance policies to a more reasonable amount and used the savings in premiums to have WiFi installed. We were slowly creeping into the 21st century at last.

My boxes finally arrived from the mainland, and I marveled that they had remained dry despite their apparent cartage by the slowest sea turtle in the world.

Cracking open the first box I found more of my shorts and tee-shirts, along with my favorite form of footwear: flip-flops in a variety of designs and colors. I squealed in glee. I had become weary of laundering my same few items of clothing that I'd brought with me.

Uncle Wally's baseball bat was in the third box. I put it in its new place of honor next to the sliding glass door that led out to the back deck. I looked out to the trees and the sea beyond and sent Uncle Wally a message of love from my heart.

When the day came that we were actually making a profit, I jumped out of my chair, spun around, and grabbed Davy up in a huge bear hug. "I think we can do it; I think we can make it!"

"Sounds like a song, Babe. Let's sing it!" He burst into a vocal with the most amazing strength – until I cut him off with a smack to the abdomen. The only resulting sound was a solid "oooof" from which I took great pleasure.

Over time, the inn's numbers steadily rose and remained solid, allowing me to calculate pay increases for the staff. My own actual salary would have to wait a bit longer, but I was prepared and still living off the small life insurance payment I'd received from Uncle Wally's policy.

Collecting Team Wally for a quick meeting, I announced a twenty percent pay raise for them all and thanked them for their dedication and hard work. Amidst much clapping and happy exclamations of appreciation from the group, I blushed and shook my head. "You all deserve it!"

As the others returned to their tasks, I pulled Bennie aside and offered him a salaried position as Assistant Manager, which would net him a raise of about 30%. His eyes misted over. "Thank you, Miss Macca, but you are too generous!"

"No, Bennie," I said with my hand on his forearm. "You are extremely important to me and to this operation. You have earned this!"

He stood in awe for a moment before shaking my hand and pumping it furiously, thanking me over and over again before returning to the front desk to resume his work.

"Well done, Babe." Davy was suddenly standing behind me. "Well done."

EIGHTEEN

No, No, No, It Ain't Me Babe
(Wrong Singer... Again)

Bennie's day off found me at the front desk checking new guests in. Mary Browning and her twenty-something daughter Jill were standing before me as I located their booking information. The older woman looked to be in her fifties with bleached blond hair and brown eyes. Her slightly sagging jowls wobbled when she spoke emphatically, which she almost always seemed to be doing. Her midsection had that spread that most women who have had kids seemed saddled with, yet her style of dress was that of a younger woman. I suspected Jill had something to do with that, picturing the "Let's go shopping before our trip" scene that most likely played out back home. Jill was a younger, slimmer version of her mother, without the wobbly jowls. She was a blonde, with pretty brown eyes and smooth skin, somewhere near my age. She had a nice figure, with a tanning booth complexion.

Davy appeared at my side, "Hey Babe, ya wanna come have some lunch when you're done here?" He whispered in my ear.

I tried to shush him away without bringing attention to myself when I noticed Jill staring at the spot where Davy stood.

"I know you," she cried out. Her mother peered at her suspiciously.

"Who are you talking to, dear?" Mary asked gently.

"That's Davy Jones of The Monkees! Right there! Oh, he's simply *amaaaaazing*." She pointed to the spot where Davy stood. I'm sure my jaw was hanging down to about my knees.

"She can see me!" Davy almost hid behind me. The whole scene was surreal. Part of me had always wondered if Davy was merely my imagination, but now I saw that he was indeed visible to me and apparently to a few others as well. But then again, maybe Jill was all my imagination too. Maybe this whole Hawaiian adventure was all in my imagination and I lay in a deep coma somewhere in Los Angeles, only to wither away after.... I was shaken out of my reverie by Davy,

70

who was pushing me closer to the two women so that he could stand behind me.

Mary gently put her arm around her daughter and looked apologetically at me. "She has a... *gift*." The older woman acted like it was more a curse. "She can sometimes see... *spirits*." She seemed to find the word distasteful. I briefly wondered why, but my thoughts turned back to Jill and Davy.

"'ello luv," Davy warmed up to her a little and came out from hiding behind me. I rolled my eyes as he sized her up and down again. "Whot's yer name, then?" I rolled my eyes but smiled and handed Mary the two keys to the cottage they were assigned.

Jill smiled – almost shyly – and giggled like a teenage girl in the 1960s might have. "I'm Jill."

"Nice t'meet ya, Jill."

"Can *you* show us to our room?" Jill batted her eyelashes. "This place is just so *amaaaaazing*!"

Davy eyed all of the luggage piled in the middle of the reception area. "How long are you birds stayin'?"

"Only a week," Jill giggled again. The sound was beginning to make my back teeth hurt.

"Bloody hell. You could stay for a month wif all them bags," he muttered and then looked up, a startled expression on his face. He quickly put his hand out in the universal sign for "stop" and spoke hurriedly, "But don't change your plans! A week is just enough."

"I'll take the bags," I jumped to his defense, "and Sam can help." I motioned to the young man peeking around the corner from the gift shop. I could see him blush as he nodded his head to the two female guests and loaded his arms with bags. I carried the two smaller bags and Davy led the way.

"But... I can't see him, Jill," her mother whined.

"Don't be silly, Mother. You follow me and *I'll* follow Davy."

She eyed his ghostly backside and I expected drool to fly from her lips at any moment. *Lascivious princess*, I thought to myself. Sam was struggling with the tower of bags he was carrying, and unfortunately we were having to hoof it all the way to cottage six, the furthest from the front desk. Jill skipped to catch up with Davy and hung on his arm as they walked, spitting out an *amaaaaazing* every

71

now and then. I saw him glance back at me and mouth the words *Help Me*, a look of near panic on his face. I quietly snorted a laugh under my breath.

"Miss Macca?" Sam was struggling under the load of suitcases. "Who was she talking about?"

I had to think fast and couldn't so I only bought some time. "I'll explain later," I whispered.

Crap. Why did these women have to choose *my* inn? There are millions of others out there, right? In all of the Hawaiian islands?

"Macca?" Davy called back to me. "Cottage six, right?" I nodded to him.

"What kind of a name is Macca?" Jill frowned and pouted. How was she able to do those two things at once?

"Be nice, dear," her mother chided her gently – too gently. It was obvious the girl had been raised by dingoes. I could feel myself growling in response, even.

"Who is she talking to?" Sam was obviously confused, and frankly, it had all become comical, except for the feelings of jealousy within myself which I was unable to explain. I mean, he's a *ghost*. But an adorable ghost. Yet… he's the ghost of a sixty-six year old man. Still, sixty-six isn't that old, and I had seen photos – he looked great. Adding to the confusion was that he had kept his "1960s Davy" look and sound ever since that first day. This was thoroughly perplexing at times. I shook my head. What the hell was I thinking? I tried to shake it all off so I could hurry away from the Dingo.

"She's delusional," I whispered to Sam and he nodded slowly. I'm not sure he bought it, but it would have to do for now.

We piled the luggage in the middle of the floor of cottage six, showed them the basic amenities – which didn't take very long because they were indeed quite *basic* – and then bade them the usual "Goodbye and enjoy your stay" wishes.

The Dingo's mother handed a few bills to Sam as a tip. He thanked her politely, stared at The Dingo as she talked to the empty air beside her, scratched his head, and then wandered away.

"But Davy, I sure hope to see you around later," the Dingo vamped for him. "That would be simply *amaaaaazing,*"

"Erm, yeah, later." He high-tailed it out of there in a hurry, the coward.

I smiled and wished them well and then returned to the front desk. Davy was nowhere to be seen. I was fairly certain I would find him hiding with Winston and Chester in our cottage.

My suspicions were confirmed a half hour later when I went home for lunch. "Make them go home," he yelled at me, and I admit it – I laughed... loudly, and with great glee.

"What's wrong? Afraid of a little *girl*?"

"That was NO little girl! That... she... oh bloody hell. I'm hiding here for the week. Tell her I went away. Please!"

I poked him in the ribs and knew she'd find him eventually.

Poor Davy spent each day hiding. He found new and interesting places to conceal himself, yet Jill always seemed to find him. He tried just staying in the cottage, but found himself far too easily bored and lonely.

"I'm a ramblin' man, darlin', and I just cannot stay in one place for that long! I'll go bonkers!"

I imitated her vamping, "Oh Davy, you're just so *amaaaaazing*!" I batted my eyelashes. "Today they're exploring the volcano, so you can relax... for now."

"Oh, that's brilliant! Thank you!"

"It's not brilliant; it's *amaaaaazing*!"

He stuck his tongue out at me.

But his relief was short-lived. He was sitting by the pool that afternoon – getting a spectral tan? How exactly does that work again? Anyway, Jill suddenly appeared beside his chair as I was sweeping up.

"Hi Davy! Wanna go for a walk with me and show me around? This is just an *amaaaaazing* place."

I swear she bounced all the time. Did she never get tired? I felt my eyes narrow and someone was growling, a low and dangerous sound. Then I realized it was me.

And I was starting to feel bad for the guy. Just a little.

NINETEEN

A Dingo Ate My Baby...
And My Patience

With three more days left in the itinerary of Mary and The Dingo, I was definitely not feeling the love. She was not only annoying but was also causing a ruckus with the other guests and at least one member of Team Wally, perhaps more. Sam still wasn't sure what was going on, although I suspect he thought The Dingo was just plain weird. He wasn't far off actually, but that was beside the point. I had to figure a way to handle that, but I decided to wait until he asked again. There wasn't any sense in inviting trouble if he ended up coming up with his own semi-plausible reasoning.

"Ohhh, Sammy," I overheard her simpering at the young man one day. "This gift shop is simply *amaaaaazing!"*

I was grinding my teeth as I hurried away.

Some of the other guests had taken to avoiding her because of her loudness and her constant whining. I appeased them with a free cocktail at night. I just hoped it worked and that they'd keep returning for future holidays.

"Oh Mother," The Dingo whined one afternoon, "I just want to stay around the pool today."

"No! I didn't come all the way across an ocean to sit by a pool." Both mother and daughter had the same annoying tone to their whine.

"But Moooooootherrrrrr!"

I speed walked away from the pool to avoid acting on the impulse to take them to Mauna Kea and push them both over the rim of the volcano.

Davy had decided that perhaps being a hermit wasn't such a bad idea. He hid inside the cottage for an entire day before finally venturing out, but it was ludicrous that he had to sneak around. I alternated between feeling bad for him and laughing like crazy, which didn't endear me to him in any case. He sulked and grumbled a lot, but I figured "This too shall pass" and got on with the daily business of running an inn.

I encouraged the annoying whiners to sightsee more by slipping various tourist brochures under the door of their cottage. Some of the suggestions actually worked too. The duo seemed to be out exploring almost daily. These were the only times I wasn't popping aspirin. My head throbbed while in their company.

"Where's Davy?" The Dingo ambushed me one morning. Damn, another day that the assassins had failed me.

"I really don't know," I lied. I knew where he was. Wild horses and dingoes couldn't pull it out of me.

"Tell him I'm looking for him when you see him."

No *please*, no *question*, no *thank you very much,* just a demand. I grunted some sort of noncommittal reply and went on about my business. I looked up at the sky and briefly hoped Karma had been busy elsewhere and hadn't listed my fib on her very long record of my offenses. "I'm sorry," I mouthed to the heavens.

"Whatcha sorry 'bout?" Davy had been hiding… and eavesdropping. Not easy to do both at once, but he managed it somehow.

"I growled at The Dingo," I whispered, worried she might still be lurking about.

"Who?!!"

Oops. Had I called her that out loud? "Jill. I meant Jill."

He burst out laughing, finally wiping a tear of amusement from his eye, "Oh my goodness, that is the most perfect name!"

"Shhh!" I admonished him, my eyes darting about. "She's near!"

He stopped laughing immediately and gulped. "Bloody hell! I'm outta here!" He dashed off and it was my turn to snicker now.

We sat in our cottage one day sipping some of Kalei's iced tea and nibbling at a fruit salad I'd prepared for us. "I swear, this is the slowest week since I arrived here," I complained. "Being nice to that ungrateful… person… just goes against every moral fiber in my body."

"Moral fiber?" Davy speared a piece of papaya and munched at it. "Isn't that a breakfast cereal?"

"Ha, ha," I deadpanned. "You've got it easy. You can just hide out."

75

"But I can hear her. I can't seem to get far away enough *not* to hear her." He shuddered a little. "Yet I cannot help thinking that someday we'll look back on this, laugh nervously, and change the subject." He knotted a straw wrapper again, four knots, evenly spaced.

"I'm not so sure about that. If I had a dollar for every time she's been rude, I'd change all of those dollars into coins, put the coins in a sock, and beat her with it."

"I'd visit you in jail." He speared a piece of pineapple.

It felt good to have a chuckle with him – sort of like a cleansing breath of fresh air.

"I'll bet you were a lot of fun back in the day," I teased him.

"Yep, more fun than a barrel full of ..." he left it hanging and winked at me.

Later that same evening I was working on my laptop, responding to various inquiries from prospective guests, and working on my online course when Davy burst into the cottage, his face flushed.

"What happened to you?" I leaned back in my chair.

"She... she groped me!" He simply stood there staring at me, his face showing all brands of shock and disgust, like he expected me to do something about her. "I feel so violated."

I burst out laughing. "I'm sorry." I truly struggled to look apologetic because the whole thing was just so absurd. Her behavior was an insult even to Dingoes. Davy disappeared into the bathroom and I soon heard the shower running. This was new. Did ghosts shower? He'd never smelled like he needed a shower. It was yet another head-scratcher for me.

He emerged a few minutes later, toweling his hair. Yep, it was wet. I shrugged and went back to my work while he plopped in front of the television with Chester and Winston, who seemed to have decided to be frienemies. "I'm not leavin' this cottage till she leaves this island," he muttered.

"Fine," I smiled. "You'll recall that I'd suggested that when she first arrived." Oh, how I loved the *I Told You So's* in life.

76

TWENTY

Hawaiian Delicacies
or How to Put on Five Pounds per Meal

It was the night before The Dingo and her mother The Whiner were scheduled to check out. The air was thick with a sense of anticipation. It was obvious that Davy and I weren't alone in wanting them gone. I was assisting Lani and Kalei at dinner since it seemed all of our guests had decided to eat in that night.

Kalei had prepared a feast that would begin with a sort of Polynesian version of ceviche called Lomi Lomi using freshly caught salmon which was cured and diced with tomatoes, onions, and peppers. The raw dish was both cool and spicy, and was served with a grilled uala, or purple sweet potato. For our vegetarian guests we substituted diced crisp cucumbers for the Lomi Lomi Salmon. Lani and I served the appetizers, and Sam helped keep an eye on the beverages, making sure to keep glasses filled.

The next course up was a chilled cream soup of daikon radish and potatoes. Fresh bread, baked by Lani each morning, was on every table.

There was a choice of two entrees, the first being the vegetarian offering of a mélange of roasted vegetables including kabucha squash, peppers, and cannellini beans. This was served with sticky rice, traditional poi, and breadfruit wrapped in banana leaves which was steamed and roasted.

The other entrée included kalua pork, sticky rice, long beans, poi, and the breadfruit in banana leaves.

While neither plate was a heaping mound of food, it was all well balanced and satisfying. I was never disappointed in any meal that Kalei and Lani delivered.

Dessert consisted of a small halved papaya filled with Haupia, which is a steamed coconut pudding, with fresh sliced strawberries sprinkled about. This was accompanied by a refreshing Thai iced coffee drink.

Serving this lovely meal – Kalei's more modern spin on traditional Hawaiian fare – was always a pleasure, and we passed all compliments back to the cook. He just grinned and stirred. Lani usually broke away for a few seconds here and there to give him a kiss on the cheek, and he grinned some more. "My wahine," he beamed, "so good to me." Lani would then wink slyly at me, both of us understanding that he was a wizard in the kitchen. It was probably one of the main reasons that the inn hadn't folded entirely over the last year. Guests loved Kalei's artistry at the stove. I knew though that if I ate this food each day I'd end up doubling my weight, so I often just made salads back at the cottage and dined with Davy after the guests were taken care of.

On this night though, The Dingo and The Whiner were quiet enough, shoveling food into their mouths and only uttering a few disagreeable remarks now and again.

"The soup is cold," The Dingo complained. I only smiled. The menu clearly stated it was a *chilled soup*.

"They really should put some meat in this vegetable dish," it was The Whiner's turn to complain. I smiled again. She should have ordered the meat entrée. Surprisingly, The Dingo shared a bit of her kalua pork with her mother. I was just thankful for small mercies.

The disagreeable duo sat fat and silent by dessert, uttering nothing either positive or negative, but The Dingo caught me as I was cleaning up the empty plates. "Will Davy be around after dinner? You know... for the drinking and music and all."

"I'm not sure, really. He's his own... man," I responded in a stage whisper.

Each evening that a dinner was served, Sam kept the bar open and played music over a fairly nice sound system that was attached to a simple mp3 player. Occasionally people would dance or sing along, almost karaoke style, but without the actual equipment or lyric prompts. It was a nice way for guests to unwind, it gave Sam a chance to earn some tips, and it provided an opportunity for Lani and Kalei to get the kitchen clean again. The noise of pots and pans being washed was hardly noticeable over the music.

78

Davy and I quite often enjoyed those post-dinner moments, but lately he'd been steering clear of all evening festivities, probably until he knew that The Dingo was back on the mainland.

Tonight though, I saw him peeking from behind a large palm tree, and I shot him a smile but kept working so that I wouldn't draw attention to him. He was hiding still, but most likely was going stir crazy. I saw him shimmer away and wondered if he was still there. He told me it was a lot of effort to shimmer in and out more than a few times, but I suspect that dire straits called for drastic measures.

"Did I just see him?" The Dingo squealed in my ear, and several guests turned to look our way.

"Um... Winston? Yeah, he's up on his perch over there." Think fast think fast!

She gave me a disdainful look as if to say "You're such a moron," but I gently led her away from the other guests.

Quietly, I tried to explain to her, "You do know that you, Winston, my cat Chester, and I are the only ones who can see him, right? Wouldn't it be better to keep this our secret?"

She flicked her hand at me as if to brush off my silly notions. "Oh, don't be ridiculous. It's a gift, and the world should know!" Then she frowned at me, a wicked glint in her eye. "I know what you're trying to do. You're trying to keep him all to yourself!"

"Um... no, I'm just trying to run a business and not look like I'm ten seconds away from a padded cell and a really ugly jacket that ties in the back." It took all my willpower to keep my hands behind my back. I sure hoped Davy had access to bail money though, just in case.

"Well, really, no one could possibly think we're crazy," she mocked me. I bit my tongue.

"Please," I begged, since we just had a few hours to go, "please give Davy the respect he deserves. Just for tonight and tomorrow. Okay?"

"What-EVER." She flounced away. I dropped my arms to my sides and sighed heavily. It was going to be a long and bumpy night. Seatbelts please, and trays in the upward position.

"Pssst," I heard from over my shoulder. "Psssssssssssssst!"

"Sprung a leak there? Better have that checked out," I grinned at Davy.

79

"Stoppit. And… thank you."

"Not that it will help, but I tried."

He gave me a quick hug and then ducked back into the palm trees, banana fronds, and other tropical foliage. I had a quick and disconcerting vision of spiders and other bugs and shivered before heading back inside to help wherever needed.

Sam was doing well. A few girls had gathered around his bar as he grinned shyly and fixed their drinks. Lani had finished bussing the dishes while I was practicing my best behavior with The Dingo, and back in the kitchen Kalai was still tackling dishes. I pushed my hair off my face and joined him. The three of us sang along to the more popular songs.

Someone must have requested the song, probably The Dingo, because I heard the first few piano notes of "Daydream Believer." I dried my hands and peeked into the bar/dining area. I could see the bushes wriggling and figured our resident ghost was doing the Davy Dance out there. The Dingo didn't seem to notice, for she was doing her own Davy Dance on the makeshift dance floor. I shook my head. *No one would believe any of this even if I tried to explain it.*

After the dishes were washed, the kitchen cleaned to health code standards, and everything put away, Lani fixed small take-home portions of the night's dinner for me and for Kalei and herself as well. We bade goodnight and I snuck back to the cottage to eat. Davy must have smelled the food, for he quickly appeared behind me.

We shared the vegetarian fare, had a glass of wine, and toasted to the fact that it was the last evening for The Dingo and The Whiner. "Been a long one," I groaned.

"Don't I know it."

After cleaning up from our lovely meal, I wandered back out to get Winston settled in our cottage for the night.

You're late! For a very important date.

I shushed the bird and patted my shoulder. He landed and rode there, bouncing a bit, as I carried his cage to our cottage. I tucked him in – or covered him up, as the case may be – and said goodnight. Winston said goodnight in his own, very personal manner.

He nani lua 'ole
Ku'u wehi o nâ lani
He kilohana 'oe
Na'u e pûlama mau
Hô'olu i ka poli e
Mehana i ke anu e.

Actually, it sounded much like bird-gibberish, but Bennie had translated it to me recently:

I can smile when it's raining
And touch the warmth of the sun
I hear children laughing
In this place that I love.

Oh what a night! But that's another song entirely.

TWENTY-ONE

Aloha `oe Dingo Dear

The words at the end of the song *Aloha `oe* loosely mean "until we meet again." I would pay money – good money – for that *not* to be the case with The Dingo. Really.

I awoke early. I mean REALLY early. Excited much? You bet! Bennie hadn't even arrived yet when I was making the coffee in the reception area, tidying up the sugar pot and cream pitcher, and replenishing the tea bags for the hot water we made available alongside the coffee.

Sam arrived first and rushed to my side. "They leave today, right, Miss Macca?" It seems I wasn't the only eager one.

I grinned, nodded, and patted his shoulder. He made a silent Rah-Rah motion and slipped off to do his chores.

"Alooooo-HA!" Bennie greeted me a few moments later. He too was grinning.

"Alooooo-HA!" I returned the sentiment and we slyly shared a thumbs-up gesture. He whistled ever so innocently as he opened up the computer, prepared the Dingo-Whiner party's final bill, and got out several pens, all lined up on the counter. It looked like the Presidential signing at an inauguration. Hell, this was better than any such an event.

I was singing a little homemade ditty in my head.

Oranges are green
Bananas are black
Dingoes are mean
Don't ever come back!

I even whistled a little as I wiped things down and swept up the leaves and debris that tend to gather in this setting where windows have no glass – only storm shutters that remain open – and where doors are rarely closed.

And then… I heard it. The clump, thump of a rollaway suitcase on the walkway. "Someone needs to get our other bags," the queen of tact brusquely stated as she rolled to a stop at the front desk.

"I'll do that!" I grabbed Sam and off we went. Our legs couldn't carry us as fast as we wanted, but we made do. We nearly knocked each other down trying to beat the other in getting the bags to the front desk fastest. Oh dear, Stanley. What, Ollie?

Sam and I crashed into each other a bit as we stacked the bags in the center of the floor. "Would you like help loading them into the car too?" Sam was one jump ahead of me. I shot him a big smile.

"Well, of course," she sneered. "I'm not doing it myself!" Ah, The Dingo was such a pleasure, she was.

Off we huffed again and stacked the suitcases by their car. We knew it was their car for several reasons. One, they had the license plate number on their registration card. Two, we always eagerly watched the parking area on the days they left us to sightsee. Three, did I mention how much we wanted them gone?

"One of us has to stay at the car with the bags," I huffed, clearly out of breath.

"Rock, paper, scissors?"

"Sorry Sam. I'll pull boss-rank for this one. You can stay." He laughed as I trotted back to the front desk. I wanted to witness them actually signing out and leaving, which they were in fact doing just as I got there.

"Bye," The Dingo said, apparently not wanting to extend any kind of friendliness – *still*, which was perfectly fine by me.

"I hope you'll visit us again soon." I smiled and inwardly kicked myself. *Why* did I *say* that? Yeah, and I wanted the plague and swine flu too. Or something.

"Jill," I heard Davy's velvety voice approaching. He reached out to shake her hand in both of his big mitts. "It was quite nice to meet you. I do hope we see you again."

How did he *do* that? He enchanted her again, just by being himself. I think. I didn't know whether to retch over his words to this bimbo who didn't deserve them or to jump into his arms and hug the stuffing out of him. So I just did what I usually do when I'm conflicted: nothing. I simply stood there, my jaw hanging open.

83

I had to give The Dingo credit though. She had some guts, or maybe it was just overconfidence. She wasn't that great-looking, and she had the personality of... well, a Dingo.

"Oh, never doubt that I'll be back, if you'll be here." She smirked and then planted a big one on him. Right on his lips. There was tongue involved too - could tell! Something bubbled up inside me. Could have just been indigestion... or vomit. Or, I was insanely jealous. Wait. What? Whoa, this was going to take some weeks – no, *years* of therapy.

Davy walked The Dingo and The Whiner out to their car, the latter keeping busy looking for keys in order to avoid having to watch her daughter talking to an empty space in the world. I watched Sam load the bags as The Whiner popped the trunk open. As soon as the last one was safely stowed, he dashed back to the inn to continue his work. He knew better than to expect another tip from them after receiving one on that first day. This pair hadn't tipped anyone else the entire duration of their stay. I know, because I asked my team.

From a safe spot behind a fruit tree of some sort – I really did need to learn my native foliage one of these days – I watched Davy help The Dingo into the car and say a final goodbye. I ducked away and ran back to the front desk, assuming a position as if I'd never left. I even whistled a merry tune and shuffled Bennie's neatly piled papers. They now looked like a team of hamsters had been playing cricket across the stacks. Bennie gave me a curious look, but Team Wally were beginning to understand their slightly weird but hopefully loveable boss. I shrugged and smiled at him as he shrugged his shoulders in return. Carrying an inventory list, he went off in search of Kalei as Davy rounded the bend of the octagonal hut.

"If she ever returns, I'm not here." He rubbed his face. "And now I must go rinse out my mouth. With antiseptic. Twice. No, three times. Maybe more." He wandered back toward the cottage, muttering and shaking his head. I snorted a little laugh and took a deep breath of Dingo-free air. I decided that I was due a treat, so I gave myself a "spa-day" in our cottage which included another coconut treatment for my hair while I soaked in a hot bubble bath. I loved my inn once again.

TWENTY-TWO

A Country Inn Is (Re) Born

One morning I took a different route from the pool area, not having had time until now to properly explore the area that was marked by a sign reading "Path to Cliffs." It began as a wooden track like the rest of the inn's trails, but soon merged with a gravel and shell-laden walkway that skirted the cliffs above the Pacific. It was peaceful and deserted in the early hours, and I smiled at the natural beauty surrounding me. I found an interesting bench made of carved stone. It was fairly large, perhaps eighteen to twenty feet long, with a gentle curve to it that fit it perfectly to the winding path. The backside of the bench, as well as the ends, was inlaid with natural volcanic rock.

As I drew closer I could see two small plaques mounted along the top.

In memory of my dear wife, Louise
Your loving husband, James

Next to that was another.

In memory of Louise and James
Together Forever

I sat down on the bench listening to the wind in the trees, the call of the birds over the sea, and the occasional rustle of leaves as geckos slithered by. I watched the clouds float by for what seemed like merely minutes, but when I checked my watch, I was shocked to see that an hour had passed!

I leaped to my feet to meet with Alex Baldwin who was scheduled to arrive at any minute. He was stopping in to check on us at the inn, and I arrived at the front desk just as he had asked Bennie to let me know he was there. He seemed genuinely pleased to see we were doing well and asked about all the changes I'd made and the ideas I'd formulated for both the near and the far futures. It was nice to talk to someone I knew I could truly trust with sensitive information. Whereas before I'd previously scoffed at attorney-client privilege (I'd been watching too much *Law & Order*), it had proven its significance in the last weeks.

We sat at one of the small café tables I'd decided to set up at the pool area. We were alone at that hour, it being prime sightseeing time, and Team Wally were busy with their tasks.

"Alex, I saw a lovely stone bench along the cliff path. Do you know anything about it?"

"Oh! The Whispering Bench!"

"Really?"

"Yes, the first owner had it made for the path but she passed on before she could see it installed. Her husband, Mr. Martinelli, dedicated it to her memory."

"I saw the lovely plaque, but who then added the other plaque?"

"That was your uncle's doing. A very nice gesture, don't you think?"

I swallowed hard. My Uncle Wally had always had such a warm heart, and I missed him terribly. Gathering myself again, I asked my next question, "Why is it called The Whispering Bench?"

He scooted his chair in to lean toward me to tell a tale that I sensed he'd told many times before, and of which he probably never tired.

"It's really quite remarkable," he began. "When you sit on one end and whisper, the sound is carried to the other side, and a person sitting on the opposite end is able to hear every word as clearly as if you were sitting side-by-side!"

I felt my heart swell. What a lovely feature! I could hardly wait to tell Davy about it. It was then I decided a new plaque would need to be installed.

"Who might I ask about making a plaque for my uncle? Do you have any recommendations?"

"Oh, what a sensational idea!" He looked in his day planner and provided me with the name of the gentleman who had done the previous plaques.

"Thank you so much, Alex."

"There is another, more important reason for my visit, Macca."
Alex shuffled through the papers in his soft-covered canvas briefcase.
I loved that particular aspect of island life, that everything was so
relaxed and casual. In the damp tropical weather, fine leather would
have required more maintenance. "Mr. Sikes has presented yet another
offer for the property," he continued.

Alex slid the paper toward me and my eyes bugged at the
amount, well in excess of a million. I found that my throat had dried
up as I tried to speak. I took a huge gulp of Kalei's iced tea and found
words again. "Is it really worth that much?"

"Technically speaking," he seemed embarrassed, "no."

"So, Mr. Sikes is being quite... persistent." My heart was racing.
I stared at the figure for several beats, blood rushing in my ears. I
thought of Uncle Wally, Davy, Team Wally, Chester, and of course
Winston. In other words, my family, both new and old. One question
kept popping up, and with it, a sense of unease. "What kind of a man
is Mr. Sikes?" I sat back and waited, toying with the straw in my iced
tea.

Alex took a few moments to choose the right words. Although
this was a very smart tactic, especially for an attorney, it had always
been one that annoyed me. Just spit it out, man!

"He's a very strongly opinionated man who knows what he wants
and will toil endlessly to obtain it."

I'm certain Alex hadn't meant to provide such a menacing
picture, but it didn't sound good to me. "At any length?"

Alex recovered quickly, realizing I'd taken his words quite
seriously. "Oh! No, no, he's a businessman, after all. He would never
jeopardize a business that had been in his family for three
generations."

"Do you represent Mr. Sikes, Alex?"

"I'm sorry. That's rather privileged information."

"Alex..." I softened my eyes and let my words trail off.

"No," he finally admitted. "He's no longer represented by our
firm."

"But he was."

"At one time, my partner represented him. They had a…
difference of opinion, and that's all I can say. I'm sorry." He really
did look genuinely sorry.

"It's okay Alex. That says a lot." I pushed the paper back to him.
"Wally's Wonderland, soon to be renamed, is not for sale, now or in
the future." I felt that renaming the inn suddenly became more
important in order to show our permanence. I'd have to give that some
further thought.

The smile on Alex's face told me I'd made the right decision.
"Excellent. I'll let Mr. Sikes' counsel know. And Macca, I'm very
pleased. Wally loved this place."

"I love it too. I feel him near me all the time."

Our eyes misted over for a moment, but both of us quickly
recovered. "And with that, I'll be on my way and leave you to your
work. The place looks wonderful, Macca. He would be so proud."

In an unusual show of affection, we hugged briefly before he
took his leave. I mentally added one more member to my family.

I sat a while longer contemplating the inn, its name, the future,
Alex's words, and only briefly, Mr. Sikes. "Tread carefully, luv."
Davy suddenly appeared in the chair that Alex had vacated, sipping
his own iced tea, another carefully knotted straw wrapper sticking out
of his pocket.

I nodded. "I will, and you'll be with me, right?"

"Every step of the way. Hey! That's a song – and the right
group!" He began to sing, and I giggled as he acted out the lyrics.

"Oh!" I jumped up and tugged on his hand, "Come with me and
see this beautiful bench!" I nearly dragged him to the cliff path and he
immediately took a seat at one end.

"A Whispering Bench, right? There's a lovely bench such as this
in Central Park!"

I sat at the opposite end of the bench from him and saw his lips
move. I gasped.

"I heard that! You said, 'Hello Macca. What's for dinner?'" I
pretended to smirk at him and his never-ending appetite before
responding to his whisper. "Fried geckos and seagull feathers."

The look on his face was priceless as he made a choking motion
around his neck.

Later that night, in the privacy of our cottage, I broached the subject of changing the name of the inn. "It's not a bed and breakfast, but it's not really a hotel or a resort either. It's more of a country inn, but Hale Haole sounds so crass."

"But Hale something Country Inn sounds pretty impressive."

"I want it to reflect the peace and harmony that you find here."

Davy looked through a pamphlet of Hawaiian words that he'd found in Uncle Wally's expansive bookcase. "What about Hale Malehuia, which means House of Peace?"

"I think there's already a bed and breakfast in the Kona area with that name."

"The swine!" He joked and went back to the pamphlet. "Oh, here's one! Hale Mele, which would mean House of Song or Poem?"

"Oh! Say it again!"

"Hale Mele."

"It sounds so… peaceful."

"It does, and it sounds so much like you." He winked.

I chuckled. "Why? I don't sing."

"No, you *are* a song."

Okay, I blushed. Deeply. And I was speechless, too. The room was quiet except for the sound of the gentle breeze blowing through the open window, but Davy soon broke the spell in a most perfect manner by jumping up and singing at the top of his lungs, "Consider Yourself" from *Oliver!* I had to laugh. No wonder so many women loved this man. Soon I joined him and we ended up singing and dancing in each other's arms, then falling onto the sofa in laughter. After the week of living dangerously with The Dingo and The Whiner on the premises, it was a lovely and much welcomed bit of celebration.

TWENTY-THREE

An Apple a Day...
Keeps the Doctor Busy

It was now well into the next week and I was feeling the lightness in the atmosphere after the previous week's misery. I bounced out of bed one morning, ready to welcome the world. I removed the draped cover from Winston's cage, already chattering good morning wishes to him. I froze though as I caught sight of the poor little guy as he huddled on the cage floor with his head down and his feathers quivering.

"Winston," I cooed, reaching inside the cage. "What's wrong, sweetheart?" His response was to ignore me at first and then snap at my hand as I reached out. This was far from normal Winston behavior! "BENNIE!" I screamed at the top of my lungs. Davy came running too, and he froze at the sight.

I ran to the reception building, still screaming Bennie's name and babbling about Winston. Bennie ran ahead of me back to the cottage and knelt at the cage.

Together we assessed Winston's behavior. Bennie dug through the bird's food dish but couldn't see anything obvious. Grabbing plastic containers from the kitchen, we packaged up both the food and the water, and then together we put Winston inside Chester's carrier. Carrying the precious cargo to the car, I settled Winston safely on the floor while Bennie tucked the food samples behind me. Davy jumped into the passenger seat of the car and braced the pet tote between his feet as I folded myself into the driver's side. We headed to Dr. Josh's office in town, using the GPS to locate it while Bennie called ahead for us.

Dr. Josh was a tall, fit, and very attractive man in his early thirties. He looked somewhat like an Asian Mark-Paul Gosselaar, from the television show *NYPD Blue*. I hastily introduced myself to Dr. Josh and thrust Winston's carrier at him. "Please help him! Quickly! I know something is terribly wrong!"

We went into one of the private rooms and he coaxed Winston out of the carrier. A full examination of the bird only brought more questions.

"There are sounds of digestive distress," Dr. Josh mumbled as he continued to carefully study poor Winston. The veterinary technician came in and retrieved the food and water samples we'd brought.

"What made you think to bring this?" Dr. Josh looked at me curiously.

I chewed on my lower lip. "Bennie did it. We had a suspicious death at the inn recently, and we're probably paranoid, but..." I left off, unable to find any other words to speak. What an atrocious week this had become.

"Why don't you have a seat and let me take Winston in the back. We'll be able to assess him more properly and perhaps take an x-ray."

"Whatever it takes, please!"

He nodded and left the room. I was barely holding it together. First Louis... now this. I didn't even want to think any further than that. Davy shimmered before me, then sat holding my hand and rubbing my fingers with his thumb.

"He'll be fine."

"But how do you know that?" I was whispering, hoping no one could hear me talking to what would appear to be the wall.

"I don't. I'm just thinking positively. Extremely positively." I saw him swallow hard as well.

It seemed like hours before Dr. Josh returned. "Is someone feeding him apple seeds? We found them in his feed."

"I... I have no idea! I don't know what he eats, only that Ming gets it from a package of parrot food. I'll call and find out." While I put in the call to Bennie, Dr. Josh left the room to check further on Winston. When I asked Bennie about apple seeds he went nearly ballistic!

"Apple seeds are toxic to many animals, including Winston! There are traces of cyanide contained in them!" Bennie was yelling to Ming, and I could hear most of their conversation. She was very upset as well, knowing full well since she first began work there that apples were among many foods that she had to keep away from Winston. "The food bag!" Bennie yelled and I could only assume they were

91

checking the ingredients list. After quite some time he confirmed to me that there was no mention of any apple ingredients.

Dr. Josh returned just then. "Should we bring the feed bag in for you too?" I asked him.

He nodded and then added, "We'll keep Winston overnight and try to flush it from him – gently of course. Call us tomorrow morning and we'll let you know how he's doing. Meanwhile, bring us all of his food items – quickly – for testing. In light of what's gone on at your inn, I'll also be calling the police."

"Oh my god," I whispered, feeling the tears begin. "Would someone really do all of this? I mean – try to kill Winston? And poor Louis…" I trailed off again, shaking my head in disbelief. This sort of thing only happened in big city life, I thought. Dr. Josh sat beside me and patted my back.

"We'll take care of him. I promise."

"Thank you. Thank you so much. Mahalo."

He walked me to the door, his arm still around my shoulders. I glanced to my side. Davy's face was dark with anger. I hadn't progressed to that point yet. I was still in shock.

We were halfway home before either of us spoke.

"Who could have done such a dreadful thing?" he demanded, gritting his teeth. "And," he continued, "did he *have* to put his arm around you like that?"

I bit my lip, not wanting to even discuss any of this, and especially not Davy's sudden jealousy.

At the inn, I grabbed the feed bag and Winston's little packet of treats and headed back out to deliver it to Dr. Josh. It was going to be a long evening.

That night, Davy and I sat together on the sofa with the television on, but neither of us was watching, and once again we held onto each other, our fingers laced so tightly together. Deep in thought, he fidgeted with my fingers using his free hand. I'd had a good cry on the way home and was exhausted, too tired to even stand up and retire for the night.

I must have fallen asleep, for I awoke with a start, and the cottage was dark around me. I was sort of slouched against Davy's chest, his

92

arm around me. Peering up at his face I could see that he was wide awake, but with that same angry darkness across his features.

For a few moments I enjoyed the little bit of cuddle, but then I pushed up to a sitting position; our eyes never left each other's gazes.

"You're upset," I began cautiously, "but I do believe that you're right that Winston will be okay."

He sighed and looked away. "Yes, but I'm worried about what's really going on here." He was silent then. I took his hand and caressed it gently with my thumb as he had done with me; it was comforting to me, and hopefully to him as well. He turned back to me with a forced smile on his lips. The darkness lifted just enough to see his old expression of content. I forced a smile, but the air was electrified and we were unable to drive away the intensity of the past days, with Louis' murder and Winston's sudden illness.

Quietly, I voiced the thoughts that had just materialized before me. "I think I just figured out why you're here."

The corners of his mouth turned up, but not in a smile of happiness. He tried to brush it off. "I told you, I'm here to help you get your life together."

"Right," I said quietly, my gaze dropping away. After several minutes of uncomfortable silence, I rose from the sofa and Davy's arms. "I'm going to get some sleep before it's time to call Dr. Josh again."

He simply blinked and nodded. I turned and headed for bed, knowing in my heart just a little more each day that Davy had indeed been sent to protect me. Whether it was emotional or physical protection, I was convinced that was it. I felt warmed and comforted and was able to get several hours of sleep.

TWENTY-FOUR

Dulled Feathers and Dark Hours

Some people treat animals as objects, and some treat them as family. Frankly, I was always disgusted by those that fell in the former category. All creatures are special, and my particular creatures were my family, right alongside the two legged creatures. Skin, fur, feathers, whatever – it made no difference.

When I called Dr. Josh that morning, he had no news for me. Winston was still in very bad shape. He suggested I call back in the afternoon. I flopped down beside Davy on the sofa and cried while he held me. I hated crying, but sometimes it was just the only outlet. The frustration and helplessness were overwhelming. Instead of feeling better afterward, I felt drained of all energy. I allowed myself the luxury of closing my eyes and sleeping again against Davy's chest, in a déjà vu sort of way. I did feel him pull the lightweight shawl over both of us, the shawl my Aunt Fran had knitted many years ago, and this was especially comforting.

But dreams can sometimes be the farthest from comfort. In my sleep, I chased a vicious rat away from Winston's cage only to be lifted up into the air in the talons of an eagle who then dropped me in the middle of the Pacific Ocean, but a handsome merman caught me in the depths of the deep blue, pulled me to the surface, and deposited me upon the beach. "Don't go," I begged him, but he only smiled and slipped back into the ocean. I awoke bathed in seawater, or so I thought. Upon catching my breath, I realized it was only sweat. Davy's arm tightened around me. I looked up at the strong curve of his jaw and smiled. Snuggling back down in the crook of his arm and the comfort of his chest, I slept again. This time it was peaceful and there were no more disturbing dreams.

The phone call that afternoon did nothing to lighten my burden, however. There had been no discernible change in our Winston. I was instructed to call back the following afternoon. This seemed like a lifetime away.

94

The next day arrived despite my exhaustion. Dialing the phone in the late afternoon was like moving in molten lava. My body felt as heavy as my mind, like pushing through sludge.

"Dr. Josh? It's Macca. Macca Liberty."

"Macca! Hello! I have someone here who wants to say hello to you!" I heard him talking quietly with someone but couldn't make out the words.

"Pretty bird. Love my Miss. Love my Miss Macca."

"Winston!" I started to cry, and Davy was quickly by my side, listening in on the telephone, his arm wrapped tightly around me.

"Never give in – never, never, never."

We couldn't help but chuckle and then cry happy tears. He was such a tough old bird. "Come home soon, Winston!"

Dr. Josh then told me that Winston was on the mend. He would require close monitoring for the next few weeks, perhaps even months, but if I treated his poisoning properly, he could very well live another twenty-something years or more. I had a momentary vision of a crotchety old Winston bossing us around and was overjoyed at the thought.

"When can I bring him home?"

"A few days perhaps, but if you would like to visit him I'm sure he'd be very happy!"

"Tell him YES! I'll come today. We all miss him so. The inn is so quiet – too quiet."

Hanging up the phone, I gazed at Davy through tear-filled eyes. He grabbed my face and planted a firm but gentle kiss on my lips. "Let's go see him," he choked out the words. I was a bit dazed by his kiss, but still my priority was Winston. I ran out to spread the word via Bennie, who was so excited to hear the news! He immediately began planning a proper homecoming for the bird, no matter when that event might occur.

Davy and I folded ourselves into the car-scooter-skateboard-skate. Yes, I'd decided to call it that again. While Winston was so seriously ill, I felt it was disrespectful, but now? It was on again. Davy sat in the passenger side of the car-scooter-skateboard-skate and off we zoomed to see the little feathered beast.

95

I was taken to the back area of the vet's office, with Davy filing in silently behind me, and saw… immediately… Winston holding court in the back office. He sat on a makeshift perch while Dr. Josh examined an injured guinea pig, vet techs drew blood from a tiger-striped cat, and another vet tech changed an IV on a large and docile Labrador dog.

"Miss Macca is in da house!"

"Hello Winston." I grinned and rushed toward him to give him our customary snuggles. He nuzzled my hair with his beak while I stroked his breast feathers with my fingers. "I have missed you so much," I cooed.

Davy gave him nose bumps and stroked his back feathers. "Miss you big guy. Needing you home soon, okay?"

"I know Dr. Josh and his pretty techs are giving you lots of healthy attention, right?" I had no idea why the word "pretty" snuck in there. I blushed and heard Davy snicker.

"Cheeky jealous li'l girl," he whispered. This caused confusion on my part. What the hell? Was he right? And… why? I was a mess of mixed emotions these days, but I pushed those thoughts back and concentrated on our beautiful grey feathered boy. I tickled his red tail feathers until he ruffled them and ducked his head before nuzzling me with a kiss on my cheek.

"I'm a sick li'l birdie." He was obviously mimicking the voices he'd heard around him the last day, I was sure, but also, he knew how to milk it for all it was worth. I only found it even more endearing.

"If you were bigger, I'd pick you up and hug you SO hard!"

He bobbed his head in response and then snuggled against me. I'd never had a bird before, never *knew* a bird, but it felt like Winston and I had known each other for an eternity. Thank you, Uncle Wally. Again.

The drive home was a mixture of happiness and sadness. Sad because Winston still wasn't well enough to come home, but happiness because he'd made it through the worst and would recover. Back at the inn, we planned a bird-style homecoming party for that one day when he'd be able to return to us. He'd been our mascot for so long that the inn felt particularly deserted without him.

96

We were all filled with contentment. It had only been a couple of days since we discovered Winston was ill, but they had been such long days – longer than I'd ever experienced. Winston was my first sick baby. Ever. It was then I realized that I had lived a ridiculously sheltered life. Is this why my spectral parents thought I needed intervention? That I had been too wrapped in cotton wool to handle these daily crises?

On the other hand, could the poisoning of a beloved pet actually be considered a daily crisis? And what kind of person could do such an awful thing? These thoughts haunted me.

Sitting on the sofa with Davy listening to soothing jazz on Uncle Wally's CD player, we discussed anything and everything *but* these disturbing subjects. We laughed and joked with each other as well. A healing process. We even made hot cocoa, despite the warm evening temperatures.

"There is something remarkably soothing about five mini-marshmallows struggling to stay afloat atop a frothing mug of hot chocolate." He blew across the top of his mug to cool the liquid.

"Have you always been this nice," I smiled and asked him, watching him closely.

He seemed to laugh, a nervous sound actually. "I've had my moments. There were times… many times, when I was very *not* nice." His eyes had a faraway look about them, and he turned his head to gaze out the window.

I let the silence hang for a beat or two until he sharply turned back to look at me. "Not intentionally though. I was just quite… mixed up, and perhaps a little too… indulged in my youth."

"But don't we all have moments of selfishness and consider ourselves as 'not nice' at times?"

"Perhaps, but I felt it was terribly unacceptable. I'd been given so much in my life. I was so incredibly fortunate – lucky. I'm still trying to pay it all back." He gave a sad smile and rubbed my hand with his thumb. "I led a charmed life in some ways."

"And tragic in others."

He cocked his head and studied my face. "I wouldn't say that."

I shrugged. I knew a bit about his childhood, his mother dying when he was young, his leaving home shortly after to learn to be a jockey, his father dying several years later. I knew these parts of his life because they were similar to mine. The difference was that I had Uncle Wally and Aunt Fran.

We eyed each other for a while, silent communication zipping between us. "Point taken," he conceded, "but I've tried not to think of it that way."

"Me too, yet it pops up in my thoughts now and again."

He nodded and pulled me close with one arm, still holding his mug in the other, and let out a long sigh. "Do you ever wonder if you're damaged goods?"

Wow, deep question, but I had the answer because I'd considered it in the past. "Yes, but I try not to think of that either."

He chuckled and squeezed me tighter. We sipped our cocoa and enjoyed the music and each other's company.

Homing... Parrot

Dr. Josh's findings regarding Winston's feed and water were disturbing. Not only were there apple seeds in the feed that had been in the bird's dish, but also in the top quarter of the feed bag itself.

"It's as if someone put them in the bag, tried to mix them up, and then stopped before they could be thoroughly integrated into the entire bag," Dr. Josh shook his head in disbelief as he delivered this news to me. "If they had succeeded, there is a good chance the symptoms wouldn't have exhibited so quickly, and he might have just died a lingering and painful death." I stood there open-mouthed. I knew Davy was beside me, listening, but I couldn't bring myself to look at him. Who could do such a thing to this innocent creature, I asked myself once again.

Dr. Josh suggested ways we could secure the feed bag and monitor Winston's dishes. "We're all ready to do whatever it takes to keep him safe," I promised, "and I thank you for all you've done."

Dr. Josh had such kind and sympathetic eyes, which is probably why he left us with his receptionist so that she could deliver the bad news in the way of a bill for services rendered. I gulped and grabbed the desk in front of me. This would pretty much eat up all of our profits so far, but we loved our Winston. I pulled out my battered credit card and slid it across to have it topped off. No room for errors now. We just had to succeed. I considered putting a black armband across the piece of plastic, but I figured it was pointless. The old quote, "It's dead, Jim," came immediately to mind, but our Winston was back.

At last we were on our way home. Davy was sitting beside me in the passenger seat with Chester's carrier on his lap. The zipper was open and he was stroking and cooing at our big boy Winston.

Home, home on the range

"We'll be home soon," he whispered at the little rascal that we had missed so much.

Wanna fly! Want.To.Fly!
Fly like an eagle!

99

"Wrong group, Winston!" Davy was shaking his finger at the bird. "Sing… Oh I could hide, 'neath the wings, of the bluebird as she sings…"

Chuckling, I reached across and presented my finger for Winston to nudge. He did so, almost as if on cue.

Sleepy Jean, Sleepy Jean

His intelligence was a little spooky, and when I turned then to smile at him, he cocked his head so that one beady little eye was looking directly at me.

"Heh," was all I could come up with. Such a conversationalist I was.

As we neared the inn, Winston became agitated.

Wanna fly wanna fly wanna fly NOW!

"Alright, alright. Hold on there!" Davy maneuvered the carrier once we were in the parking lot and unzipped it. Winston trotted out a few feet, ruffled his feathers, stretched his wings, and launched. He soared over our heads, arching a wing now and then to bank and curve around us. Awestruck at the beauty of his flight, I trotted down the steps without ever taking my eyes off of him completely. I grappled with the banister but found my way to the deck where his open cage and his freestanding perch awaited. Winston took several more laps, enough that Davy had a chance to catch up with me. We stood there, dumbfounded but smiling, our necks craned and our eyes keen on our little friend as he soared above. At times he was just a speck in the azure sky, but then he'd swoop down and skim us with his feathers before ascending to great heights again. I shivered in excitement and felt Davy's arm go around me and pull us close together. I could see he was reacting similarly, a huge grin splashed across his face.

After several high-altitude excursions, Winston swooped down again and I patted my shoulder. He landed ever so lightly upon it and nuzzled my ear. His chest was heaving with the exertion, but I think a large part of it was the thrill of the voyage.

"Good boy, pretty bird," I whispered against his feathers, stroking his wings. I believe both Davy and I had tears in our eyes. I could tell he wanted to comfort me, but it was I who needed to comfort him. We were at an impasse and it took the ever comical Winston to break the spell.

Honnnnney I'm hommmmmmme

Bennie, Sam, Kalei, and Lani rushed out to greet our feathered sweetheart. Above the front desk was a small banner that read, "Welcome home little buddy, Winston!" Ming and Alberto joined us, and Team Wally took turns welcoming our mascot personally and reading the banner to him. My battered credit card was temporarily forgotten. Every cent had been worth it to have our Winston back.

TWENTY-SIX

A Hurricane by Any Other Name… Is Still a Hurricane

We began to get reports of a tropical storm approaching the islands. Never having lived through such a storm, I was a bit apprehensive. I did extensive research on how to provide for guests during hurricanes since forecasters claimed that this storm was indeed picking up speed. By the time it hit land here on the Big Island, it would be categorized as a hurricane. I didn't care what they named it; I just wanted it to go away.

Fortunately, Team Wally were old hands at this, and they guided me along the way. We made sure that all the shutters in the cottages, the dining area, and the reception area buildings were in working order and easy to access. Any necessary repairs were made by Alberto. We prepared to move all outside furniture to the inside protected areas. The generator was tested and all propane connections were secured. An extra supply of bottled water was brought in and extra batteries were stocked. Each cottage had handheld flashlights along with battery operated lanterns. First aid kits were replenished and placed in each cottage while larger first aid kits were placed in the communal buildings.

Kalei and Lani made sure that food was stocked that would not require much preparation but would be tasty and healthy enough. There was an almost comical debate about whether Spam fell into the category of healthy. After much laughter, I gave in to their traditions, but the brief moments of levity certainly eased the tension. However, all these additional safety measures were hastening the depletion of our funds. I added money worries to my weather worries.

Davy made himself quite scarce during some of these preparations, often returning late, his face darkened with a frown. When I asked what he'd been doing each day, his responses were vague, or he would simply change the subject. All this served to add yet another layer of tension.

102

Several bookings were canceled ahead of the impending storm. Bennie assured me this was normal. Also, if guests were not able to leave because of the weather, they could extend their trip at the same rates they had been paying. Additionally, if guests were unable to pay at that time, we remained open to negotiations to extend payments over a period of time. I was told that this was pretty much the standard practice in the Hawaiian Islands. Even though this courtesy often created financial hardship for the smaller inns like ours, Hawaiian culture prided itself on extending good will, and I was determined to do the same.

The group of guests we happened to have at the time were a jovial bunch who didn't seem to be too worried about an impending hurricane. Several claimed they'd "been there, done that." I was hoping they would hold my hand through this since it was my first time.

The winds picked up during the night and the power went out. Everything had been shuttered up, battened down, and prepped. Employees who didn't need to go home stayed on, for it would be safer than driving in these conditions. Some of the guests were playing marathon card games and board games in the dining hall, each table lit by a battery operated lantern.

I huddled in my cottage with Davy for I was not as laid back as the rest of them yet. Every time there was an increase in noise outside, I flinched; a couple of times I even yelped. We sat by the light of a lantern reading. Uncle Wally had quite the library, and we were making it our goal to explore every book and magazine.

I was shamed by Winston, another old hand at storms.

Don't be scared. Don't be scared. It's just wind. Who farted?

Of course I never said he was tactful, but he did keep us laughing.

Chester seemed determined to sleep through the entire event. Davy lounged back on the sofa, his arms stretched across the back, legs upon the coffee table. But then again, what did he care? He was already on "the other side" and I reminded him of that whenever he jokingly chided me. Poking him in the ribs was becoming a habit, and it never failed to make him giggle. I don't know if the guy ever did

103

grow up in his day. He was like an adult-sized kid. Well, almost adult-sized.

"I've lived through many earthquakes, but this is far different!" I admit that I sounded a little whiny.

"Earthquakes are like having your teeth knocked out with a single punch," Davy laughed, "and hurricanes are like root canals... long and painful."

I stared at him for a moment and then burst out laughing. He'd nailed it!

When morning came, I waited for a lull in the wind before scurrying to the dining hall for two cups of hot tea and then scurrying right back. We were exhausted. I had kept us both up most of the night with my anxiety. Davy was rubbing his sleepy face when I set the tea in front of him, pushing milk and sugar to within his reach. He fixed up his cup with the appropriate amounts of each and took a sip.

"If tea were liquor, I'd be an alcoholic," he muttered under his breath.

"I'd risk it, myself," I responded. We sat in a companionable silence, letting the liquid gold wake us up.

Eventually we made our way into the communal dining hall. The path was littered with fallen greenery along with a bit of trash here and there. I picked up whatever I could hold until Davy placed his hand on my arm. "You're basically shoveling the driveway while it's still snowing. I mean... really?"

I grinned and nodded but held onto what I'd captured already, tossing it into the main garbage bin behind the kitchen.

There were guests sleeping soundly on the floor in the dining area, a pillow and light blanket their only bedding. Some of the hard core gamers were still playing poker, their eyes red rimmed but their laughter still echoing against the walls. It really was a happy sight, in a rather peculiar sort of way!

I sat with the bleary-eyed staff and munched on yogurt and fruit with them, along with more tea, of course, and when that didn't work, I switched to the more heavily caffeinated Kona coffee. I even saw Davy sneak a cup and hide in the kitchen to drink it. I silently thanked him for that, although I do believe that every person in that room was

104

so weary that the sight of a cup moving along on its own in the air wouldn't have surprised anyone.

I found an excuse to wander into the kitchen to find Davy. He was leaning against the counter, the cup of Kona to his lips when he saw me in the doorway.

"Babe." He grinned.

I smiled and leaned beside him and motioned to the poker playing guests. "I think most of them are pretty smashed."

"As they should be. I didn't want to take a chance on floaty things being seen. Your Dingo did enough damage while she was here."

"I could have gone all week without being reminded of her, you know. And she's not my Dingo. She's yours."

He grinned. "Jealous of her flashy send-off?"

"Enormously so."

He seemed surprised. "Really?"

I blushed. "Really, and I'm not proud of it."

His shoulders shook with laughter, and I heard the slightly raspy chuckle deep in his throat. "Good to know," he snickered and turned back to his coffee.

"Hmph," I said under my breath, not straying from my spot as we leaned against the counter together. I think we were pretending to be lost in our coffees.

"Miss Macca!" someone called from the other room, and I went off to see what was happening. As I turned the corner, I caught Davy looking after me, a grin still on his face.

Oh, dear therapist, where art thou? I will be in need of thy services... soon.

TWENTY-SEVEN

The Cleanup...
or Time to Snoop

"After the storm." How many times had I heard that on news reports but never thought much of it? "After the earthquake," sure, I was used to that, but "after the storm" was different. We hadn't any remarkable damage except in the landscaping. We pitched in to help Alberto clean things up and then branched out to check on neighboring residents and businesses. Our little area seemed to have escaped any severe damage.

Winston was just happy to have his bit of freedom once again and flitted from perch to trees to roofs to... well, you get the idea. He was in constant motion it seemed.

It then occurred to me that I could use this time for some valuable snooping. I wasn't a snoop by nature, but I had a strong desire to become one on a certain neighboring property.

"I'm going to make sure our good friend Mr. Sikes hasn't sustained any major damage," I casually mentioned to Davy while downing a cup of tea in the cottage. "Wanna come?"

"I really don't think this is a good idea, Babe. I think he's... dangerous."

Sighing, I set the mug down harder than I intended. "Well, I'm going. Come with me or stay here; it's your choice."

His face darkened. "I really mean it, darlin'. I don't think you should go there."

I stared him down and then turned on my heel. My keys jingled as I marched towards the car-scooter-skateboard-skate. Imagine my surprise when I arrived and saw Davy already perched in the passenger seat, looking smug and so very pleased with himself. I was chuckling as I jumped in and we peeled out, heading up the road a piece.

Royal Aina (meaning homeland) Resort was only a mile or so away from our place, as the crow flies, but driving was another issue. There was one main road and then several smaller roads we had to travel, dodging fallen palm fronds and other vegetation. A couple of

106

times we actually stopped and moved debris out of the way. Being neighborly was the Hawaiian way of life, and it felt quite natural to me, unlike living in Los Angeles where people were in their own little worlds, permanently hooked up to iPods, iPads, and phones.

Rounding the last bend in the road, a broad expanse of dark wood and rough stone loomed ahead with a fairly large sign declaring we had arrived. It did indeed seem very welcoming. Why did I think it would be anything but? I let out my breath in a whoosh.

"This place is huge! I wouldn't even try to compete with this!"

"No, but... stay safe, Babe."

We cautiously parked and wandered through the grounds. There were a few people out and about – tourists, seemingly without care, sipping drinks by the huge pool area as if no hurricane had ever ravaged the area, and various workers cleaning up storm debris. I could tell they were employees by the brown uniforms they sported.

"Remind me to never require uniforms, or at least not uniforms that make people become invisible to guests."

"Don't worry. I'd hog-tie you and hide you away if you tried."

We grinned at each others and pressed on. The reception area was massive, with the center attraction being a enormous tiki statue. I grimaced slightly and gave it wide berth. There was such a sense of hustle and bustle here. At first I thought I was jealous, but the feeling was fleeting for I soon realized that our little inn had a much more relaxing atmosphere. We wandered around, peeking into community areas, getting a glimpse of a room here and there as the maids did their work. It was quite impressive and obviously successful as well. The pool area had an extraordinary sunken bar at one end with a swim-up extension attached.

"Wow," I said several times under my breath. It was then that I noticed a tall bald man leaning against a pillar and watching me quite intently. He was wearing dark glasses, a brown Hawaiian print shirt, and khaki slacks. I smiled briefly but kept surveying the grounds so that I wouldn't allow myself to stare back at him, and then it dawned on me. Could this be the notorious Mr. Sikes? I felt a sudden chill. He was one scary-looking dude. *Nonsense*, I chided myself. *Grow up, Macca.*

107

Taking a seat at the bar next to several bikini-clad girls, I felt truly overdressed and outclassed. I noted Davy taking in every detail of the scenery, and I don't mean the vegetation or the décor. I subtly poked him in the ribs as he stood behind me at the bar. He was completely distracted by the sunbathing beauties. I briefly wondered if only women stayed at this place until I spied a few hunky types in board shorts in the pool.

When the bartender approached, I ordered an iced tea. Mr. Baldy was suddenly at my side, leaning just a tad too close for comfort. He knocked on the bar.

"Ms. Liberty's drinks are on the house, Mano."

"Yes Sir," the man with the name tag "Mano" bowed and presented me with a beautiful drink with a fruit decoration.

"Thank you." I smiled at both of them and took a sip. I was relieved to find that although it was pretty, it was rather tasteless; in that respect, Kalei had nothing to fear in the way of competition.

"Gilbert Sikes," Mr. Baldy said as he extended his hand in a goodwill gesture. I shook it firmly, wondering why it was so soft and dry. Did he never have to do any work around the resort? How nice for him. I smacked my inner sarcastic bitch away and smiled again at Mr. Sikes.

"Macca Liberty," an inane response, considering he somehow already knew who I was. "I'm sorry for your loss." It seemed mechanical, for I saw no actual sorrow in his eyes. "Your uncle was well respected in the community."

"Thank you." I felt Davy's hand on my lower back and relaxed a little. He had that remarkable ability to calm me with just a touch.

"Is there anything in particular you were looking for?"

I frowned briefly, having forgotten for just a moment my fabricated excuse for being there. Recovering quickly, I said, "Actually, we cleaned up at our place and have reached out to other neighbors in need. I just came to see how you had fared in the storm, but I see you're doing well."

"Yes, the staff has been cleaning up. We're just fine." No warmth in his eyes. I felt a chill again.

I smiled and nodded, suddenly eager to leave. I sucked up the last of my iced tea. "I received your latest offer and I apologize, but the inn isn't for sale, so I'm afraid you're wasting your time." I really did try to say it nicely. Really.

"Everyone has a price, Miss Liberty." He smirked; I swear he smirked. "I'll discover yours."

He straightened up from leaning on the bar, and I stepped away from my barstool. "Suit yourself," I said, this time not the least bit nicely. "And now I'll be going. There may be others who could use some assistance."

"How very… neighborly of you." He said it with such obvious disgust. I felt compelled to get out of such a toxic environment as quickly as I could.

"I'll be going then. Thank you for the drink."

"Anytime. Our doors are always open."

He watched me walk away. I know because I kept giving a quick look over my shoulder. As he began to walk in the opposite direction, Davy casually stuck his leg out and tripped him. My hand flew to my mouth as I watched Mr. Sikes recover his steps and whirl around to see whatever had the nerve to get in his way. He never gave me a second glance.

Davy was already waiting in the car-scooter-skateboard-skate when I got there. How *did* he keep *doing* that? When I folded myself in beside him and locked the doors, I let out a huge whoosh of breath.

"Oh my god, that guy is… is…"

"He's a bad man, Babe. Please stay away from him. Please?"

"Oh I will. I definitely will." I shuddered and he patted my thigh as I backed out of the parking lot and took us home. I was no longer feeling up to visiting neighbors, even though I doubted that any of them were as disagreeable as Mr. Sikes.

TWENTY-EIGHT

Early Morning Blues and Greens

Quite early the next morning, I brewed our own pot of Kona in the cottage and took a mug of it out to the private deck on the back side of our space. It faced the tops of tropical trees and vegetation, with the sea on the horizon beyond. The air was cooler than before the storm, with stronger breezes than usual. I sat with my feet on the railing, sipping the warm beverage. The coffee was not as good as what Bennie made, but it still warmed me as I was underdressed in my usual shorts and tank top. The door behind me opened and Winston fluttered out, alighting on the railing.

Oh what a beautiful morrrrrrning. Oh what a beautiful daaaaaaaaaaaaaaay.

"Wrong show, bird," Davy playfully reprimanded him and took a seat beside me. He had helped himself to a mug of the coffee I'd made as well and had taken several sips, testing its heat. I couldn't help but notice though that he wrinkled his nose a bit at first taste.

"Are you alright this morning?" he gently asked me. I was lost in a brief thought – reminding myself to brew a pot of tea for him each morning as well – and almost missed his question. I froze for a moment and performed a sort of mental rewind before I was able to respond.

"Yeah. Mr. Sikes gives me the creeps though."

"As well he should. Please, and I cannot stress this enough… stay away from him. For me?"

"You have my word," I promised and took a deep relaxing breath, watching the ocean in the distance. "I love it here. I love the green of the trees and the foliage against the dark blue of the sea, and the bright blue of the sky. It's breathtaking… every single day."

"It *is* a really beautiful place to live." He rolled his head to the side and looked at me from under heavy brows and dark lashes. "Despite your tragedies, you are one very lucky girl." He pronounced it "gehl" and my heart fluttered. It's amusing how so many women fall for that lovely British accent, especially when it's attached to a guy as adorable as Davy.

110

"I know, but luck can be a double-edged sword I suppose." I sipped the last of my coffee and got up to get the day rolling.

Winston fluttered to my shoulder, hitching a ride. I moved his cage and perch back out to the main building's front deck. We were still taking no chances with our little buddy. He flapped his wings a few times and landed on his stand once I'd properly positioned it. I gave his chest a few little strokes, and he bobbed his head at me.

Looking at the guest register, I saw Bennie had made a notation for a small family who were scheduled to arrive in the afternoon.

"Good morning, Miss Macca," Bennie greeted me in a lively manner as he arrived for the day. He really was a gem I thought to myself.

"Good morning, Bennie!" I moved aside and let him put his backpack behind the counter. "It's so surprising how quickly the weather sprang back after that storm!"

"The rain renews us, Miss Macca," he said with a grin. Such simple words, but they gave me something to think about as I went about my tasks.

I watched as Bennie fixed the first pots of Kona for the morning. When he reached for a small tin decorated with hand-painted plumerias, I put a hand on his arm to pause his actions. "What is that?" I felt excitement at his impending response. Could this tin contain the magic that separated Bennie's Kona from all others?

He smiled and spoke as he took a pinch from the tin and sprinkled it on the freshly ground coffee beans. "This is my mom's secret to what she considers perfect Kona. She has never liked the bitterness, so she adds a pinch of cinnamon, a pinch of nutmeg, and one cocoa nib." He showed me the contents of the tin. I sniffed gently and salivated. It was like a blast from childhood – like the smell of baked goods from a grandmother's kitchen.

"Bennie, your mother is my hero." I sighed in pleasure as I sipped the finished product.

"Mine too." He grinned as he cleaned up the area before continuing with his other opening tasks.

I was nearby when our latest guests arrived, and I was thrilled to greet the Drake family. I guessed Adam and Laura to be in their early

111

thirties. Their son and daughter, fraternal twins, very boldly introduced themselves as Billy and Emily, both 8 years old.

"It's wonderful to meet you all." I shook the children's hands first, then their parents. There was a lot of luggage for the four of them, but it was a week's worth, and children do seem to go through clothing faster than adults. Together, Bennie and I took up all the bags and showed the family to the first cottage, which happened to be the largest. It even had a small kitchenette much like my own. This was ideal for families with young kids because milk and a peanut butter and jelly sandwich were never far from reach. The kids ran for their own room as Bennie pointed them to it, claiming their respective beds. We left the family on their own then to get unpacked and settled in.

Within the next hour though, the kids had persuaded their travel-weary parents for a swim in the pool. Those kids could swim like fishes! I took a seat nearby to watch them dive, cannonball, and play Marco Polo. Then they stunned me with races, led by their parents: backstroke, freestyle, and breaststroke, ending with what seemed like a lesson in the butterfly stroke. I cheered them on from the sidelines.

"They've been water babies since the age of six months," Laura explained. "We just can't keep them out of the water," she ended with a light laugh.

"They are on the peewee swim team at our local YMCA," Adam joined in. The parental pride was strong and very obvious.

"Well, they certainly surprised me!" I got very wet high-fives when the kids emerged, dripping. "Well done, both of you!"

Later that afternoon Davy and I were sitting on our private deck again, this time sipping Kalei's iced tea. Winston was sitting on my shoulder, and Davy was knotting another straw wrapper. I looked at him questioningly, but he smiled and shook his head. I guessed he'd tell me in due time.

He suddenly leaned over and exclaimed, "I forgot to show you! Look what I learned to do!" He pulled his boots off and wiggled his bare toes. I laughed so hard while he grinned up at me. "Now if I could find some swim trunks, I'd have it made!"

"I'm sure there are some men's swim clothes somewhere."

"I'll look around later."

112

It was then we heard voices – little voices on the path below our deck. We leaned over and smiled as we saw Billy and Emily smelling flowers and chattering on about the birds and lizards.

"Hello!" I called out and their adorable faces turned up to peer at me. I saw their eyes go back and forth, like they could see Davy. I looked sideways at him. "Can they see you?"

"I believe they can, yes." He was grinning down at them and waved. They waved back and we both chuckled. "The innocence of children…"

"Hey," Billy said, "I've seen you. On television."

"Well, perhaps you have. What show was it?"

"The Monkees. We watch that show every weekend."

"That's very good! I always love to meet fans of all ages." Now it was my turn to put my hand on his back. He seemed so happy at that moment. He pointed to the bird still on my shoulder, "Have you met Winston?"

"No! Can we pet him?"

"Of course. Come on up here," He pointed to the path that would lead them to our front door and then ran to meet them there. Winston flapped a bit and landed on the back of the sofa, closer to eye level with the kids. "This is Winston," Davy proudly introduced him. "Winston, this is Billy and Emily."

Trick or treat smell my feet gimme something good to eat.

This tickled the kids, and they laughed about it not being Halloween. We showed them how to pet him, and they took turns giving him strokes. He preened and stretched his neck, bobbing now and then in happiness.

"He likes you," I volunteered. He was such a great entertainer.

"I've been trying to teach him to sing a special song," Davy told them. "Let's see how he's doing."

Davy sang the first few lines of "Daydream Believer" and then waited.

Cheer up, sleepy Jean.
Daydreeeeeeam believer.
Homecoming queeeeeeeeeen.

"Bravo!" Davy clapped for the bird, who took little bows for his audience.

113

Thank you thank you I'm here all week.

I joined Davy in a good giggle.

"There's a new one, yeah?" Davy turned and winked at the kids.

TWENTY-NINE

Running with Scissors

I saw the Drakes leaving early the next morning, most likely for sightseeing. I let Davy know that the kids wouldn't be around for a few hours and was surprised to see his face fall, contradicting his next words. "Oh good; less chance of people seeing them conversing with invisible friends." He smiled, but it didn't reach his eyes.

I put my arm around him in a gesture that he was usually showing me. "What's wrong?"

He gave his head a few shakes, as if to erase an Etch-a-Sketch in his mind. "It's nothing, but I do hope they come to visit with us again at some point. I like those kids."

"You like kids in general."

He nodded, showing me the impish little kid side of himself. "I love that innocence, the sense of fun and all-abandon."

"They will come and play; I'm pretty sure."

"I also love that they're not in awe of seeing me on television. It's so matter-of-fact."

"You probably didn't get that too much, did you?"

"No. Wherever I went, it was a mob scene... a train wreck."

"But so many people love you. Do you realize that?"

"They love the image."

"No!" I was adamant. "No. It's so far beyond that. You changed the lives of so many – improved their lives because you made them happy and gave them a bright little ray of sunshine to hold tightly when all around them their worlds were crumbling."

He frowned, but with a hint of smile. "How..." he frowned again. "How do you know this?"

Grinning slyly I said, "I have my ways of finding things out." I was proud of my secret bit of research. The less he knew of what *I* knew the better to surprise him. I was starting to think we were *both* in need of each other.

And sure enough, when mid-day rolled around, the family had returned. Laura had tried to get the kids to lie down for a nap, but they were bouncing off the walls at the front desk.

"I would love to take them down to the beach if you'd like some quiet time," I suggested. "I promise I won't let them go into any big waves or anything. It's a very calm little cove." It didn't take any acts of persuasion from me; Laura and Adam readily agreed. The kids changed into swimsuits and romped along behind me, flip-flops flapping noisily on the walkway. At the cottage, the kids piled on top of Davy who had been lounging on the sofa while watching television. "Ooof!"

"Snap to it! Get some beach clothes on," I playfully ordered him while I tossed some food into a picnic basket. He grinned and jumped up, tossing a kid here and there, and taking great joy when they would squeal in delight and run back for another assault. He ducked into the other room and emerged wearing some Hawaiian print swim trunks and flip flops on his feet.

"You look great! Where did you find those?"

"The Lost and Found box. I'll put them back; I promise."

I giggled and shook my head, admiring him. He was quite a fine specimen of a man, albeit in a compact body. I decided then that height was highly overrated.

Grabbing the picnic basket and towels for all of us, we dashed out of the cottage and made our way down the walkway, then down the steps, then down another walkway and some more steps. Hey, these were volcanoes we were living on! Beaches here weren't flat open areas like in Southern California. Davy lugged the picnic basket and blanket for us to sit on while I carried a bag of necessities such as extra sunscreen, my phone, and the towels.

"All right then, kids," Davy warned as he led the way, "hold the railing! I won't be carrying anybody back if they fall. You'll just have to lie there until you grow up."

I chuckled, bringing up the rear.

"Emily! Billy!" Davy called to them as he reached the bottom. "It's your job to find the very perfect spot. Hop to!"

The kids giggled and scuttled about, pointing out potential picnic sites. Davy would go to each, bend over, playfully find something wrong – the wrong sized rock, a seashell that was broken, anything – and wave them on. I just strolled along, catching up with them occasionally. He was a marvel with children! Then I realized yet again

116

that it was just because he was a kid at heart himself. When at last they had found the very perfect spot, we spread the blanket and anchored the corners with our flip flops and the picnic basket.

"Race you to the water," Billy yelled to everyone and off we went. We played in the gentle waves for a while, Davy diving past them a few times and then sneaking underwater to tickle the kids' legs.

After a while I got out to sit on the blanket and take some photos, leaving the playtime to the kids – all three of them. I watched the children closely though and began to have interesting flashes of déjà vu. Puzzled, I put my chin in my hand and tried to hold the fleeting near-memories still so I could identify what it was I was seeing. I kept whispering to myself, "I've seen this… I know this…"

The tears pricked hard behind my eyes at the moment it suddenly all became clear. I quickly brushed those tears away to further concentrate on the memories, for they were indeed actual memories. It wasn't déjà vu at all. I could see it clearer each time I saw Davy pop out of the water and laugh with the kids, seeing him give the occasional glance and wave to me as I sat onshore. He was having a blast – just as he had perhaps twenty years ago – on a beach in the Los Angeles area. I was having trouble separating my memories from scenes from the Monkees television show romps on the beach that had been filmed further south in San Diego, but not twenty years ago – more like forty-something.

All those dreams I'd had were pieces of memories. They were now forcing their way to my consciousness – memories from early 1997. I was about nine-years old and had gone to a Los Angeles beach with my mother while my dad was working. I remember she was tremendously excited because something was happening at the far end of the beach from where we'd planted our blanket and chairs.

She and I had run down along the waves to watch, my hand held firmly in hers. I really couldn't understand much then, but was remembering now that they were filming a Monkees reunion television show, and it had been my mother's dream to meet Davy Jones. I remember her chatting with a man and that we had all ended up playing together in the sand and the sea. It was only now that I truly understood. I had met Davy that day so long ago and we had

117

played together on the beach. My mother had been so thrilled, happier than I had ever seen her, and her happiness had been contagious.

There is a lot of downtime on a television or movie set, sometimes hours. Every time props needed to be moved, or cameras and lighting reset, the actors sat in chairs on the sideline or in their dressing room trailers, waiting to be called back. All except Davy. He spent his downtime with people. Always the entertainer, always the friend. As I recalled a kiss goodbye on my forehead and a kiss on the cheek for my mother at the end of the day, I realized that this was the connection that had brought us together now.

My tears were falling steadily then, my chest heaving with intense sobs. I put a pretend smile on my face and ran towards the waves, diving into the first one I met. I swam until the salty seawater had washed away the salty tears, mingling them in the Pacific. When I surfaced, I was near Davy and the kids, and he was grinning at me. His face fell for a moment though.

"Are you alright?" he whispered, brushing wet hair off my face.

I nodded, averted my eyes, and dove to tickle the kids' legs below the surface, their laughter making me buoyant both in the water and in my spirit. As we played, I looked at Davy in a new light. While his physical appearance was not like when he had met my mother and me, he still looked like the young man she had fallen in love with in 1966, and to add further comparison and confusion, his spirit was actually that of a sixty-six year old man. Taking all that into consideration, I felt he was still quite true to himself in that he never really had grown up, only grown older, yet he had been wiser than his years for most of his living days. These were characteristics that endeared him even today to his fans of all ages, young and old.

"I'm stahhhving," he roared as he and the kids caught a small wave in on their bellies, bodysurfing to shore. "Let's eat!"

The kids ran ahead to the blanket while Davy hung back and casually slung his arm around me, pulling us close enough so that he could whisper, "You alright then, luv?"

"I'm great actually." I smiled, truly warmed by my earlier revelations.

118

He looked at me curiously, gave me a soft kiss on my forehead – exactly where he had planted one nearly twenty years ago – and we plopped down on the blanket.

I passed out cheese sandwiches and small containers of pasta salad with veggies. "Eww!" The kids were underwhelmed by the vegetables in the pasta salad.

"Whatcha mean 'eww' there, ya daft dwarfs!" Davy teased and put a huge spoonful of veggies in his mouth and crunched a few times before he was able to speak again. "Veggies are wot make ya grow strong and tall. Look at me! I didn't start eating me veggies 'til I was an adult and see what happened? Stunted me growth, I tell ya." He teased them, winking at me as he egged them on to try the vegetables. "Try the cucumber at the very least then!"

Each kid put a thin slice of quick-pickled cucumber in their mouths and tried so hard to scrunch up their faces in distaste, until it dawned on them that it actually tasted good.

"See?" He put another bite of food in his own mouth, talking around it. "I told ya, didn't I? I'll never steer ya down the wrong road, little mates."

The kids giggled and ate pretty much the entire serving I'd given them, tackling their cheese sandwiches at the same time. There was a jug of cool iced tea, compliments of Kalei, and for dessert, a cupcake each.

"Oh my." Davy nearly swooned over the cupcake, his eyes almost rolling back inside his head. "This is heaven." The cupcakes were devoured in no time at all, and only a little of the pasta salad was left behind. All in all, it was a very successful picnic.

Davy picked up a few pieces of corkscrew pasta that had landed on the blanket and threw one at each kid. They threw it back at him, dissolving into laughing blobs of tickled children. "FOOOD FIIIGHT!" Davy picked up a handful of the rest of the pasta and flung a few pieces at the kids and at me, an innocent bystander!

We were all laughing and scrambling for pieces of pasta to fling right back at him, finally collapsing in a heap of oily food-covered bodies. "To the sea, mates! To the sea!" Davy led the brigade as we all trooped down to rinse ourselves off.

119

The sun had sunk low into the mountain behind us. Before packing everything up though, Davy gathered us all in a line.

"Right... Now," he instructed, "put your arms around each person next to you." He showed us how. "Now, when I say 'go,' lead with your left leg, and instead of walking straight, stick it out to the left, like you're crossing over in front of your neighbor's leg." He gave a little exhibition and then got back in line. "On three, now! Everybody!" He counted to three, and we all tumbled laughing onto the sand in a tangle of legs. He was a persistent instructor though, and after a few minutes, we had done it. We had mastered *The Monkee Walk*. There was much cheering before we packed up our picnic things and headed back to the path and the stairs.

"Hold the rails again! Remember that I'll leave ya where you fall." He was such a sweet character and made the kids laugh at every turn. They knew he was playing with them and seemed to love it. At the top of the stairs, he squatted down to their level.

"Oi, I just want to remind you," he whispered conspiratorially. "I am your secret. Right? When people grow up to be adults, they lose their ability to have fun sometimes, so they don't understand. And when they see or hear things that they don't understand, they get very worried, and we don't want that, right?"

Both kids shook their heads. "No!" they spoke nearly in that unison that often exists between twins.

"Good then." He hugged them both and planted kisses on their foreheads... that same spot I knew. "Go with Macca, and I hope to see you tomorrow, okay?" He took the picnic basket, the blanket, and the bag from me.

A harmony of goodbyes from them and I took them "home" to their room. They squealed with delight, telling their parents all about the wonderful day at the beach they'd had, exclaiming about the weird vegetables they'd enjoyed too. I simply smiled and allowed them to thank me. The kids gave me hugs goodbye too, and I thought to myself, *they'll sleep well tonight!*

120

Confessions of a Gentler Kind

When I returned to the cottage after dropping the kids off with their parents, I found Davy in the kitchen washing the dishes and such. The sandy blanket and towels were in a pile on the deck, ready to go to the laundry. "Aww, thank you, sweetie. You didn't need to wash up."

"You cooked and you made delicious cupcakes, so it was my turn."

"By the way, there are more cupcakes in the fridge."

He stopped what he was doing and turned to look at me, his face full of happiness and surprise. "Dinner!"

I laughed. He truly was like a little kid sometimes.

I sat at the dining table while he finished up. There wasn't room enough for both of us in there.

"So, tell me..." He was wiping the last of the small plastic bowls I'd served the salad in. "Something happened out there."

I swallowed hard and said nothing for a while. I opened the fridge and found an open bottle of Chardonnay. "Want some?" I was delaying my answer. He nodded and I poured two glasses. He pulled the tea towel from his waist and gave the dishes a quick drying wipe before sitting down with me. We clinked glasses, our usual toast, and sipped.

He set his glass down, crossed his arms on the tabletop and leaned in. "So?"

I took a large gulp of wine and poured more for both of us before answering.

"You knew, didn't you?"

"Knew what?" He toyed with the condensation on the bottom of his wine glass, not looking at me.

"That we had met before. You knew."

He closed his eyes for just a moment, then turned his face to look directly into my eyes. "I didn't know how to tell you without bringing up painful memories." The look in his own eyes was nothing but softness and love.

121

I had to smile then, which released the floodgates once again. "I'd blocked it out," I cried and choked the words out. "I don't know why I blocked it out though. It was beautiful."

He reached across and held my hand. "*You* were beautiful. You still are. You and your mother made an impression on me. She wrote me a couple of times. I responded when I could, and then I learned of her passing shortly after we'd met. It chilled me to think of this beautiful little girl left without a mother, and then it was worsened when I learned your father followed her soon after. I never stopped thinking about you." He gulped. "We're kindred spirits, Macca."

I nodded, for that was all I could manage around the knot in my throat.

"I wish I'd contacted you," he continued, perhaps thinking he needed to fill the silence. "I am sorry for that. I hope you'll forgive me."

We let a silence hang for a bit, broken only by my occasional sob.

"Macca," he finally said again, for I was incapable of words. "I've never forgiven myself... so I'll understand if you aren't able to forgive me either."

I shook my head and covered my face, then used one hand to wave off his words before covering my face again. To his credit – and so many credits to him already – he stayed there with me. No words, no sounds, just his presence, albeit spectral.

Tissues had been placed in front of me when I came up for air. I used several of them to wipe my face, refusing to look Davy in the eye quite yet. I wasn't ready. I got up and went to the kitchen sink, rinsing my face with cold water and using a paper towel to dry. I let out a ragged sigh as I braced my arms on the counter for a moment to calm myself. When I stood and turned toward him, I saw the distress on his face. I truly had not meant to cause him any worry or upset. I sat back down and reached out to take his hands.

"I'm not upset with you. I hold no grudge, no feelings of being cheated... by you." I swallowed hard. "That you would even think you'd upset me, is upsetting enough." I laughed but it came out as a hard sound. "I'm only upset that I had not remembered all of this sooner."

122

He let out a whoosh of a breath. "Oh, Babe." He shook his head and smiled. "I understand that. I just feel terrible for holding the information back."

"No, I think I needed to have the memory on my own."

He tilted his head and smiled ever so sadly at me. "I'm sorry, luv. I really am. I wish... well, there are so many things I could wish for – for both of us. But it is what it is. Right? And now, together, we can help you learn to live with the memories... and the regrets."

It was then I realized that any regrets he had would remain just that – regrets. I needed to make peace with my own, accept them and move on.

"I need to change the way I think. I need to NOT have regrets. If I make a mistake, I must consider it a learning experience."

In one movement it seemed, he stood up and drew me close in a hug. "I think you've got it, Babe. I really think you do." He squeezed me hard and it was then I panicked and pulled back a little bit to look in his eyes.

"Does that mean you're leaving me?" I felt the sadness and the tears wash over me again.

"Oh, bloody hell no! You need me." He pushed me toward the living room, grabbing our wine glasses along the way, and led me to the sofa where we sat together. "You are in such need of a guiding hand, my darlin' and I'm that hand. I am no expert, but I'm a good listener, shall we say."

I grinned and leaned my head on his shoulder, snorting some laughter of sorts through my nose. (I admit, it might have been mixed with tears – again. Good thing that velvet shirt of his was impervious to such things.)

"I know that some day you might have to leave, but I hope it's a long time away like... never." My words were muffled by the velvet fabric as he rubbed my back.

I heard the chuckle deep in his throat. I'd come to love that sound and the accompanying vibration. "You're sort of stuck with me, luv."

123

THIRTY-ONE

The Fuzz Returns

I saw them arrive before they noticed me watching them from my cottage. Davy peered over my shoulder as Detective Green and two police officers entered the reception building. My stomach tightened in anticipation and dread. Squaring my shoulders, I let out a sigh and grasped the door handle. Davy covered my hand with his.

"I'll be with you."

"I know." It was almost a whisper, my throat suddenly dry.

I moved swiftly out the door and was at the front desk in mere seconds.

"Detective Green." I stuck my hand out automatically and he returned the gesture. Robotic handshakes – the business world had trained me.

"Miss Liberty," he nodded. "I have a few more questions. Is there someplace we can talk?"

"Here is fine with me." I waved to the two loveseats.

"I was thinking of something more private. It's a… sensitive subject."

I think a sound that was remarkably like a "harrumph" came out of my mouth as I turned and led them all to our tiny cottage. I wouldn't be offering any hospitality though. They could stand around for all I cared. This was the first time they'd contacted me since that awful day that Louis had died. I'd left several calls asking for updates, but each had been ignored.

I sat in the center of the sofa while the police officers stood by the front door and Detective Green leaned against the entrance to the kitchenette.

"How well did you know Louis Cabral?"

"Not well at all. I didn't even remember that was his last name. I'd only seen his employee file once. My uncle hired him, and I met him on the first day we reopened. The next day he was floating in the pool."

He wrote in his notepad.

"How well do you know Gilbert Sikes?"

At the mention of Mr. Baldy's name, I frowned and sat up straighter. "I... I... what the hell is this all about?"

"Just answer the question, Ms. Liberty."

"The Fuzz," Davy sneered, sitting behind Detective Green. "I don't trust this dude."

Ignoring Davy, I sat back again, my irritation building. "I had the displeasure of meeting him for the first time a few days ago. The meeting lasted less than ten minutes. However, he has been trying to buy my inn. It's not for sale, but he seems determined to change my mind."

He wrote in his notepad again.

"Does Mr. Sikes have something to do with this?" I demanded.

"I'm not at liberty to say whether he was involved or not. At this time, it was simply a question." He smiled, but without any joy behind it. I'd be really surprised if this man had any joy in his life... ever.

"Fine, then. If that's all, I need to get back to work." I rose from my seat and showed them the door.

"I'll call you if I have more questions," he promised. Or threatened, maybe.

When I was certain they were well gone, I turned to Davy, both of us with our eyes wide. "Oh my god," we yelled in unison. We plopped onto the sofa, me with my legs crossed half-lotus style, him hugging his knees to his chest.

"Now you'll definitely stay away from Sikes, right Babe?"

I nodded my head vigorously. "You bet! Holy crap! That man creeped me out before. Now he just plain scares the pants off me!"

He briefly looked me up and down before deadpanning, "I'd quite like to see that." Bum-di-bum.

125

THIRTY-TWO

Mahalo Car-Scooter-Skateboard-Skate Aloha R2 D2

With our little inn finally doing well, profits rising, and the vet bills for Winston being paid down, I felt it was time for some more improvements. I turned in the rented car-scooter-skateboard-skate – complete with Auntie Agony and her agonizingly annoying GPS voice – and purchased a slightly used model from the previous year, sans GPS. I could read a map as well as the next person. In addition, I arranged to have a mini charging station installed at the end of the inn's parking lot. Some people might consider this foolish business, but I felt that encouraging people to use more environmentally friendly vehicles would allow me to sleep better at night as well as provide the business with a good tax break. As I was driving the new car-scooter-skateboard-skate home, I realized he needed a name. I couldn't be calling him car-scooter-skateboard-skate for the rest of his life.

"I hereby dub thee… R2 D2. R2 for short." I patted his dashboard. "Hey, it's better than Tin Can Harry."

I also had the exteriors of all the buildings painted, removing the previously peeling and flaking paint and having a few fresh coats applied. It would extend the life of the construction by protecting it from the elements.

I was finally able to begin drawing a small salary for myself. Putting my name on the payroll spurred something inside me as well. I found myself working longer hours, doing a lot of small upgrade tasks myself, and ordering new bedding and bath towels for all seven cottages through an online lodging supply catalog. One afternoon, after I'd finished filling in for Ming on her day off, Davy and I hopped into R2 and sped off to town. I bought myself a couple of soft cotton sundresses and skirts. I wanted to look more presentable than I usually did in my old shorts and tee-shirts. I also bought some items for Davy so that he wouldn't have to borrow things from the Lost and Found box any more. He simply pointed to things and I found the correct size and then included them in my purchases.

When we returned to R2, he rummaged through the bag. "Thanks mom! Groovy threads!"

I laughed and smacked his arm, then quickly looked all around me to make sure I hadn't been seen. I pretended to be batting at an insect. Getting increasingly comfortable with Davy was causing me to drop my guard more. Not a good thing at all. And there Davy sat, looking at me swatting imaginary flies before he burst into laughter, doubling over and holding his stomach. I stuck my tongue out at him and then again looked all around me to be sure no one was watching.

"Y'look like yer workin' out on a bloody speed bag, punchety-punchety-punch-punch-punch," he laughed, which just made him giggle harder. "They're coming to take me awwwwaaaaaaaaaaaaaaaaaayyyyy…"

"Stop it! Just… stop…" I couldn't even finish before his laughter took over again.

He turned to an imaginary passer-by and pointed to me, "Watch out for that one there. She's gone round the bend, y'know."

Soon though, his giggles became contagious, and I was laughing at myself right alongside him. It was one of those moments when we'd start to calm down, then look at each other and set off again. We both had tears rolling down our cheeks.

"Oh my god! Let's get out of here before they lock me away," I choked out between guffaws. I put the car in gear and zipped away, hitting a pothole in the process. Poor R2.

My next stop was the grocery store to stock up on personal supplies for our own cottage – fresh fruit and veggies and some staples. We were starting to cook mini-meals more and more in private to avoid the luscious meals in the main dining area. After all, I wanted to be able to continue to fit into my new clothes.

Returning to the car, Davy was "dancing" in his seat to some music I could not hear. I began to giggle again. He was far too good at egging me on.

Back at home, we washed our new clothes in the inn's main laundry facility. While we waited to do the washer-to-dryer transfer, we returned to the cottage and watched a little television. It was so nice to have some valid downtime without feeling that I was neglecting things.

"Hey look!" Davy grinned and pointed at the television set. "The Monkees are on in ten minutes!"

"Oh, let's watch it, please? My mother and I never had the chance to watch together before she died. I've watched since then though," I smiled, "but it sure would be fun to have someone to laugh with."

"Babe, you are in the right place then because we were a daft bunch," he chuckled and shook his head. I think of us back then and laugh a lot. It was a crazy time."

"But if you had the choice today, would you go back and do it all over again?"

"Oh, bloody hell, YES! But I'd be a little smarter – one would hope – and I'd take it all in and still enjoy every bloody moment."

"So you had fun?"

He looked at me, surprised. "Oh yes! It was a gas! But I let some selfish people take advantage of me. That wouldn't happen again." He was shaking his head, letting me know it stung deeply still.

Reaching out, I touched his shoulder, "You made such an impact on the world. I still don't think you understand the depths of it all, or how many people you helped... how many you influenced."

"It was just a two-year whirlwind for the show, another year or two of touring. Then it was gone."

I sat up. "But that's just it – it was never gone. Those that loved you never left you. Even when they couldn't follow you because there was no internet in those early days to give them all the latest little news, or they had families of their own, or they were broke and couldn't afford to attend shows, they never stopped loving you. Sure, many couldn't follow you around to watch the shows you gave in later years – but it doesn't mean they loved you any less. I think you'd be surprised at how many people kept you in their hearts all throughout the years and even now."

His brows were knit together as he studied my face, but he was silent. I was hoping he was taking it in.

We got comfortable on the sofa then and watched as the episode called "Success Story" began. We laughed, and he pointed and

128

laughed at himself, but he alone had the right to do that. At the farewell scene, I sniffed and dabbed at my eyes.

"Come on..." he chided in a gentle manner. "It's just a show." He brushed the hair back from my face.

"But..." I was having trouble finding the air to speak the words, "I don't want you to ever leave me."

He sat up straight and faced me, taking my face in his hands. They were so warm and calloused, but not in a bad way.

"Darlin', I'm here for as long as you need me."

"But... there are so many other people who need you."

He smiled and kissed my nose. "And I'm there for them as well! That's the beauty of this gig, Babe! I can be so many places at once, and each place and person gets my full attention. It's really quite remarkable – and a whole lot of fun!"

"So... I don't need to feel guilty that you're here and others..." I was specifically thinking of his family.

"You aren't to worry about me. The universe is so much bigger than you can know for now. Some day though. But that's a long way off. Right this moment though? It's your job to live your life to the best of your abilities, with the occasional boost from me." He grinned.

I leaned against him and took a deep breath. Between the scent of him and the weight of the words he'd just spoken, I needed time to absorb it all, and Davy needed time to realize the impact he had made in the world. I vowed then to help him see that.

THIRTY-THREE

Daydream Believers Forever

One day after all the work was done, I called Davy to my side. I had my laptop set up and the Wi-Fi connection was strong enough that I was able to have several tabs open onscreen.

"Remember when we were discussing your impact?"

"Or lack thereof, yes." Oooh, he was in a bit of a snippy mood. I would soon turn that around.

"I want you to sit here and look at this, read everything, look at the photos, and soak it up. I'll be here on the sofa." I showed him how to access each item that I had set up for him, and then I backed away.

There was nothing but silence in the room for a very long time. I glanced up occasionally to see how far he had gotten. He was moving slowly. Good. That meant he was taking it in.

The websites, the pages, the testimonies from fans and friends and co-workers were all there. I could hear him occasionally watching a fan's video. He sat back at one point, his arms hanging at his side. I wondered briefly if he was upset, but I had decided to leave him be unless he asked for me. He seemed to collect himself and returned to the task with which I had challenged him. I went back to the book I was reading, but kept an eye on him. I think I must have read the same page forty times, but it didn't matter. He was reacting as I'd hoped. He'd underestimated himself and his impact.

As I saw he was nearing the end of what I'd set up for him, I moved to sit on a stool beside him. I put my arm across his shoulder and kissed his temple.

I watched him sift through the final few pages I'd lined up. There were more, but I had tried to just hit the broadest highlights. As he came to the last, which was simply a dedication page from fans, I put my forehead to his temple. "Do you see now what I meant?"

He nodded and swallowed hard. When he turned away from the laptop to look at me, his eyes had welled with tears. I smiled at him and we leaned our foreheads together.

"I... I..." he let the words hang, unable to speak.

"Don't talk. Just *breathe it in*, okay, and let it settle in your heart?"

He nodded against my forehead and we both closed our eyes. I felt him relax little by little. When I felt he was quieting, I kissed his brow and went into the kitchenette. I popped the cork on one of Uncle Wally's lovely bottles of Chardonnay, saluted the man for his love of wine, and poured two glasses. Carrying both the glasses and the bottle to the living room, I found Davy sitting quite sedately on the sofa, staring out the large window that looked upon the tops of the trees and the sea beyond. As I neared, I saw little tracks that his tears had made down his face. His eyes were red and very wet. Sitting beside him, one leg tucked beneath me, I set the bottle on the coffee table and handed him a glass.

"I thought we could both use this right about now," I spoke quietly.

He simply nodded and took the proffered glass. We clinked them and I took a sip. He downed his in two gulps and I refilled it.

"No one ever showed me any of that before," he said through a choked voice.

"They should have. Whoever 'they' were. I don't question your activities, so I'm just saying this in a broad way there." I put my hands up. "Maybe someone tried, sweetie."

He was very quiet as he sipped his wine and stared out the window. "I think..." he swallowed hard, gathering composure. "I think you're the first I've interacted with so closely." He picked at a thread on the sofa, anything to take his attention away from our discussion, but I wasn't letting him off that easily.

"So, you're still learning how to 'do' this, right?"

He nodded. "I wish there was a 'How-To' book or something."

I snickered quietly. "*How To Be A Ghost*. Yeah, that'd be a bestseller."

He looked up at me, the sadness in his eyes still there, but a hint of the smile from his lips was creeping into them. "I'd buy it."

I laughed softly and put my head on his shoulder. He rested his head on top of mine. We just sat like that for a long time, each lost in our thoughts. The level in the wine bottle kept going down though as I refilled our glasses.

131

"So..." I had given him several minutes of 'space' to grasp the reality he'd not been privy to previously. "Do you understand now that you've made quite an impact on the world?"

He straightened up beside me to look directly into my eyes. "I had no idea," he said so quietly I could barely hear him. "I was 'told' by my family, in an otherworldly way, of the incredible outpouring of love, but seeing it myself... I'm shocked."

I felt an immense relief and a joy too, deep within my heart. There were so many idiots out there who were so full of themselves with absolutely no reason to be, yet here was a man with a heart of gold who never realized how much he was loved. The world – and the otherworld – were indeed mysterious places.

THIRTY-FOUR

Chip and Egg Butties

As part of my continuing efforts to become a true Hawaiian resident, I purchased a new phone at a discounted price and low monthly fees. I needed it mostly for business now, which was a sad statement of my personal life.

It was in the first week of the new phone and new plan when I got my first unusual wrong number in the way of a text.

Hey, u busy 2nite? Need help w/laundry. Call me

Looking up the area code, it seemed to have originated from Illinois. I was having a little chuckle when Davy peeked over my shoulder.

"Who's that from?"

"I have no idea. But I think she'll be doing her laundry alone."

I slipped the phone back into my bag and turned around to face him. He was standing there with a plate of French fries in his hand. He grinned and waved me to follow him to the kitchen.

"I'm making brekkie for us."

"With *French fries*?"

"Actually, I call them chips, but yes! You'll love it!"

I sat down at the little table and watched him work.

"So, why this sudden desire to make breakfast for us?"

"I've finally figured out how to cook again! I've always liked to cook. Also..." he tossed a guilty smile over his shoulder before turning back to his task, "I ate the last cupcake. I'm sorry. It was in the refrigerator mocking me, so I ate it, and it was glorious. But I'm sorry... so this is my penance." He winked then.

I burst out laughing and watched him put four slices of bread on the cutting board and then slather them with butter. He placed hard-fried eggs on top of two of the slices and carefully laid the French fries/chips on top of each. He squeezed ketchup all over them both, then put the remaining slice of bread on top.

"Come on then. You must eat it over the sink. It's quite sloppy!"

He grinned while I grimaced and joined him at the counter as he spoke

133

again while munching his creation. "Oh, you'll love it! If you don't, I'll eat your butty as well!"

"Excuse me?"

"Butty! It's a sarnie! A sandwich! I couldn't find any pickle relish though, so we must do without."

I shook my head and laughed. This man never failed to make me laugh and scratch my head at the same time. Squeezing next to him to lean over the sink, I took my first bite, fully expecting to spit it out. But as I chewed, I realized he was right! There was a hint of vinegar on the fries too. While not the healthiest choice of breakfast, it was oddly delicious!

"I love it!"

"I told you so," he said between bites, wiping ketchup off his face, then wiping it off mine as well. I grinned, and he then wiped the ketchup-y napkin on my nose. In return, I dipped my finger into my ketchup-y sandwich and wiped it on his nose. We chuckled and then bent over to finish breakfast.

"I need a shower after that," I teased him.

"The sink didn't fare well either." His chuckle echoed into the old porcelain basin as he leaned over to clean up the drippings.

I popped into the bathroom and looked in the mirror. I had a big red blob on my nose, nearly identical to the one I'd gifted Davy. Smiling, I washed my face and hands and returned to the kitchen. I put on a pot of Kona coffee as he finished doing the "washing up" as he always called it. When he turned around, he had his standard tea towel tucked around his waist, which he then pulled off and used to dry the dishes he'd just cleaned.

"All right then, luv, all done. What shall we do today?"

I had to smile at the pure innocence in his question. "Well, I don't know about you, but I've got to fill in for Ming today, so I'll be cleaning rooms and doing laundry, although not with my new bestie in Illinois, apparently."

"Perhaps then I'll go see what the tots are up to." He draped the tea towel over the counter to dry and went off in search of his new playmates, Emily and Billy.

134

I stopped him a moment before he left. "Hey, I arranged for them to join us for another beach picnic tomorrow. Are you up for it? They leave for home the day after, you know."

"I'll be there with bells on!" He turned back to the doorway then stopped abruptly. "What the hell does that actually mean? With bells on?" His infectious chuckle got me going too, and he went off to play with his little friends.

My phone twinkled its merry "You've got a text" tune.

Hey, can I borrow your red lace dress and wicked woman shoes for my date Friday night?

This time it was from a Nevada number. I deleted the text and chuckled. I'd given up replying with "You've got the wrong number" because the rude people on the other end never bothered with an apology. Oh well. It was their half minute, not mine to worry about.

THIRTY-FIVE

You Can't Tie a Mustang Down
You Can't Keep an Ocean in a Cup

It was a cold, dark, and stormy night… actually it was really just another hot, breezy day of sunshine on the Big Island. But we were in a silly mood, the four of us – Davy, Emily, Billy, and I. I'd packed another picnic lunch, and we were headed down, down, down the path and stairs to the beach far below. Once again the kids were in charge of finding the perfect spot to spread our blanket.

"No rocks! Remember that, mateys!" Captain Davy was at the helm again. This time, however, Emily and Billy used their flip-flops to spread the sand smooth and even. "Aren't you the clever ones," he stood grinning at them, hands on hips, the pride beaming on his face.

Once the blanket was spread and anchored, we raced to the water's edge and romped. Occasionally I would stop and just watch them. It was a far lighter mood for me this time as I drew upon the memories of that beach trip from my childhood so long ago. I snapped photos while sitting on the sand as well. I wanted to remember this time with the kids. Suddenly I wondered how odd the photos would look without Davy in them, even though the kids were playing off of him. I couldn't really see the screen with the sun so bright, so I knew I'd have to wait until later.

"Come have some lunch," I called to all three of the kids, for Davy seemed just as youthful as the children were at times, and almost their size too.

"Hey, no short jokes," he sneered and flicked water in my face from the droplets still clinging to his fingertips.

"Hey! Get outta my head!" I buried his feet in the sand.

"Oh no!" He pretended to be sinking in quicksand. "Emily! Billy! Hellllp meeeee!" as he sunk to the ground. The kids giggled and climbed on top of him before trying to haul him to his feet. Instead, he simply crawled to the blanket and collapsed, his arms reaching for the food I was laying out. I smacked his hand away.

"Not yet. Let me finish getting it ready."

136

"Geez, Mom, you're mean. And slow. Very slow. C'mon, we're stahving!" He egged the kids on until all three of them were begging for the first morsel of food they'd had in at least three years. Or so it seemed.

There were egg salad sandwiches, cherry tomatoes, potato salad, and carrot sticks with Ranch dressing for dipping. The kids had no complaints about vegetables this time, and most of the food was devoured quickly.

"What's for dessert?" Davy was peering into the picnic basket.

"Strawberries and…"

"Please say cupcakes."

Sipping iced tea, I nearly snorted it out of my nose. The kids laughed and joined him in chanting "We want cupcakes. We want cupcakes."

"Oh all right, but this time they're not chocolate." Three faces fell. "They're peanut butter and chocolate!"

"Yay!" There were cheers and eager hands reaching for their cupcakes. Happy faces surrounded me, frosting on their lips and chins. Yes, even Davy's.

That evening he made a pact with them, that he would visit them occasionally, but only for as long as they wanted him to. Of course, as children, they insisted it would be forever. I found it very touching and hoped they realized what lucky kids they were. Maybe some day they'd get it. There were hugs all around and bouncy goodbyes. I was hoping the sugar would wear off before their bedtime though, or their parents might never forgive me.

Back at the cottage, I uploaded the photos on my camera to the laptop and watched, mesmerized, as they popped one by one across the screen in that magical way of the digital world. And then, one by one I studied them, laughing as Emily appeared to be jumping, when in fact I knew she had been climbing on Davy's back. Further photos showed Billy suspended sideways over a wave, but I remembered that I'd caught Davy in the act of tossing him into the briny sea.

"Wotcha laughin' at, luv?" He peered over my shoulder and was soon laughing right along with me in that deep chuckle that was so infectious.

"These must never leave this laptop," I choked out the words between giggles.

"Never."

But I saw a certain twinkle in his eye and shook my head. Hopefully he would forget about them. Soon.

THIRTY-SIX

I'm Gonna Buy Me a... Guitar

I woke up when Chester sneezed in my face. My phone buzzed with a text – another wrong number – that said simply, *cooking pb&j for dinner 2nite u better be on time!*

The call was from an area code in D.C. Your tax dollars at work. I chuckled, tossed my phone onto my bed which I'd just made up, and headed for the shower. As usual, I did my quick routine while deep in thought. One problem though – I'd gone so deep in thought that I'd forgotten if I'd washed my face. So I washed it, perhaps again. Who knows? One little trigger can ruin a really good routine, you know?

Five minutes later I was whistling a tune when I opened the bathroom door. There – sitting not two feet away on a kitchen chair he'd dragged over from the table – was Davy, arms crossed and with one ankle crossed on top of the opposite knee. I jumped at least ten feet. Well, in my mind maybe.

"You scared the crap out of me! What are you doing there?"

"Waiting for you. What'd you *think* I was doing? You said I could never, never, EVER follow you into the bathroom. I think those may have been your exact words even."

He looked so serious that I struggled to suppress my laughter. "Okay, then." I bit the inside of my cheek to keep a straight face. "Did you need me for something?"

"Yes, I do, as a matter of fact. I want a guitar."

I blew out a long breath. "That's it?"

"Yes. That's it. But I have a problem. I don't have money, nor any means of acquiring any."

I smiled then and cocked my head to the side. "Oh sweetie, you should be pulling a salary. How about I pay you retroactively?"

He frowned and made a face like he'd just eaten a bug. "I don't do anything to earn a salary!"

"But you do. You're my confidante, my right-hand-man, my protector, and you keep me smiling. And you wash my dishes. That's more than most of Congress does and they pull a salary – a HUGE salary!"

That made him chuckle. "Well all right then – but minimum wage! What is that in this country again? About 35 cents an hour?" His eyes twinkled as he toyed with me.

"Actually," I sniffed, "it's up to 36 cents now." I turned on my heel and went off to make up guest beds, clean bathrooms, and vacuum six rooms plus the common areas. While I was taking a tea break though, I made some calculations to come up with a number I might owe him and wrote up a "note" of sorts. It was indeed enough to buy a guitar and more.

Early that afternoon I was able to present him with the figure.

"Noooo..." His face showed his total disbelief.

"Yep. You, my dear, will be teaching me to play guitar... soon."

"But they're so expensive. And you're so... *you*."

"HEY!" I gave him a soft punch on his shoulder. "I'll even pay you a fee for each lesson. How's that?" I stood with such a self-satisfied look on my face that I could even feel it!

He deadpanned and then suddenly poked me in the ribs and grinned. "Oh stop that smug look. It's not becoming."

"Becoming what?"

His sound of "Tsk" was enough to set me off into giggles and chuckles.

Just a few minutes of research on the internet revealed that there was a music store with a "Wide Selection of Guitars and Ukuleles" in a nearby town. Davy and I hopped into R2, ready for a little shopping.

"Hello little guy," I cooed to the tiny mechanical beast as I turned the key in the ignition. He started right up and purred for me a bit before I put him in gear and off we went. As we toddled along, I avoided the potholes and bumps I'd grown to know by heart; I was becoming a true wahine.

The music shop was small but packed with guitars. Davy simply pointed to a few and had me strum them. He would touch the neck a couple of times, pressing certain strings as I strummed. I was thrilled to hear an actual chord emit from the piece of wood, but when the store's clerk began walking toward us, I quickly covered Davy's fingers with my own.

"Hello! Shopping for a guitar?"

140

"Yes," I smiled, keeping his attention on me instead of on the strings that Davy was plucking. Putting his ear to the hole, Davy listened intently, oblivious to the clerk watching me oddly.

"Great resonance... the suspended chords sound good... single notes are... adequate," Davy muttered.

"Have you been playing long?" the sales clerk asked me. He was probably judging my degree of knowledge to determine how expensive a guitar he could sell me.

"No, I don't play. This is for a good friend of mine who is extremely talented. He's giving... *given* me some ideas."

"Nice cover." Davy grinned and winked at me. He looked up at more guitars and exclaimed with delight, "Oi! They have three-quarter size guitars in stock!"

I stood up and joined him, pretending that it was me who was perusing a potential instrument, but I admit, I knew nothing about whatever the hell a three-quarter size guitar was. Davy pointed to a guitar hanging on the wall high above our heads with what seemed like a million other guitars. I then pointed to it as well.

"Could we... Could *I* see that one please?" I needed to concentrate on the number of people in my little group – ONE – according to the general public and our sales clerk too, who by then must have thought I was nuts. He probably wasn't far off. The clerk used a hook to retrieve the guitar from the wall, which, by the look on Davy's face, was an absolutely horrific way to handle the instrument. The sheer terror on his scrunched up face made me want to laugh. It was just a guitar, you know?

"I heard you thinking that." He looked at me out of the corner of his eye. "No guitar is *just* a guitar." He shook his head, most certainly disgusted at my lack of respect for The Guitar. Apparently I had a lot to learn. I bit my lower lip to keep from laughing.

Taking the proffered guitar, I started chatting with the sales clerk again as I covered Davy's fingers on the neck of the instrument with my own and strummed with my right hand. We went through the entire process several different times before Davy stood back and looked at the five different guitars we had lined up. His arms were crossed, but one hand tapped his lips. He was deep in thought.

"So..." I started a little bit of small talk with the clerk while I made a show of inspecting each guitar from a distance. "How long has this store been here?"

"We opened in 1994."

I was impressed and wondered how it had stayed in business these twenty years. "You must have a lot of musicians in the area then?"

"Actually, our biggest sales are over the internet." He grinned so proudly. *Ahhh, the way of the future,* I thought to myself.

"That one." Davy pointed to a pretty guitar of a deep rose hued wood, with a nice faux tortoise shell panel. "It's called a pick guard," he corrected me. "And add a capo and some picks, please." He was nearly jumping up and down with excitement.

"Well, I think I'll take that one." I pointed to the same guitar and repeated Davy's words. "And please throw in a capo and some picks."

"Very good choice, Miss." He took the guitar to the register and flipped a book open. "This is on consignment." He found the item in his book. "And it comes with a soft-side case."

I nodded. "Very nice, thank you." I looked to Davy, who had a big grin on his face and was nodding enthusiastically. As I was handing my credit card over to the sales clerk, Davy planted a big smacking kiss on my cheek. I blushed but quickly recovered by fanning myself.

"It's quite warm today, isn't it?" I added to my sales clerk chit-chat act.

"Yes, the storm rolled in, dumped on us, rolled right out again, and now it's back to business as usual," he joked with me as he zipped the guitar into its cool looking black canvas case and handed it to me. He slipped a small paper bag into my other hand. "Your capo and a selection of picks. I hope your friend enjoys the resulting music!"

"Thank you. I'm sure he will."

Davy climbed into R2 and we wedged the guitar between his legs and against his chest. Tin can cars don't have much room, but we made the most of it.

As I folded myself into the driver's seat, Davy was grinning and peeking into the paper bag. "This is SO cool, man!" He fanned out about ten or twelve picks on his palm and touched each one before tossing it back into the bag. Then he pulled out the capo, a small and odd contraption covered in a blue and green plaid fabric, rather like what they use to make shoelaces. "Sooo cool," he repeated, like a little kid with a new electric train set.

"And you still have money left! How did you manage that? I was shocked at some of the prices in there!"

"Well, the Gretsches are very pricey, but worth every cent. Gretsch used to give us instruments way back in the day. I had a beautiful three-quarter size that they custom made for me. It was quite special." He gazed out the window, and then said so quietly that I almost missed it, "Those were some good times."

"You miss those days?" I asked, matching his tone and volume.

"Somewhat. They were also tumultuous." He laughed then, a sound devoid of mirth. "I would never have used the word tumultuous back then, but I felt it."

I reached over and touched his arm, sliding down to grasp his hand in mine. "I would love to hear you tell me all about those times... and other times too." I wanted to be a soundboard for him, to somehow give back what he had given to so many in the past.

He turned to look at me, a sad smile on his face. "Maybe. A lot of what happened back then would be better served to remain unspoken, if you know what I mean."

I nodded and was certain that he had skeletons, just like the rest of us. The difference was, no one wanted to write tell-all books about the rest of us.

"I would never do anything to harm your girls. I promise." We caught each other in eye contact just at that moment and the gaze held. I felt he could see inside me. He nodded once and smiled. The message had been passed. Everything was safe with me. He reached over, still smiling, and squeezed my hand as it rested on the console, then kept that contact between us the rest of the ride home.

"Davy... David..." I spoke softly. "We may be new friends, but I consider our friendship to be solid and everlasting. I dread the day you have to leave."

I let it all hang there, because frankly, I didn't know how or when we would part, but I was fairly certain that some powers that be – or some situation – would wrench him from my life. I hated that idea. I often refused to even think of it, but there were times – those times when I would lie in bed and stare at the ceiling – when I knew he'd have to leave me someday, but then I'd arise and push those thoughts from my mind.

Good one, Macca, I'd chide myself. *You finally have a delightfully solid relationship with someone and he's a ghost. Yeah, you're so good at this.... NOT.*

"I heard that, you know."

I turned to him, stuck my tongue out, and blew raspberries at him. "No privacy," I mumbled. "No sense of personal space," I muttered some more.

"I can give you a lot of personal space, if that's what you really want."

I gulped. "No, never mind. Forget I thought any of that or said anything. It's all good."

I hated that he smiled so smugly, but then he squeezed my hand again, and I felt the warmth return. He was there to guide me, yes, but he was also there to be given some insight from me as well. There was much to do… for both of us.

THIRTY-SEVEN

Making Music

As soon as we arrived home, Davy's inner sixteen-year-old took over. I'd barely gotten the door closed before he was unzipping the case and pulling his new guitar out. He ran to the kitchen, clutching his new "baby" in one hand, and then rummaged in the drawer of tea towels. Pulling out a particularly soft flour sack cloth, he perched against the dining table and gently rubbed every inch of the instrument.

"Would you two like to be alone?"

He chuckled quietly under his breath. "Of all the things I've missed – my daughters, my animals..." he paused, concentrating on the area underneath the strings before he continued. "Music is up there as well."

"I can only imagine." I didn't know what else to say.

He tossed the cloth aside and moved back into the living room, perching on the armchair. I sat on the sofa across from him, Chester joining me and wanting attention. Davy strummed the guitar a bit, the smile stretching across his face. He tuned the instrument for several minutes. When it was to his liking, he chose a few chords and then began to sing a song about a ceiling in his room. As I listened, I realized it was telling a story that sounded remarkably like his early days as a Monkee.

I didn't recognize the song, but I admit to being somewhat in the dark about a lot of the music from his past. However, the poignant words went straight to my core. Davy's sweet face betrayed no emotion other than the joy of singing and playing his new guitar.

"That's so lovely," I whispered when he ended.

"Thank you. Believe it or not, I wrote that with some mates way back in the day."

"Then that makes it even more lovely."

"Semi-autobiographical. Rough times. Good times. Wild decades." I left his cryptic comment alone. He would discuss those times if and when he was ready.

"So, when you gonna show me how to play that contraption?" I used my best imitation of a hillbilly, which I admit wasn't very good, but it worked to lighten the atmosphere.

"First lesson, right now." He scooted back in the armchair and patted the cushion in front of him. I sat down where he indicated between his legs, and he scooted close behind me, balancing the guitar across the front of us. He showed me how to tuck the guitar against my body with my right arm, and how to hold the neck in my left hand.

"Place these fingers here... here... and here." He put my finger tips on the strings. "These dividing ridges are called frets. Now hold those strings down tightly and strum."

A plunkety-plunk-plunk sound came out. "Yikes," I cringed.

"Never fear. That just means that you aren't connecting the strings to the neck tightly enough. Press a little harder," and he pushed down on each of my fingers.

"Ouch."

"Yeah, you'll get callouses eventually and get used to it. Now strum again," he said when I'd increased the pressure.

A lovely melodic blending of notes resulted. I squealed in delight. "I made that noise!"

He chuckled, and his mouth alongside my ear and his warm breath tickled my hair and skin. Between the heady sensations of my sudden ability to create a musical sound, and the enticing closeness of this incredibly sexy man, I was completely lost in a fog. I shivered, and Davy pulled me closer.

"Cold?" He grinned at me, our faces so close.

"No, rather overwhelmed," I whispered.

"Music mingles souls," he whispered back.

I swear, if I'd been in a bodice-ripping romance novel right then, I would have swooned. But I'm a level-headed person... sometimes. And I could look at situations objectively... usually. And I wasn't one to get my feathers ruffled... most of the time. But hell, who was I kidding? I couldn't even finish a coherent thought or catch my breath. I cleared my throat. "Show me more!" I nearly choked on the words, but it managed to clear my head.

He chuckled and began placing my fingers for another chord. After four such chords and having me practice switching from each,

146

he gave me a little hug. "I think you're ready for a song! Do you know 'Scarborough Fair'?"

"My mother sang that to me when I was little! Yes!"

He nodded as if he already knew this, and we began to very slowly play and sing. I admit, he helped me through most of it, but I was getting the hang of this newfangled contraption – and loving it.

After what seemed like several hours but was really only about sixty or so minutes, my fingers were screaming to stop.

"Owwww," I moaned and shook them. "Ow, ow, owwww!"

He chuckled at me. "I strongly suggest ice. Ice and keep playing. The more you play, the faster your fingers will become accustomed, and the less they'll hurt."

"So, in the words of Ringo Starr, 'I've got blisters on my fingers!'" We pulled apart from each other, laughing, and I handed the guitar back to Davy. I retrieved a bottle of Chianti, two glasses, and a small bowl of ice for my fingers, and then returned to the living room. Davy sang and played through most of the night, breaking only once for some leftover pasta salad. The level of wine in the Chianti bottle went down pretty quickly. It was one of the most comfortable evenings in my life, and I wish I could have recorded it to view it over and over again.

"This has been the best night in a bloody long time," Davy declared.

THIRTY-EIGHT

Wishing Detective Green
Would Turn Blue

One afternoon while I was bent over the task of scrubbing a table in the main dining room, two loafer covered feet came into view on the other side. As I looked up with a smile, it turned quickly into a grimace when I saw it was Detective Green... again. Two police officers stood flanking the doorway, my only escape. What? Did they really think I'd try it? This island might be the biggest in the chain, but in the larger scope of things, it's pretty damned small.

"Miss Liberty." No greeting, no *go to hell*, just my name. The man had such a way with people.

"Detective Green." Two could play the rudeness game.

"Sit down." He pointed to a chair while taking the opposite seat.

"Excuse me, but this is *my* domain. I'll sit when I damned well want to sit, thankyouverymuch."

He gave an exasperated sigh. "I have questions... and I have news."

I dropped into the chair he had pointed to, my jaw slackened. *News? And he was going to actually share it? Wow.* Davy appeared beside me and perched on the back of the other chair, his elbows propped on his knees, his chin in his hands. How did he do that?

"In the course of our investigation, it has come to our attention that there seems to be a connection between Louis Cabral and your neighbor, Mr. Sikes."

"W-w-what?"

"Mr. Cabral was Mr. Sikes' estranged illegitimate son... from an affair many years ago."

I gulped. "Mr. Sikes is married?"

Davy snorted in laughter. "That's all you got from that statement, Babe?"

I glanced at Davy, then back to Detective Green. "What does this have to do with me though?"

148

"We're not yet at liberty to tell you more except that it was Louis who poisoned your bird, and also, there is a great deal of evidence that he may also have been the one who ran your uncle off the road."

My vision blurred for a moment, and I felt a deep coldness seeping into my body. I grabbed the table to steady myself, now very relieved I'd actually taken a seat. Davy was right beside me, rubbing my arms and whispering assurances in my ear. I nodded, just a barely perceptible movement of my head.

"Are you all right, Miss Liberty?" Perhaps Detective Green actually did have a heart, for he looked concerned for a moment.

"I... yes... I could use a glass of water though." My throat had seized up and the words came out in a hoarse whisper. I tried to stand to pour a glass from the pitcher on the sideboard at the end of the room, but Davy held me down in my seat, and Detective Green instructed one of the officers to pour a glass for me. "Thank you," I whispered as it was set in front of me. The poor officer looked sympathetic. I drank steadily until the water was nearly gone. The tightness in my throat eased which seemed to bring the warmth back to my body as well. Davy was crouched beside me, his arm around my waist, and then my silent tears began to fall.

I had accepted that Uncle Wally had been the victim of a freak accident. This was a whole new kettle of fish to fry. Fish. I was suddenly hungry, and I had been a vegetarian my entire life. It's odd how the body reacts to unwelcome news.

"I'm unable to give you any more information at this time though," Detective Green continued.

"But, that means Winston is safe again?"

"It would appear so. There are no known accomplices, and his motive isn't clear yet. We did find your uncle's laptop in Mr. Cabral's possessions as well. I apologize, but it's evidence at this point, so it will have to remain in our custody for now."

"Why would he hate us all so much..." it wasn't really a question they could answer so I let it trail off. Wiping my eyes, I stood again and extended my hand to shake Detective Green's. He seemed startled at first, probably unaccustomed to being treated civilly, but he took my proffered hand and shook it guardedly, like I was going to attack

149

him or something. "Thank you." I couldn't smile through my tears, but I tried. "Thank you for taking the time to let us... me know."

"Just remember, we don't know who killed Mr. Cabral yet, so be careful."

I pulled my hand back. I hadn't even thought of that part. My brain must have been stuck in the frozen hell of Uncle Wally's death. "I will," I promised, though not very sure of myself.

I walked them out to the parking lot and then hurried back to our cottage. Davy was waiting for me, standing in the center of the living room.

"Bloody hell, Babe, I'm so sorry."

I began to shake again, and he enveloped me in his warm embrace, the velvet of his eight-button shirt so comforting against my own bare arms. We rocked back and forth until I regained my composure enough to speak.

"Poor Uncle Wally. He just wanted to have some fun in the tropics." I wiped my face on Davy's velvet. Hey, I was taking advantage of the fact that spectral clothing is immune to tears. I'd seen proof over the last months.

THIRTY-NINE

Paper Trails to You, Until We Meet Again

The twinkle of my phone for an incoming text message woke me at half past I'm-going-to-kill-the-sender. Bleary-eyed, I pushed the button. Sure enough, another wrong number. If this kept up, I was going to throw this phone into the Pacific.

"Hey, u there? Why u no pick up when I call? Lazy ass," was the lovely voice mail left for me. The number was unfamiliar, of course, but I recognized a New York area code, where half of the day was gone already. Asshole. I threw the phone across the room but got zero satisfaction when it landed on the pile of clothes from Uncle Wally's closet.

I peered at the bedside clock. 5:09. Yes, AM. I closed my eyes and tried to fall back to sleep, but thoughts kept invading my mind, and I just couldn't turn it off. Groaning, I gave up and jumped in the shower. I pulled on my favorite type of clothing: shorts and a tank top. In Hawaii, that had become a sort of uniform for me. Even when it rained, it was warm.

What to do, what to do. I decided at last that the phone landing in the soft pile of Uncle Wally's clothes was a sign. I went out to Winston's cage and let him welcome the morning.

I love Macca. I love Davy. Sleepy Jean.

"I love you too, Winston. You're my favorite birdie!" I made a kissy sound at his cage, which he fervently matched before fluttering to the separate perch outside his cage.

Back in the cottage, I tip-toed to the kitchen and brewed an entire pot of Kona, complete with Bennie's secret ingredients. I selected a mug that was imprinted with the word *Aloha*, added some half and half, and then poured the rich, dark brewed coffee into it. Taking the steaming mug with me, I returned to the bedroom.

Sitting cross-legged on the floor, I picked out each item of Uncle Wally's clothing, holding it up to view it before shaking it out. Many of the garments landed in a pile I was creating for charity. There was another pile to keep – mostly for sentimental value. For example, my uncle's old college sweatshirt looked soft and inviting. My fingers

151

brushed against something with corduroy, and I was overwhelmed by memories of Uncle Wally and Aunt Fran. I held up the old corduroy blazer with suede patches on the elbows. He'd had that since I was just a child. I pressed it to my face and took a deep sniff. "Yep," I sniffed again. "That's my Uncle Wally." The fragrance was a combination of soap and shaving cream. "I love you Uncle Wally, wherever you are... and you too Aunt Fran." I decided to keep the jacket for now. I needed it as a sort of security blanket.

I finally whittled the pile down to just two items. One was a wacky looking tee-shirt that declared the wearer to be Dolphin Friendly. I had to chuckle at that, and tossed it onto the "keep" pile. Tee-shirts are always good to have, even if you simply use them for sleeping, and since I'm dolphin friendly too, I felt I could comfortably wear it in public.

The final item of clothing was a pair of khaki slacks – old, faded, and worn. I checked the pockets, for Uncle Wally had been notorious for stuffing things into them, and I pulled out several pieces of paper and two quarters. Cool. Quarters were good to keep in the car – you never knew when you might need a Kona coffee while you were out and about, and with enough quarters, I'd be able to purchase one.

The tattered paper was folded several times. I carefully opened it, then opened it again, then opened it some more. Before me was a faded, dog-eared letter.

Dear Wally,

Forgive me for not writing to you sooner, but I've been really busy. I met a wonderful lady here on the big island. We'd been seeing each other for several months, and I finally did it – I popped the question! Me! I even got down on one knee. You would have laughed – hell, you're probably laughing now. Especially since she had to help me back up after. Hahaha. Old knees – you feel that pain too?

Well, we got married. And low and behold, we're suddenly owners of a little hotel here in Hawaii! Me, the platoon cut-up! Ha! Seems her daddy owned a whole bunch of land, and it had two hotels on it. He split them up and gave her the smaller of the two. It's perfect! She showed me the letter from her dad, too. Wally, you'd never believe it but she keeps all this stuff about owning the place inside a book, for gods sake!

But now I'm living the good life, and I really hope you will come visit us very soon. We have an extra bedroom too, and don't even begin to think that you would be a problem or a third wheel. Remember all those rooms we all shared back in the day? Just know that Louise and I want you to come stay with us. We will show you the good life that you and I used to dream about in the dark times.

Sincerely, your army buddy and good friend forever,

Jimmy The Beak Martinello

The weary gears in my brain started to turn. Louise? Inheritance? Two adjoining properties? To the south of us was a state park, and to the north was... Gilbert Sikes.

"DAVY!" I tried to scramble to my feet but my legs were locked in a pretzel. I leaned forward, unfolded my legs, and boosted myself to a standing position. "DAVY!" I kept yelling, because I was getting absolutely no response. I ran to the living room – it was empty. I ran to the extra bedroom that we'd called his own – empty. I stood in the center of the living room and yelled one last time – "DAAAAAVID THOMAS JOOOOONES!!"

His shimmer showed up in front of me before he did. "What? What's wrong?"

"Where *were* you?" Even I could hear the panic in my voice.

He grasped my shoulders and forced me to look directly into his eyes. "Calm down, Babe. I'm right here. What's wrong? And... by the way... few people in my life ever called me by my full name... and lived to tell the tale."

"This!" I thrust the paper in his face, my chest heaving with gasps of breath, and ignoring his idle threat.

He took the paper from me far too calmly, turned away, and read it with great deliberation, and then he had the nerve to stop, scratch his chin... and read it AGAIN! I squeezed my eyes shut, shaking my head. This couldn't be happening. His total calm was infuriating.

"Don't you SEE?" I pointed at the paper, tapping it and making it jiggle in his hands. The look he gave me perfectly conveyed that of a patient yet irritated parent.

153

"Let me study this, please?" His seeming serenity was overwhelming. I yelled nonsensical words, turned my back, and stomped out to the deck, throwing myself into one of the deck chairs.

"Damn," I mumbled under my breath. "Damn, damn, damn, and damn some more" – an oath I'd long ago heard my father say. I heard the chair beside me scrape the deck as it was moved closer to me. Davy planted himself in it.

"You're cute when you swear."

I glared at him. "And you're infuriating at times."

He blinked slowly. "So I've been told."

That stopped me for a moment. Sometimes he divulged so much, and it slipped past me too easily – far too easily. I must have been staring at him with my jaw open, for he smiled and used his hand to make an act of closing my mouth for me. I snapped it shut and was quiet. What the hell do you say to that? And then suddenly I was incensed again.

"See? How do you *do* that? How do you distract me from my focus? And *why* do you do that? What does it accomplish?"

It was his turn to be quiet for a while. Slowly, he raised the letter still clutched in his hand. "This... explains a lot."

"Not to me," I huffed.

He turned to look at me, his patience finally wearing thin. "I've been over at Sikes' place a lot the last few weeks."

"What?!" I stared at him in shock.

"When things are quiet here, I go to Sikes' and watch him." He looked away from me, gazing out across the ocean.

"Just watch?" My eyes narrowed in suspicion.

He grinned quickly, but it disappeared almost as fast as it had materialized. "I admit I like to torment him with little irritants."

"Good. But tell me the rest."

"I've been watching him, and he acts suspiciously. A lot." He turned in his chair to give his undivided attention to our conversation. "I don't trust him, Macca. There's something off about him. And this," he shook the letter still grasped in his hand, "this gives me something to go on, to prove there is more to this than people would think."

"So... what should we do?"

154

"Research. All night if necessary."

"Sounds great to me." I jumped up and booted up the laptop.

"Good. You go high tech... I'll go old-school." He sat cross-legged on the floor in front of Uncle Wally's grander-than-a-cottage-deserves bookcases. One at a time, he pulled Uncle Wally's books out and leafed through the pages, carefully, and not haphazardly.

I began searching for any records of Louise Sikes and her family, and I threw in Jimmy "the Beak" Martinello as well as Walter Collins, aka Wally.

"I'm finding receipts for clothing, groceries, and books even – dating back to 1998. This won't be quick," Davy moaned from the floor.

"I'm finding very little on Louise Sikes," I updated him. Her mother was Louise, Sr.? Who does that?" I shook my head and kept going. "Her father was Gilbert, Sr. What the hell?" Whenever I came across a Louise or a Gilbert Sikes I had to stop and figure out which one. It was frustrating, and after a while my head felt like it was spinning on my neck. I took notes as best I could.

"Okay, Gilbert, Sr. – Daddy – was born in 1898. Louise, Sr. – Mama – was born in 1930. Oooh, Daddy robbed the cradle. They were married in 1945, Gilbert was born in 1950, and Louise followed in 1955. Mama died in 1997 – cancer. Daddy died in 1999 – at the ripe old age of 101. Wow!" I heard Davy whistle.

"He must have been living right!" Davy chuckled. *"Ever eat a pine tree? Many parts are edible.* Euell Gibbons' famous last words."

"Who?" What the hell was he talking about?

He shook his head at me sadly. "So young..." and then he *tsked.* I hated when he *tsked.* "The old Grape Nuts guy? Swore that eating natural health foods would make him live forever?" he trailed off and shook his head. "But I digress. Continue!"

I waited a full beat before I went back to my research notes. "Louise, Jr., now just Louise, married Jimmy The Beak – who makes up this stuff? – in 2000, one year after her Daddy had died and left her the inn. Then *she* died in 2004 – an accident. An accident?" I looked up at Davy and shook my head. There were too many accidents for this to be coincidental. I continued, "The inn then transferred to Jimmy, who died in 2010 from another accident. He left the inn to his

155

best friend and old army buddy, my Uncle Wally." I flopped back in my chair, exhausted. "I feel like I've run a marathon."

Davy tossed a stack of receipts at me. "Time to run another one. Go through these and see if any are worth keeping."

"Ugh." I pushed the laptop away and started sorting through the slips of papers. "She liked to shop."

"That she did."

"And eat. Lots of groceries. Oh! Could it be she was personally buying all the Spam for this place, instead of using a business account?"

"Could be. Perhaps Daddy's little girl never got schooled in the operation of an inn." He stopped shuffling papers for a moment, gazing out the window but not really seeing anything. I could tell.

"Hello?"

"Oh, sorry." He shook his head. "I was lost in thought. It was unfamiliar territory."

I snorted a laugh at his self-deprecating humor and saw him grin back at me as he went back to the papers. I pulled the laptop back and looked up accidents in the area, going back several years. The police reported everything to the local paper, so I had to wade through years of everything from simple falls on the sidewalk in front of the grocery to a fatality involving two cars and a mountain. At first I tried putting the last name Sikes in the search field but soon realized she would have used her married name. Using Martinello instead brought up several items, all associated with Louise and The Beak. There was a report of vandalism here at the inn. I clicked the link and read the details.

"Two years before Uncle Wally inherited this place there was $10,200 worth of vandalism reported!"

"Wow, what happened?" He had dumped a huge stack of papers in a box that I had retrieved from the main supply closet in reception and was now using as a filing cabinet, bidding farewell to Louise's very eccentric filing methods.

"The swimming pool was emptied using a hose that ended in the dining area. The water flooded the entire room, plus the adjoining reception area. The report says that if there hadn't been a drain in the kitchen floor it might have been worse."

156

He gave a low whistle again. "The plot thickens. Did they catch anyone?"

"No, and no suspects were named."

"Listen to you, going all *Law & Order* on us." He chuckled when I stuck my tongue out at him before we turned back to our tasks again.

It's Clear as Black and White, Dynamite

After a couple of hours of research, I felt like I was going blind from reading web pages. I stood and stretched. We'd skipped breakfast. "Hungry?"

"I passed hungry an hour ago. I'm in the homestretch to stahving."

I smiled and shook my head lightly, wandering out to the main dining area to see what sumptuous lunch items Kalei and Lani had provided on the buffet. I found some luscious sesame coleslaw, a cold quiche, and a fresh fruit bowl of sliced mangoes, papaya, and strawberries. I loaded a tray, thinking briefly that people who saw how much food I'd often take back to the cottage probably thought I ate an awful lot. Oh well. Being the boss had big advantages, as they all kept their silence about it.

"Lunchtime!" I called as I placed the tray upon the kitchen counter.

"Wow, Kalei has outdone himself once again," Davy marveled as he filled a plate. "This looks fabulous!"

We decided to take a full break and eat at the dining table. "Oh my gosh. Kalei sure has a way with quiche, right?" I asked Davy, but all he could do was nod emphatically as he stuffed more into his mouth, causing me to give a bit of a giggle.

Within a few moments, it was all gone. I rinsed the dishes and replaced them on the tray, returning it all to the kitchen and loading them into the large commercial dishwasher I'd only recently learned to use. So pleased with myself, I returned to find Davy already at work again in front of the bookcase.

"I made a pot of tea," he mumbled, and I did indeed see that he had a mug beside him.

"Thank you!" A cup of tea was just the stay-awake juice I needed. I fixed my cup and then returned to the laptop. Sighing loudly, I leaned my head in one hand while I scrolled through the stories. I stopped now and then to make more notes.

158

"Bloody hell!" Davy leaped to his feet, holding out a paper. It appeared to be a letter – actually more like a sinister note – to Louise. I glanced down at the signature. It was from her brother!

Louise –
You stupid bitch. I told you we needed to combine these properties for maximum profits. I warned you! You'll be very sorry. Accept the partnership or pay the price. Father was right. You never were very smart. One way or another, I'll own it all.
Gilbert

We just stared at each other, our jaws slack and our eyes rather glazed over for a moment as we took it all in. Finally, I began to stutter over my words. "I-I-I think this is an ominous threat, don't you?"

"It's not good, Babe, and as much as you don't like him, I think you need to call Detective Green."

"I think so too." I shook the cobwebs of evil out of my head. "But shouldn't we make sure there are no others?"

"Perhaps you're right." He pulled books out and stacked them in two separate towers. "You take those and I'll continue with these. Be careful though. Some of the smaller papers hide."

I nodded, absorbed in really ugly thoughts, but began again to leaf through the pages of the books. It took several hours, but in the end we had amassed seven similar threatening letters from Gilbert to Louise, as well as love letters from sweet Jimmy the Beak to Louise, and one last nasty-gram from Gilbert to Jimmy, presumably after poor Louise's demise.

"D'ya wonder if Evil Gilbert ever sent something wicked to your Uncle Wally too?" Davy's face was creased with a frown of worry and sympathy at the same time.

"I do wonder, but Uncle Wally would have put it in a file. I've yet to find any personal files – if he even had any. He must have had his tax info some place too."

I sat and chewed my thumbnail, racking my brain for an answer. Suddenly, I flashed on Uncle Wally and Aunt Fran's home when I

159

was younger. They didn't use filing cabinets, but they did use file folders! And where did they keep them?

"Oh my gosh," I whispered and sprinted to the closet in Uncle Wally's – *my* bedroom. There on the top shelf was what I had thought was the empty box for the printer, but upon nudging it I determined it was heavy. I couldn't get a good hold on it.

"Come on, Babe!" I heard Davy cheering behind me. "Stretch higher!"

I reached so hard I even heard something pop in my shoulder.

"Oh," Davy chuckled, "that didn't sound good."

"It didn't feel so good either." I stretched as far as I could without toppling over. Pulling with my fingertips, I was able to scoot it closer and closer until I was able to let it tumble to my feet. It was filled with file folders. "Uncle Wally, you scamp!"

We plopped on the floor with our legs crossed and went through them. The were labeled clearly – Taxes/Finances, Correspondence, Bills, Deeds, Legal Docs, etc.

The first thing we did was look inside the Deeds folder, and we saw reference to the fact that Alex Baldwin had the ownership documents on file for the family. In the Taxes/Finances folder were basic tax filings and bank statements. Nothing looked out of the ordinary there. However, in the Correspondence file we found a jackpot – several love letters from Louise to Jimmy the Beak that Uncle Wally had perhaps found and kept. The only thing those proved was that it really was a loving relationship. More importantly, we also discovered two nasty-grams from Gilbert Sikes to Uncle Wally dated after his inheritance of the property. Why hadn't he gone to the authorities?

For several minutes we just sat on the floor, looking helplessly about at all the papers we'd pulled that were to be given to Detective Green. Finally, I heaved a sigh and got to my feet. "I'll call him now."

Surprisingly, I reached the disagreeable man on the second ring of his phone.

"Green."

"Hello Detective Green. This is Macca Liberty." Dead silence on the other end, so I plowed ahead. "I've found several documents and

160

letters pertaining to... the various relationships between Mr. Sikes and this inn. I thought you should see them."

Various relationships? What the hell was that? I just got tongue tied. I mean, what I really wanted to say was, "I think I have proof that Mr. Sikes is indeed an asshole who wanted to terminate the lives of anyone who he considered to be in his way." Yeah, that would have resulted in a swift hang-up or a trip to the state mental institution. Did Hawaii actually have one of those? I really didn't want to find out.

"What kind of documents?"

"I mean the kind of documents where Mr. Sikes had been threatening Louise, Jimmy Martinello, and my Uncle Wally."

To his credit, Detective Green didn't respond with some smart ass comment. In fact, he remained silent. That, in itself, was just a bit... uncharacteristic. But I can do silent too, if need be. Of course, it wasn't as easy for me because I wanted to shout at him, "You asshole! Turn on the light, get your ass over here, and look at these letters!" but instead, I remained calm and silent. I swear, I deserved a medal. Or two. Maybe even a statue that didn't look like me... on a pedestal. Okay, now I was just yanking my own chain – but that's what happens when I'm freaked out over stuff pertaining to my loved ones.

"Do you have these documents in your possession now, Miss Liberty?"

Oh, man, I sure hoped no one tripped over the pole that was up this guy's butt. "Yes, I'm looking at them right now. In my hands. Now." As in, *get yourself over here now*? *Patience, patience*, I chided myself. I picked up a magazine we'd unearthed and threw it toward the picture window that looked out on the serene Pacific. Yeah, right – serenity on the surface, turmoil beneath. I identified with that at times.

"Will you be there for an hour or so? I can have someone pick it up."

"You know what?" This was an impulsive decision, but I was sick of his treating me as if every question I answered was a lie and anything I offered was inconsequential. "I'll be in the area in the next half hour. I'll bring it all by." I ended the call before he could come up with any more lame comments.

"Mini-road-trip!" Davy was on board, figuratively speaking. I filled my arms with all we had found and trotted out to R2, Davy

161

beside me, and off we went. The police station was a small cinder block building with double-doors of glass in the front and very high-placed windows. In short, it was so ugly that I was certain criminals tried to live on the straight and narrow just so they wouldn't have to visit the place.

I parked R2, marched inside with Davy at my heels, and told the receptionist I had an appointment with Detective Green.

"Go, Macca," Davy quietly cheered behind me.

The receptionist briefly spoke into an outdated telephone and then asked me to take a seat.

"No thank you. I'll stand." Hey, I was on a roll. I wasn't about to give up now.

It was only about ten minutes before Green appeared and led me back to his office. Davy floated beside me with a big thumbs-up aimed in my direction. I shooed him away and composed myself, the overstuffed folders in my arms.

"Have a seat, Miss Liberty," Detective Green directed me as he took his own place behind his battered desk. I briefly considered continuing my stubborn act but decided sitting was better. This might take a while. However, once I was sitting I realized the error of my ways, for the chair was hard and rickety and had curves in all the wrong places. Still, I rocked forward on its rickety legs and placed my folder on Detective Green's desk.

"This is everything we found in Louise Sikes-Martinello's books, and in Walter Collins' files." I opened the front cover and pointed to the first document, then leaned back for him to take in the rest on his own. "As you can see, that is the first of the threatening letters. There are many, some so chilling that I felt you should see for yourself."

He read the top letter, and to his credit, reacted with a frown and a glance at me before he turned to the next, and the next, and so on. I felt relieved that I'd gotten his attention at last. Poor Uncle Wally. Poor Jimmy and Louise too.

When Detective Green had finished reading everything, he closed the file and folded his hands over the front of the folder. "I thank you, Miss Liberty, for bringing this to me. I assure you we will go over each document. Let me ask you... to your knowledge, are you the

162

only one, other than the recipients, to have touched these papers? As far as you know, I mean?"

I gulped. Do ghosts leave fingerprints? I made an executive decision and hoped it was the right thing to do. "Yes, only me."

He arose and held out his hand. "Thank you again. This will be quite helpful. We'll let you know when our investigation is complete. And remember to be careful. Don't let anyone know that you've seen these." I nodded, promising to be vigilant. We shook hands, civilly, and said our goodbyes.

In the car on the way home, I felt quiet, but I also had a million questions that had no answers yet. Davy rested his hand on mine on the console. It had already been a long day and I was ready for sleep.

FORTY-ONE

Lookout Point, Here Comes Tomorrow

I decided that today was a well deserved day of rest. Finding the letters and documents, and seeing my uncle's personal feelings laid out for strangers to analyze had served for a highly emotional day.

I put on my typical Macca uniform – pink shorts and a white tank top – and stretched out in the shady part of the deck with my Kindle. It was time to vegetate with a good old easy-going mystery novel. While I usually leaned toward a book by Janet Evanovich or Sue Grafton, today I had a new author to read – Amanda M. Lee. A bit of frothy snarky dialogue from a hot-shot reporter kept me entertained, while the mystery wasn't taxing enough to keep me awake at night. However, I began to think of our own mystery. There were pieces missing, and I was sure the police held those pieces in a most-miserly manner.

I soon found my Kindle abandoned face down on the chair beside me as I gazed out to the Pacific, not really seeing it, but instead using it as a crystal ball of sorts. There were no answers though – only more questions and doubts.

The cottage was silent and the inn relatively quiet. I zipped up my windbreaker, grabbed a steaming cup of Kona in a commuter mug, and went for a walk, heading north away from the state park. With one hand in my pocket and the other holding the brew, I sipped occasionally while I peered out at the misty Pacific. The sunrise was just emerging on the horizon, a muted golden reflection on the mist and the nearly black sea.

I sat for a few moments on the Whispering Bench and idly smoothed my fingers over the words on the newly installed plaque.

In loving memory of Fran and Walter Collins
In loving memory of Jude Liberty and Willow Bodhi
A loving tribute to David Thomas Jones

Davy had been very touched when he first saw it, and I smiled at the memory.

164

My coffee nearly gone, I walked as far as the marker for the Sikes property and rested a bit at the Lookout Point Cliffs viewpoint. The albatross were coasting along the air currents, putting them near to eye level, the rocky coast far below. There was a small wooden barrier at the edge, but I was able to peek down at the gulch below. There were trees on either side of the viewpoint, and even a few volunteer branches poking out from the rocky sides of the cliff – seedlings trying desperately to take a solid hold and grow up to touch the sunlight above. How they managed to survive the sea spray and the rocks all the way down to the bottom was beyond me.

It took a mere twenty minutes to get home, for it was more direct than using the road. Driving time from our inn to Sikes' place the other day had been twenty minutes as well. I rinsed my cup and placed it in the main kitchen's dishwasher before returning to the cottage.

"Where have you been?" Davy ambushed me when I opened the door.

"I went for a nice walk along the Lookout Point Cliff path. It's good for thinking."

He visibly relaxed then. "Thinking is dangerous, y'know."

I grinned and hugged him briefly. "Yeah."

I took to making that same walk early each morning. It was a great way to get a bit of exercise but also gave me time to clear my head in preparation for the day ahead.

165

FORTY-TWO

Cuddly Toys and Other Creatures

Despite the rather frightening discoveries of the previous days, I was still marveling at how Hawaii, in general, seemed to agree with us all. Chester had taken to wandering out to the back deck and watching the butterflies and other insects that flitted about. He seemed so much more content than he had been in Los Angeles. The change of residence seemed to have added some kitten behaviors back into him as well.

One day, a butterfly landed on Davy's folded hand as he rested it on the arm of the deck chair. We both sat still, amused. Chester, however, was beside himself. He did the old wiggle-butt and pounce thing, but years of the complacency of apartment life had caused his hunting skills to become a bit sluggish. The butterfly floated up to the trees, and Chester leaped up onto the railing to watch. I held my breath, for it was quite a drop to the pavement below.

"Chester?" I said quietly, not wanting to startle him but trying to distract him from the butterfly quest.

He turned and gave me a slow blink. I chuckled, interpreting his expression as, *Please, Human, give me some credit.* Then he ever so lightly jumped back onto the deck. I let my breath out and hadn't even realized I'd been holding it.

The young feline had also developed a few new habits, such as sleeping beside me on the bed, and sometimes on top of me. Cats don't follow the normal rules of physics. They have no inertia. A cat in motion can stop at a moment's notice and change directions as if he had been running that way the entire time – until they fall asleep, at which point no human force on Earth can move them. I often thought Davy might find me some morning, suffocated by the pressing of sixteen pounds of cat on my chest.

And who said that cats and birds can't get along? Winston and Chester had become best buddies. I often found the crazy bird grooming the purring feline with his beak. Other times, Chester would lick Winston's feathers – and always in the correct direction, never "against the grain," so to speak. It had come to be a very normal sight to see the big orange cat greeting guests quietly and accepting a skritch or two, while in turn, the big grey bird chatted them up. They were the darlings of Hale Mele.

Hale Mele. Our new sign had been commissioned to a local woodworker and put in place. We christened it, not with a bottle of champagne (Who would waste such good stuff?) but with a glass of Kalei's now nearly famous iced tea. Team Wally cheered with me and hugs were shared when I declared in my best Queen Elizabeth imitation, "I now declare this bridge... erm... inn... OPEN."

Davy had taken to playing the guitar on the back deck, especially in the early evening hours. Chester, Winston, and I were his rapt audience. I liked to imagine that somewhere along the auditory stratosphere, the melodies reached other ears as well.

FORTY-THREE

She Hangs Out

I continued my early morning walks but also added an early
evening run most days, unless we were slammed with guests and the
demands of the business. I was slowly getting in shape again.
Occasionally Davy would run with me, his spectral feet never hitting
the ground, his brow never breaking a sweat. I envied that at times.

Taking my daily walk early one morning, I stopped at the
Lookout Point Cliffs to watch the albatross soaring over the gulch.
The screeching cries they made were so melodic, singing a happy
morning tune to the world. This had become one of my favorite ways
of greeting the day.

"Miss Liberty." I hadn't heard the footsteps approach and the
sudden presence of another person gave me a fright. I sidestepped
quickly, letting out a little yelp.

"Oh." My hand went to my heart. "Mr. Sikes. You startled me."

"You shouldn't stand so close to the cliffs, Miss Liberty."

His gaze was dark and intense, and the slight smile on his face
made me shiver. "I was just... watching the albatross dance."

His eyes darted to the birds, then down to the rocks below before
coming to rest on my face yet again.

"Yes, well..." he spoke so quietly I could barely hear him against
the sound of the waves below and the albatross at our shoulders. "I've
been told you delivered some interesting documents to Detective
Green."

I felt the blush rise from my neck to the top of my ears. "Yes,
we... I mean, I found them in an old book." I nervously glanced up
and down the path, but I knew there'd be no one there at this hour.

"Frankly, Miss Liberty, you should mind your own business."

"I beg your pardon! The inn *is* my business!"

"No, you silly little fool, that inn and the land it is on is rightfully
mine." He glanced down at the rocky shore again and then at me once
more. I frowned, realizing that the man was indeed dangerous, and I
felt a tingly sensation, as if the world had suddenly slowed too much
on its axis. I edged to the side slightly, hopefully just enough to get a

168

running head start. I sent a mental appeal to the universe, directed at Davy. I sure hoped he was "listening" – or whatever it was that usually guided him to people and places.

Sikes grabbed at me in a move that caught me off balance and I tumbled to the ground. Ignoring the scrapes on my knees and palms, and the gravel that was burrowing into my skin, I screamed and fought to regain my footing.

In our scuffle, Sikes alternated between pushing me and pulling me closer to the edge of the cliff, muttering, "You've made yourself an irritant to me. You're that little something I have to stop and scrape off the heel of my shoe before I move any farther forward. You should savor that level of accomplishment, because it's going to be the high point of your short existence."

The edge seemed to creep closer to me. *Hello Albatross, can you catch me?* I thought silently in a brief moment of mental clarity. The idea of an albatross catching me seemed so absurd that a sound rather like maniacal laughter burbled up from inside me.

"You dare to laugh at me?" He was suddenly incensed and threw his weight into tossing me over the side.

I somehow was able to catch the small wooden post with one hand while using the other to hold onto Sikes' arm for dear life. I screamed then and heard the echo bouncing back and forth along the cliff walls and out to sea. "No!" I cried again as he tried to pull my fingers from the wooden post. As I felt my grip loosen, I put every bit of my life's strength into a good hardy tug and sent Sikes over the side of the cliff behind me. As he slid down my body, he grabbed onto my leg, and I used both of my hands to hang onto that post with all I had.

"DAAAAAAAAAAVYYYYYYYYYYY!" I screamed at full volume. I'd never known I could make such a sound.

I felt Sikes trying to claw up my bare leg, and I squeezed my eyes shut to tune out the pain as his nails shredded my skin. Hot tears escaped my closed lids and pooled in my ears as my face turned to the sky and the path that was now above my head. I tried to kick out to loosen his grasp, but all that did was intensify his talons on my skin.

"Over here! Over here!" I heard strange voices on the path. Opening my eyes in shock, I desperately searched my limited view, hoping I hadn't been hearing some new and cruel imaginary friends.

Hey, I loved a ghost, and anything was possible, but no, Detective Green and the two patrolmen from the other day appeared before me, arms reaching out.

"Ropes! Get ropes!" I heard the words being shouted but had no comprehension, no understanding of their meaning. "Anchor us!" I saw ropes being tied to the barrier, to trees on either side, and then suddenly someone was rappelling down the side while Green and the patrolman held onto my arms.

The Hero Rappeler, for that's what I saw him to be, hollered to those above, "I'm securing Sikes." I felt tugging and then was horrified to see my attacker being hoisted to safety first.

"NO! He... he... he..." I was trying to explain that he had pushed me, but I was nearly incoherent.

"It's okay," Detective Green said softly and smiled warmly at me. I held my breath to hear him. "We've got you. You're safe. He can't hurt you any more."

Letting out a whoosh of air, I bit my lower lip to keep it from trembling as I hung over the cliff, four arms holding onto me securely. "Don't let go, don't let go," I kept whispering. Out of a fog filled with hope and despair I saw Davy floating beside me. "Why are they leaving me here?" I began to cry again.

"Shh, shh, luv. They're not leaving you here. They've got you secured. You'll be fine. Just smile and think of England," he joked with me. I laughed faintly and he kissed my cheek. "I'm so proud of you." He put his arm around me and rested his forehead against mine. I loved that closeness, and it seemed to make me feel lighter. "You're incredibly brave, luv. Always remember that for me, all right?" I could only give a slight nod. I felt as if I was fading away, mercifully escaping this reality.

"I'm tired," I whispered.

"Hey!" Davy shouted in my ear. "Wake up, perk up, and be ready. Do not give up. Understood?"

It was the first time he'd ever been rather gruff with me, so I did indeed perk up just a little. I peered above. I was still secured by two sets of hands, and one officer was rappelling down beside me again. This time he stopped at my level. Davy shimmered and disappeared. I frantically searched the path above me for a glimpse of him but saw no brown-haired boy, no red velvet eight-button shirt, no tight bell-bottoms, nor white boots. I briefly thought he might have changed into beachwear, so I tried to refocus my search, but my eyes failed me. There were so many bodies above my head, I wondered who they all were and why they were there before I lost consciousness.

FORTY-FOUR

Oompa Loompas, Heffalumps and Woozles, Dancing Hippos, and Other Things That Go Bump in the Night

Standing in the middle of a supermarket, I saw giant pink hippos dressed in tutus pirouetting down the aisles. Oompa Loompas applauded. Heffalumps and Woozles laughed. Above me, the ceiling fell away and a lavender cloud floated by, but then I realized it wasn't really a cloud but rather feathers that began to flutter. Upon the cloud was a man with a hookah and a sitar. He was dressed as a clown with a yellow wig and bright red nose. The fluttering lavender feathers suddenly moved away from their formation, causing the clown to fall in slow motion. The feathers surrounded me in a menacing manner, trying to suffocate me. I knocked them away, and they flew back to the yellow-wigged clown who smiled wickedly. A flock of African Grey parrots chased the lavender feathers and their passenger far from sight.

The ground below me began to move, rather like a conveyor belt, snaking me through a forest of short blue trees and smiley faced flowers. The conveyor belt turned into a chariot that was blue as ice, being pulled by fifteen gold and silver horses. No one held the reins; no one needed to, for they were well-behaved, yet spirited.

"She still back there?" One of the silver horses asked a golden friend. "We're not supposed to lose her, you know."

"I know, I know. I heard him." There was a hint of irritation in his words, but all fifteen of them pulled me along smoothly.

"Quiet up there, you two," a larger golden horse huffed, shaking his head but never breaking his gait.

Standing between the blue trees, I saw my Uncle Wally and Aunt Fran waving happily. I waved back. They were both dressed in shimmery clothing of the forties – she in a gown that looked like

172

molten silver, much like something Ginger Rogers might have worn, while he wore top hat and tails.

On the other side of the path were my parents, also waving happily, but dressed in tie-dyed and gauzy clothes, wearing head bands and love beads.

Looking back to the left, Uncle Wally and Aunt Fran seemed to be following along, still waving, and keeping up with my parents on the right. I felt warm, loved, and suddenly motion sick. I retched and awoke to find myself in a hospital room, nurses bent over me as I tossed my cookies into one of those ugly pale green plastic kidney bean-shaped basins. One of them applied a large sticker to my neck.

"This will help with the vertigo and nausea," she said with a smile. "Good to see you awake," she added.

A man in a white coat appeared to the left, and I worried he was going to take me to a mental institution, far from gold and silver horses and nasty clowns with yellow wigs.

"Hello, Miss Liberty." He, too, smiled. "I'm Dr. Lee. You've got a nasty bump on your head and a slight concussion that's causing the vertigo, but it should subside in time."

I tried to move, but my limbs weren't responding to my demands. Pain shot up my left arm from my wrist to my neck, which left me panting and fighting nausea again.

"Your shoulder was dislocated, as well," Dr. Lee continued. "We've immobilized it and are keeping it iced for now, but you should take care not to try to move it around just yet. If you'd like, we can give you something more for pain."

I nodded and squeezed my eyes shut. A needle was plunged into my IV tube and darkness fell in the room. I hoped the clown would stay away, but the horses were more than welcome to return.

173

FORTY-FIVE

Beat Girl

I awoke after a while with no more remembered dreams. Perhaps I didn't dream at all, but I did feel a little better. It hurt to move, but I knew I must or it would just increase the pain – I'd been in that catch-22 before. Very slowly turning my head a fraction to the side, I saw the familiar red velvet eight-button shirted young man sitting in the chair beside me. He looked up as I moved, and he leaned forward to grasp my good hand, taking care around the IV tubes and pole and such.

"Hello, luv," he whispered, his eyes soft but his jaw tense.

I smiled then. "Hi. Where have you been?"

"Right here. I rode in the ambulance with you. Secretly, of course." He smirked and cocked his head to the side. "How ya feelin'?"

"Sore. Tired. Relieved."

He squeezed my hand gently. "I'll take care of you."

"Just promise me there'll be no more cliffs, okay?"

"Not without a lifeline, a helmet, several thousand carabiners... oh, and a parachute."

I chuckled then, but the movement made me wince, and Davy put his finger to my lips to shush me. "People will think you're laughin' at yourself, y'know." I did love his teasing and his laughter. Especially his laughter.

The door opened and a nurse peeked in. "Oh! You're awake! I'll be right back," she promised... or threatened. It depended on her reason. Dr. Lee returned with her which wasn't so bad, but then Detective Green followed shortly thereafter which wasn't anything close to pleasant.

"The detective has a few questions for you," Dr. Lee spoke in his gentle manner, "but I warned him it was to be short and that he is not to upset you."

I smiled at the kind doctor and the nurse too. I moved my eyes so that I could watch Detective Green take the visitor chair that Davy

174

was in. Davy jumped up and scampered to the foot of the bed, wrinkling his nose in distaste.

"Miss Liberty," Detective Green began, "I'm glad to see you are well."

"Thank you."

"We have Mr. Sikes in custody for the murder of Louis Cabral, Louise Sikes Martinello, and James Martinello."

My eyes widened. "He killed Louise and Jimmy too?"

"We have a full confession. Louis knew the truth and apparently killed your uncle to gain favor with his estranged father, but Sikes wanted nothing to do with him. The young man then poisoned the bird because he'd been a witness. When Cabral then tried to blackmail Sikes, the young man paid with his life. Sikes also confessed to trying to murder you."

"Is he here in the hospital too?" I looked warily at the door.

"No, he's in custody in the county jail. He only had minor scrapes."

I frowned. "Bastard."

Detective Green nodded, seemingly in agreement, before continuing. "Could you please tell me your version of what went on at the cliffs yesterday?"

"Yesterday?" I frowned, not understanding what he was asking.

"Yes, the day you and Sikes met."

My eyebrows shot up. "That was *yesterday*? I thought it was today!"

"You've been sleeping for quite some time," Dr. Lee interrupted.

It took me a moment to grasp that I had lost an entire day. I saw Davy's sad expression as he leaned on the foot of the bed. No wonder he'd looked a little stressed. I would have been too, had the tables been turned.

"Miss Liberty," Detective Green spoke again, "if you could tell me what happened?"

"Oh! Yes." Dragging my mind back to the current time, I related the entire chance meeting with Sikes to him, but now I was beginning to wonder if it had indeed been just a chance meeting or if something more sinister had been afoot at the time. I decided I didn't really want that question answered. "Detective Green, will Mr. Sikes be going away for a very long time?"

"He will most likely get a life sentence. It depends upon the judge's decision after his allocution."

Okay, now I was feeling better!

I do have one more question, Miss Liberty." He pulled out a piece of paper sealed in a plastic bag, and I heard Davy utter a string of curses under his breath. "What I would like to know though is who put this on my desk, and how did that person know?"

I took the paper in my good hand and held it up shakily.

Macca Liberty is in danger.
Go to Lookout Point Cliffs NOW!

I knew the handwriting, but if I told Detective Green the truth, he'd think I was lying. On the other hand, I'd suffered an injury or two. After all, who knew if I were in my right mind at that moment, other than me?

I cleared my throat, handed the plastic encased paper back to him, and looked him straight in the eye. "A ghost." I heard the nurse gasp.

The detective stared at me for a long while before tucking the note back in his folder. "A ghost," he repeated my words.

I could tell he thought I was pulling his leg, but I nodded very gently in response. He glanced at the doctor, who shrugged his shoulders. The detective sighed and stood up. "Perhaps we will talk again when you're feeling... stronger."

Sure, I thought, *and then I'll tell you all about the unicorns in my closet and Santa Claus in the attic.*

Dr. Lee and the nurse followed the detective out of the room, leaving Davy behind with me. "You have unicorns in your closet? I had no idea." He grinned and patted my knee, but I cringed. I then remembered Sikes' nails scraping the backs of my legs as he tried to hang on.

"Oops, sorry Babe." Davy smiled and patted my good shoulder instead.

176

We held each other's gazes for a while, comfortable in the silence, but I broke it with, "So how did you manage to write that note to Green and leave it on his desk?"

He looked away a moment as if trying to remember, but I knew he had the answer right away. I let him play the stalling game, and just as I was about to yell at him, he responded. "I went to his office, picked up one of his pens, and scribbled on his notepad. Then... I went back to you."

"So, you've learned that little trick now too? Writing?"

"It's amazing how fear can drive one's actions."

"There's another area of confusion for me. Were you with me on my whole walk?"

Now he turned back to me with darkness in his expression. "No. I figured you were safe on your little walks, and I liked the idea of giving you space. Believe me – it won't happen again."

I stared at him. "I like having a little space," I whispered, "but I'm glad you found me."

"We need a safe word, a word you can scream inside your mind so that I'll be there."

"You choose. All I can think of is SAVE ME." We chuckled together, he with that nearly raspy, contagious sound, me with a soft sound so that it didn't jiggle the rest of my pain-racked body.

"How about 'Goldfish' for a safe word?"

I grinned. "It's perfect – so offbeat – just like us."

He swaggered a little in his chair, and I briefly wondered how he managed that. He was the only person I'd ever known who could strut while sitting down. "I don't know about you, but I'm a Cool Cat," he grinned.

"I always wanted to be a Beat Girl. Teach me?" We simply smiled at each other for several minutes. My eyelids grew heavy. "Wait, what's a Beat Girl?"

He kissed my forehead, "I'll teach you, Babe. I will." He stretched back in his chair and watched me as I fell asleep.

177

FORTY-SIX

I'll Be Back Upon My Feet

When I awoke, Davy was in the same position I'd left him, except his head was resting on his fist and his eyes were closed. I simply watched him for a while, noticing that when he "slept" he shimmered a bit, rather in between his solid and transparent state. He seemed to have finally figured out how not to hover. I smiled. In the last few months life had bounced around between good and bad. It felt good again now, but I was quite guarded for that very reason. Would he be leaving soon? I didn't want to think about it.

The nurse came in and checked my vitals again, waking the sleeping prince.

"Okay, Miss Liberty. Let's get you up and moving around. It will hurt less if you start working out the soreness – or the kinks as some people call them." She helped me out of bed and guided me halfway into a robe of sorts, my right shoulder immobilized in a brace that strapped around my back. We shuffled about the room, Davy softly encouraging me from his chair.

When she led me back to the bed, I pointed to a small gym bag on the third chair in the room. It was my gym bag, but I didn't know how it got there.

"Who brought that?" I asked the nurse.

"Oh, your Bennie from the inn brought you fresh clothes to go home in."

"Aww... That was very kind of him!"

"He's a nice boy. His mother works here in the hospital, in the cafeteria, you know."

Well, there's something I hadn't known. I needed to know my Team Wally better!

The nurse left me alone, and I inspected the scrapes and cuts down the backs of my legs. It wasn't pretty, but I carefully slid my feet back under the light blanket and lay back to rest.

I must have fallen asleep again because I woke with a start. The room was dark, and I felt scared and alone. My chest heaved in fear and someone whimpered. Then I realized it was me.

178

"I'm here, Babe," Davy spoke quietly from the dark corner his chair occupied.

Relieved, I let out the breath I'd been holding. Davy stood and crossed the room to take the chair closer to the bed. He covered my hand with his, stroking my knuckles with his thumb.

The door opened and the lights from the hallway shone in, the shadow of the nurse falling upon my bed as she entered. "Hello," she said so brightly. "How are you feeling?" She was the same nurse who had gasped at my mention of a ghost when Detective Green had been here.

"Much better, thank you. When can I go home?"

Davy moved back to the chair in the dark corner, his eyes on the nurse. I gave him a curious look but was distracted by the nurse's next words.

"Dr. Lee will check up on you later this morning and you can ask him then."

This morning? I'd lost yet another day? The nurse checked my vital signs. I watched every move, suspicious of almost everyone now.

She caught me watching and smiled cheerfully. "Would you like the lights on now?" she asked.

I nodded. "Yes please," and she flipped the switch before making her way back out to the bright hallway.

"What time is it?" I asked Davy.

"It's half seven."

I grinned. "Is that 6:30 or 7:30? Or perhaps 3:30? Half of seven..."

He stuck his tongue out at me and crossed to stand by my side. "You know what it means, you wee li'l wallaby."

"Wallaby?!" I burst out laughing and then suddenly covered my mouth, not wanting to be heard outside the door. "Wallaby?" I whispered it that time. "What's a wallaby? It reminds me of a song from childhood: *Willoughby Wallaby Wee, an elephant sat on me. Willoughby Wallaby Woo, an elephant sat on you.*

"Just keep that up, Wallaby, and I'll dislocate your other shoulder," he teased and kissed the tip of my nose.

"Oh, but then who would fetch you food from Kalei and Lani?" I teased right back.

179

"Well, it certainly won't be you, my dear, at least for a little while," as he pointed to my injured arm.

"Oh yeah." I shut up then.

"Yeah." And he looked so smug then, satisfied he'd had the last word.

Dr. Lee and the nurse chose that time to come check on me. Davy sat in the corner again, biting his nails this time. This was a head-scratcher. I'd have to ask him about that some other time.

"I think we'll be able to let you go home today, Miss Liberty!"

"I'm ready!" I was more than ready.

"Do you have a way to get home?"

"We... I'll call a cab."

"Very well. Let me get you discharged, and Nurse Jones will bring your aftercare instructions."

"Nurse Jones?" I smiled and bit my lip to keep from laughing.

"No relation," Davy snarled quietly from the corner.

"It was a pleasure caring for you, Miss Liberty." Nurse Jones smiled, too. "I'll be back as soon as we're all ready, and we can get you a cab then."

"Thank you."

The doctor and nurse left the room and I laughed. "No relation, eh?"

"Shaddup," Davy grinned.

"I meant to ask you – was it yesterday that you looked at her sort of funny? Why was that?"

"I saw her name tag, and also, I think she's a sensitive."

"A sensitive? What's that?"

"She might sense my presence, or if she's open to it, actually be able to see me."

"Whoa! Are there are lot of people out there like that?"

"A good number. Sometimes they're easy for me to spot, but not always."

"Like Jill the Dingo. She caught you completely off guard didn't she?"

"Oh bloody hell, yes! Let's not discuss her. Ever. Please."

I laughed again.

Davy plopped the gym bag on the bed and opened it for me. A note was inside.

Hello Miss Macca,
I gathered these clothes for you and Bennie delivered them. I hope I chose well enough. We miss you and will be happy to have you home.
Ming

Davy unpacked a pair of my shorts and a baggy tee-shirt that must have been my uncle's. He then pulled out a pair of bikini panties and waggled his eyebrows.

"Turn around," I ordered him. "Or better yet, shimmer away somewhere and let me do this."

"Call me if you get stuck."

I laughed, picturing myself with one arm in the tee-shirt and the other stuck on my head or something. "Okay."

He faded in a shimmer and I sat on the chair. I moved very slowly, not wanting to tweak my muscles any more than they already were. The panties weren't a problem, nor were the shorts. I pulled the hospital gown off and studied the huge brace. Deciding to go the easiest route, I slipped my head into the tee-shirt and put my good arm through the sleeve.

"Okay, I'm done. You can return. And you had better not have been watching from... wherever it is you go." I heard him laughing before he even shimmered back into the room.

He tossed my yellow flip-flops on the floor, and I slid my feet into them.

"There, good as new." I made a silly face to match the absurdity of that statement. I shuffled over to the mirror and grimaced at the reflection. Oh well, the rest of my toilette would have to wait for another day.

I slowly lowered myself back onto the chair and heaved a sigh of relief.

"Exhausting?" Davy was grinning at me.

I just nodded. It was some time before Nurse Jones returned, pushing a wheelchair. She handed me my instructions and a bottle of

181

pain medication, and then she walked me through it all. Basically, it was going in one ear and out the other, but I was hoping my friend in the corner was listening.

"And your taxi is waiting outside. Let's get you out to it so you can be in your own home."

That sounded very nice so I did as I was told. "And you come along too," she said toward the corner where Davy was sitting, and she winked at me. "Our secret, yes?"

"Yes," we said in unison.

"You take care of her, okay?"

"I will," Davy smiled and touched her arm. "Thank you."

We waved goodbye to her from the taxi and sped off for home sweet home.

FORTY-SEVEN

Throw Off the Chains That Bind
and Leave the Past Behind

There was a homemade banner greeting me at the beginning of the walkway to our cottage. It was stretched across two trees, and as I hobbled closer I could see they'd taped several trash bags together to connect it, and then taped paper placemats to it, each containing a part of the words "Welcome Home Miss Macca" in bright greens, blues, and reds.

"Aww, look at that!" I had just gotten the words out of my mouth when I heard them cheer and clap just outside the reception area. "Thank you. That's so kind of all of you!"

They gathered around me, giving me gentle hugs and warm words of good wishes.

"I took care of your Chester," Ming told me, "and we all cared for Winston too."

"Thank you! I didn't even realize how long I'd been gone until late yesterday. I really appreciate it. You're all wonderful!"

Their faces beamed, but they scooted me off to my cottage to rest. "I'll bring you dinner later," Lani said. "Don't you worry, okay?"

Once inside the cottage, Davy helped me into bed. I bit off a half of a pain pill and took it with the water he had brought me. Chester snuggled down beside me, purring loudly and making biscuits on the summer weight blanket. I vaguely remember Davy tiptoeing out but leaving the door open before I escaped into a deep and dreamless sleep.

Hours later, waking up in a dark room once again was completely disorienting at first, but sitting beside me in a dining chair he'd pulled from the other room was my rock. Davy leaned forward as I began to slowly move around.

"You slept long and deep," he said quietly, a smile in his voice. I could see that same smile reflected on his face as he leaned forward, elbows on knees, with the dim light from the hallway falling upon him.

183

"I feel refreshed for the first time since…" I had no idea what to call it, for it wasn't an accident.

"Armageddon?" He grinned and I saw that twinkle in his eye again – I'd thought we'd lost it in the last few awful days.

"That'll do." I grinned right back at him and tried to sit up. My body screamed and fought against me.

"Wait." He jumped up and assisted me. "Just ask for help, you silly Wee Wallaby."

"I wish you'd stop calling me that," I chuckled. "It's not very flattering."

"All the more reason to use the name when you behave like a daft twit."

I lifted my eyebrows. "I think I like daft twit better."

"Boo hoo," he mocked me and helped me swing my legs over the side of the bed. "And Lani brought a lovely spread for dinner. She left it in the kitchen. There's enough for four people. She must think you're quite the competitive eater or something."

I smacked his velvet covered arm. "That's your fault!"

He grinned and shushed me, supporting me only slightly. "Well, you need to fend for yourself or you'll end up being dependent and depressed."

"Whoa, Dr. Jung-Freud-Jones, when did you get your psych degree?"

"Sharp tongue there, Silly Wee Wallaby and Daft Twit."

"If you don't stop calling me those names, you'll be very sorry!"

"Gimme a second. Let me put on my scared face." He spoke softly with a gentle smile that I might have interpreted as mocking my little fit. "I know – it looks a lot like my bored face," he continued. "Oh wait, sorry, it *is* my bored face. Let me give you a tip, Little One. If you're going to threaten someone, make it believable."

I froze and looked up at him, seeing the compassion in his eyes. "I'm sorry," I spoke softly because he was right. "I'm just grumpy and sore."

He kissed my forehead and we said nothing more until we were seated at the table. He brought me a cold plate of fruit, pasta salad, and a tomato stuffed with wild rice. It was heavenly, but eating with one hand wasn't easy. I struggled a bit now and then.

184

"Just pick it up in your good hand and eat it without the fork or spoon. I promise not to tell Miss Manners."

I chuckled and picked up the hollowed out tomato. It tasted like a sweet and salty piece of happiness. Looking across the table, I noticed that Davy was eating with his left hand as well, picking it up and taking big bites. "When in Rome," he chuckled, but it made me feel quite loved.

"Were you always this solicitous?"

"No. I would have liked to have done more for those I loved."

"Don't you think everyone has regrets like that at some point?"

He wrinkled his brow a moment. "I have... had... a lovely, caring family. I just wish I'd shown them more love than I did. In some cases, a *lot* more."

"It's human nature to look back and wish for more..."

He raised his eyes to mine then, and I saw a deeper sorrow. "No, it's more than that. If only I had taken more time with them..." He shook his head. "It doesn't matter at this point. What's done is done. I try to help them now... I hope they know that."

I reached across the small tabletop and squeezed his tomato-y hand with my own tomato-y hand. "I cannot even begin to think that they don't know that, that they don't feel you around them. Hell, I can't even pee without you there," I teased, but it seemed to fall short. I squeezed his sticky hand. "But I cannot imagine my day without having you there, and I think they must feel the same. They must."

He drew a deep and shuddering breath, blinking back tears and nodding. It seemed as though he knew it in his head but didn't feel it in his heart. At that moment, I was certain that we needed each other. I would find a way to help – someday, somehow. I squeezed his hand and he looked up at me, hearing the thoughts in my head. He nodded again, and at that moment we heard the fluttering of feathers as a large grey bird arrived and landed on the table.

"What's for supper?"

Laughing, I tossed a bit of fruit to Winston and he gratefully obliged by eating it.

FORTY-EIGHT

It's Hard to Believe

As I began to heal, I was able to remove the shoulder brace for a few minutes at a time. The deep scratches on my legs were healing as well, with very little scarring, thanks mostly to thick layers of oil I applied to relieve the itching and discomfort. I attended physical therapy sessions three times a week, with Bennie and Lani taking turns driving me as I still didn't have full use of my arm. It gave me a chance to get to know them better.

I helped Kalei with menial tasks in the kitchen, further increasing the use of my arm and fingers.

Helping Sam in the pseudo gift shop one day, I was surprised when Bennie announced I had a visitor.

"Miss Macca? Mrs. Sikes is here to see you." He fidgeted, clearly nervous to have our competitor, and the wife of my attacker on our property. I dusted off my hands on the knees of my capris and went out to welcome her.

Rounding the corner, I took a moment to check her out. She was in her mid-fifties with a chic look about her. Short pale blond hair was carefully in place, but not sprayed to oblivion with lacquer like some women did. She wore a lightweight pair of grey slacks, heeled sandals, and a polished cotton blouse. Pearl studs were at her ears, with a short matching pearl necklace.

"Hello, Mrs. Sikes?" I stretched my still-tender arm out to shake her hand, "I'm Macca Liberty." She looked at my hand for a moment as if no one had ever taught her what to do in these types of situations, then she reluctantly grasped it and we shook gently. A smile lit up her face.

"Hello, Miss Liberty, I'm so very pleased to meet you," and then her face darkened. "And I'm so very sorry for the pain my husband has caused you."

I put my other hand over hers, still grasping it momentarily. "Please, don't you fret. I'm doing well, as I hope you are too."

She fidgeted with her purse that looked vintage, and I suspected she'd bought it when it was brand new for its style many years ago.

"Is there someplace we can talk?"

"Of course. Come with me please," and I showed her to the cottage. "Would you like some coffee?" I asked as I gestured to one of the more comfortable chairs in the living room.

"Oh! That would be delightful, thank you!'

I poured two cups of Kona, set the cups on old fashioned saucers and a tray, and balanced them precariously as I set out for the living room again. My arm wasn't at full speed yet, so this type of activity was quite good therapy.

Sitting across from Mrs. Sikes, I felt her nervous energy and tried to soften her unease.

"I know you must be going through a difficult time," I began in the most feeble of fashions, but it was all I had in me. "Is there anything that I can do – or that we can do here at the inn to help you?"

She shook her head, her smile suddenly very sad. "No, it is I who came to help you, to... thank you, actually. My husband and I have had a... difficult marriage. I truly do think he is where he belongs right now." She took a sip of coffee as if it would give her strength, and it gave her a chance to shield her eyes for a moment. "It's just that he's harmed so many people," her voice caught, and she paused to catch her breath. "I'm so very sorry." Her eyes were soft and sweet as she brought herself to look at me once again, and I saw such despondency there.

"Mrs. Sikes, you are not responsible for the actions of your husband."

She alternated between looking at her hands in her lap and looking into my eyes until she found the strength she seemed to require to finish what she'd come to say. "Thank you. Nevertheless, I've come into a good deal of money, thanks to a very effective pre-nuptial agreement and Mr. Sikes' incarceration." She fumbled in her handbag and finally drew out a check. "I want you to have this. I know it's not nearly enough to make up for your personal losses, but I do hope it will help you in some way."

I looked at the amount and nearly choked on my own spit. "Mrs. Sikes! This is... this is far too much." I tried to push it back to her, but she stood then, her hands clasped around her bag.

"No, it's not even near enough, I'm sorry to say." This time it was she who held out her hand to shake mine. I grasped it firmly as she smiled just a bit sadly. "I do hope we can be friends someday, and that you won't hold his actions against me?"

"Oh my goodness, of course! I would never hold his misdeeds against you!" I glanced down at the check in my hands and tried to count the zeroes. "Does this mean you own the hotel now?"

She smiled calmly for the first time since she'd arrived. "Free and clear... yes."

I squeezed her arm then and gave her a brief hug. She acted almost as if it were very out of character for her to receive one, but she relented and put an arm around me in return. "Congratulations, Mrs. Sikes. I know you will do well."

FORTY-NINE

But How Much, Baby,
Do We Really Need?

Staring at the check in my hand, I almost forgot to close the door behind Mrs. Sikes. Davy peered over my shoulder. "Whoa. That's a lot of zeroes."

I was speechless. It was a lot of zeroes, and I felt wrong in accepting it, but she'd left me little choice, short of stuffing it back in her pocket when she wasn't looking. Oh! Perhaps that's what I should have done! Damn! But maybe that would have insulted her. I picked up my phone and dialed Alex, my attorney, to ask his advice.

"By all means, Macca," he chuckled when I told him my dilemma, "you should take it. You will have medical bills, and Mrs. Sikes must know that. It's her way of assuaging her own guilt, and paying for her husband's misdoings."

"I hadn't thought of it that way. So," I swallowed hard, looking at all the zeroes again, "it looks like I'm going to need some financial advice."

Alex chuckled and gave me the name of the CPA that Uncle Wally had used, one who already had the financial information on the inn. We set up a time to meet the following week.

I tucked the check away in a safe place and then moved it to a safer place. Vowing to purchase a small safe, I moved it yet again. Davy leaned against the doorframe, an amused look on his face.

"Where should I hide it?"

"I have the perfect place," he grinned. "In honor of your Uncle Wally's passion... we should keep it on ice. Literally."

The only passion I could think of was... oh my gosh, "Genius!"

Davy grinned, so proud of himself. We encased the valuable slip of nondescript paper in a reclosable plastic bag and slipped it into the bottom of the wine cooler.

"I think the occasion calls for a little celebration," I pulled out a bottle of Soave.

"I'll drink to that."

189

"You'll drink to anything," I teased him.

"I'll drink to that too."

"Well," he laid on an extra thick Mancunian accent, "I figgah me livah's alrea'y gone and me tickah's ticked fair enough, right?"

I lifted my glass, "To your freedom then." We clinked glasses and sipped before he began to sing.

I wanna be freeeeeeee

But I had to laugh because he was singing it in an imitation of Winston's voice.

Rawwwwwwk!

And quite suddenly we heard a responding *rawwwk* from outside, and Davy joined in my laughter. He opened the door and Winston flew in, alighting on the back of the sofa.

Sing a song, singsong!

"You are a character, Winston," he stroked the beautiful grey feathers and the bird made little chirpy noises, rubbing his beak on Davy's hand. "But I love you too." He made kissy sounds and Winston imitated them, sounding rather like a cranky infant, but I had come to know that he was showing affection.

I looooove you! Love you. I love me, pretty bird.

"And we know you do, yes. And yes, you're pretty," I joined them on the sofa, glass of wine in hand, setting the bottle on the coffee table.

Drink up, me hearties!

We had to laugh at the little guy again, but he always seemed to interpret our soft laughter as love, just as we intended it.

I plugged my mp3 player into the stereo and let Billy Joel tell us his stories for a while.

"Any ideas for the money?" Davy asked me.

I blew out a breath of overwhelming awe. "Mostly investment, I would think, and some renovations."

"You have such a level head, Macca, but what about something for you?"

I snorted quietly, and Winston turned to give me nuzzles as well along with his little coos. "Pay my medical bills?"

"Still level-headed. I meant something to reward yourself for all the work you've done here – the good work. For those times when

190

you've gone without new belongings for the sake of the inn or your employees."

Looking off through the window, gazing into the distance, I could think of nothing and told him so. "But I'll think about it."

"Good." He patted my knee. "Just don't rule it out."

"Okay, Dad," I teased. He smirked at me.

"Way to make me feel like an old man," but there was still a twinkle in that eye.

I poked him in the ribs and kissed his cheek. "You're welcome."

"That wasn't a thank you."

I grinned and scooted away from him before he could retaliate with a tickle or something.

Winston wants a tickle!

I gave the sweet bird a skritch and let him nuzzle my face with his beak while he made sweet cooing noises again.

The following week I felt ready to face the world and I prepared myself for a long boring meeting with Calvin – my new financial advisor. I'd carried the icy check in its freezing plastic pouch to his office and handed it over as if it were a great find from Stonehenge or something. Calvin took a photocopy of the check and then had a courier whisk it off to the bank. It was all rather surreal to me. I sat in my chair and concentrated on absorbing my surroundings.

Calvin was old-school, but of the Hawaiian native variety. From the waist up, behind his desk, he wore a starched short-sleeved dress shirt with a dark tie. But when he stood up and moved from behind his desk, I saw that he was dressed in khaki shorts and flip-flops. I barely contained my laughter until I felt Davy suddenly beside me, pinching me to shut me up. I squirmed in my seat as if the principal had reprimanded me way back in third grade. I flashed Davy a withering look. He did not fit my image of any *principal*. At all.

After the dull, dry, boring meeting – wherein very few of my questions were answered – we climbed into R2 and headed out of town… slowly.

"So, the only thing we really accomplished was to list a few funds I could invest in. I don't want to invest. I just want to protect that money but use it when I need it."

191

"I think he got that, luv," Davy tried to soothe my ruffled feathers. "I think you can basically do whatever the bloody hell you want. Just tell him, and he'll magically make the funds appear."

"Really?" I was skeptical.

"Really. I've seen it in action... long ago. Perhaps it wasn't in my best interest at the time, but things are different now. You're more protected. You have rights, and the financial advisor has a responsibility. Still, you must remain vigilant. When you get statements of accounting, review them carefully, okay?"

"I will." I bit my lower lip. For a minute, I thought this was more than I'd bargained for until I realized that it wasn't at all the same as poor Davy and his past financial issues. I had not earned this money. It was only given to me.

"It doesn't matter," he said quietly.

"Stop doing that!"

"I can't help it. If it's in your thoughts, it's in mine. And still... it doesn't matter any more. It's water under the bridge. You cannot change the past, but you can learn and use that knowledge to protect the future. Hopefully. Okay?"

Who could deny that smile and those deep brown eyes? "Okay," I replied with a smile.

FIFTY

O' Tannenbaum O' Paina

Life certainly became easier, and while I didn't squander a penny, I did use the funds provided to us in a way that could only benefit the business.

December arrived bright with warmth and sunshine. I'd always thought it was odd to celebrate the winter season in Southern California, and this was no different. In the past I had spent most of my Christmas holidays in shorts, with the occasional rain slicker, but here on the Big Island, it was all sun and sand. I still lived in shorts and flip flops and realized I should have been born to it. Each day the sun shone for at least six hours. Winston sang, Kalei and Lani cooked delectable feasts and served them to our guests, Bennie managed the inner workings of the inn while using his natural friendliness to welcome the guests, Ming cleaned, and Sam and Alberto tended. We were a well-oiled profit machine. Of course they weren't huge profits, but we were in the black. And while I briefly wondered about expanding our operations by building on more rooms, I realized that would have compromised the close comforts, the sense of family we provided to our guests. Instead, we concentrated on making the most of what we had.

And during those times when Winston sang, Kalei and Lani cooked, Bennie managed, Ming cleaned, and Sam and Alberto tended, Davy continued to tie knots in his straw papers. One day I saw him sitting with a large file box. I peered over his shoulder and saw that it was filled to the brim with his knotted straw papers.

"Whatcha got there?" I asked tentatively, for I was concerned that I'd invaded a privacy of sorts.

"Nothing. Just decorations. We need to get our tree."

"Tree?"

"Yeah. Like Christmas tree? But island style..." he broke off, letting the idea hang between us. The problem was, I didn't know what Hawaiian style Christmas trees were. "C'mon." He stood and waved for me to follow him.

193

We went outside and he led me around to the far side of our private deck, behind the generator, an area I never had explored. There, in lovely green pots on wheels were two evergreen trees like none I'd ever seen before. One was about six feet tall, the other about four.

"These are beautiful! What are they?"

"I heard Alberto and Bennie talking. These are Norfolk pines, grown in many parts of the islands. This big tree here," he caressed the needles on one of the branches, "is wheeled into the reception area every year for Christmas, and the smaller one was always reserved for the owner's cottage. And, as luck would have it, that's you!"

I clapped my hands like a little kid discovering a new bike. "Oh! Let's do it now!"

We rolled the smaller tree through the back door and positioned it near the large window that looked out upon the sea and the greenery around us.

"And look!" Davy ran to the small coat closet which actually never had coats in it, but instead beach equipment. He reached up toward the shelf and jumped a few times to use his finger tips to jiggle a box over the edge. It slipped neatly into his arms and he brought it to the floor in front of our tree. He pulled off the lid, and I could see strings of lights and several ornaments. One caught my eye and I lifted it gently out of its protective nesting of tissue paper. It was a small replica of a silver blue 1966 Mustang.

"Oh," I choked a little. "I gave this to him when I was twelve." I pressed it to my heart and closed my eyes for a moment to pay my respects to Uncle Wally.

"Are you okay?"

I nodded and reached to hang the 'stang on a middle branch of our tree. We continued pulling out the decorations and together dressed the tree in tiny multicolored lights and various baubles and ornaments. Then Davy retrieved his box of tied straw wrappers and began to gently pull them out in one long strand.

"When did you connect them all?"

"I did it that night you first came home from the hospital when you slept so much. Perfect distraction." He secured the end of his tied papers to the top of the tree and then carefully draped the remaining

194

footage as a garland. It wrapped all around from top to bottom and looked almost like ribbon.

"It's beautiful," I slipped my arm through his and snuggled as we stood there admiring the fairy lights and decorations. "Where did you get the idea for the garland?"

He smiled, sighed, and led me to the sofa facing the tree. "I miss my girls, so every knot was a message of love I was sending to them."

I looked back at the tree and the yards and yards of garland. "That's a whole lotta love."

He grinned. "And not nearly enough."

FIFTY-ONE

Silent Night, Lonely Night

Christmas crept up on us. The main tree was beautifully decorated by the staff, and our guests were thrilled to see it as they arrived, some squealing in surprise at the Hawaiian decorations and the unusual shape of the branches of the Norfolk Pine.

I took an afternoon off and went shopping for employee gifts – just a little something to thank them. Their main gifts were to be sizeable bonuses slipped into cheery cards, but I found a small shop that would make personalized coffee mugs for each of them, with their name on one side and the new logo for the inn on the other. I placed the order and was promised they'd be ready well in time for Christmas. I would then fill each cup with candy. But the big dilemma was Davy. What do you get a ghost? I'd already included him in the coffee mug order, which we would keep in the cottage for him, but that just didn't seem like enough.

I stopped in the music store to look for ideas, but I could only come up with a collection of cool guitar picks and a book of sheet music from Broadway shows. As I turned, I nearly bumped into a large plastic Christmas tree heavily decorated with tiny ornaments for sale. Grinning like a kid, I selected a tiny tambourine, a guitar, and teeny maracas. I also picked up a small horse ornament from the local pharmacy and gift shop.

Feeling good about my purchases, I headed home to an empty cottage. I had no idea where Davy was. He'd been disappearing a lot lately, but I assumed he was busy elsewhere with other people he watched over. It made me smile to think of him patrolling his "wards." I took advantage of his absence and wrapped the few tiny packages I'd brought home with me, placing them under our little tree.

While each of the guest cottages had little plaques on their respective front doors, ours – the owner's cottage – had nothing. I designed a plaque in a manner similar to the others, but the number on this one was 7a, a little nod to a running joke in the world of Monkee fans. In the recording of "Daydream Believer," the young men had been tired from long hours of filming and then recording. At the beginning of the song, someone announced that it was take "7a" but Davy had lost track. He asked again, "What number is this?" and all present had repeated in unison, "7a!" The plaque had been installed, and I looked forward to surprising Davy.

It was Christmas Eve, and still no sight of Davy. While I chalked it up to more important beings needing his guidance, I still kicked myself for feeling selfishly jealous that he wasn't around. Granted, my life had settled down to a serene vista, as the camera of everyday life panned across, but it seemed empty without him.

All of my employees' gifts were wrapped, and the mugs with candies were under the main tree in the reception area. I held the bonuses in my hands when we gathered that evening. We shared Lani's luscious rum punch, which I deemed to be far better than any egg nog ever, and we listened to the old crooners sing about the holiday on our nicely enhanced sound system. (Thank you, Mrs. Sikes!) I'd made more of my cupcakes, while Lani and Kalei had created a luscious pie for the occasion, accompanied by ice cream! I nearly drooled on the bonus envelopes I was clutching.

"Open mine first please, Miss Macca," sweet Sam implored. I ripped open the paper from the little box he'd handed me and found a lovely ceramic rendering of an African Grey parrot on a pin – a broach of epic proportions.

"Sam," I exclaimed, "he's wonderful! Thank you!" And I proceeded to pin the handcrafted item on my shirt. "Did you make this?"

"Yes, miss, I did!" He was so sweet, and always quite eager to please.

And then the others clamored to deliver their gifts to me as well. I was so very touched by the deep messages of comfort, love, and gratitude in their gifts. Gifts were exchanged between each other as well, and the amount of warmth then far exceeded that of any barometer. I handed out my little tokens of candy in personalized mugs, and squeals of delight were soon muffled by sweetly stuffed mouths.

"I've had such a wonderful time with you all, and I've been quite grateful for your guidance and support. Here's to another year – and many more – of success and happiness." I handed each their envelope filled with the bonus cash, and accompanied every gift with a hug. We toasted more with our rum punch and enjoyed the festivities. Still, I wondered where Davy was. I tried really hard not to miss him, but he'd become such an integral part of my family.

That evening, I had a long talk with myself. I chastised my inner child for the jealous feelings, I throttled my inner teen for the desire to make enough of a ruckus to bring him back, and in the end I just sat and enjoyed the lights on "our" tree, his sweet knots for his girls, and the holiday music on the stereo. Chester snuggled with me, his purrs in direct opposition to the music. Winston bobbed his head to the music while he perched on the back of the sofa. I raised a glass of Barolo, thanks to Uncle Wally's stash in his improvised wine storage in the second bedroom. Davy and I had been unearthing much of his hoard each month. It was a source of laughter, merriment, and respect for the man who left us too early.

And speaking of such men, I passed Christmas Eve solo, for Davy was nowhere to be seen. I began to wonder if he'd seen that I was headed in the "right" direction (whatever that direction was) and had moved on, despite his promises he'd always be with me. The music changed and Davy's voice sang about winter wonderlands of snow, reindeer with shiny red noses, and dreams of white Christmases. But it wasn't until he sang "Mele Kalikimaka" that I began to cry. This should have been our song. I polished off the entire bottle of Barolo, and spoke to the ceiling as I poured the last glass. "Here's to us!" Then I trudged to bed.

When I awoke the next morning, there was still no white Christmas – there never had been in my life, so that was no surprise. But sadly, the gifts I'd wrapped for Davy remained untouched under the tree. I chided myself for selfish feelings and then went about my day.

The guests needed tending, and I'd assigned shorter hours to Team Wally to allow them time with their own families. So I showered, dressed, and ramped up my activity for the day. By evening it was just me bussing dishes for a satisfied group of tourists. I had been sure to flip the stereo system on so that canned Christmas music from Bing Crosby, Dean Martin, Frank Sinatra, and all the greats was being piped in to our guests.

198

In the kitchen, I scraped plates and placed them in the commercial dishwasher, but I heard an odd musical sound from the main dining area. It sounded like Davy's recording of "Mele Kalikimaka," yet I hadn't even included that in the playlist. I peeked around the corner and saw guests sitting in our comfortable rattan chairs around the makeshift dancefloor, engaged in quiet conversation amongst themselves. I let my eyes glide along the panorama of the scene until they rested upon one very lovely sight. Davy sat on one of the half-walls, leaning against the post. He was dressed in his usual white boots and dark pants, but had an ivory Mao jacket on, which was trimmed in a gold-thread embossed design. I let my breath out in a "whoosh" and ran back to the kitchen to compose myself. However, he'd seen me already... or sensed me, as he was so inclined to do. He immediately appeared then as I leaned against the dishwasher.

"Didya miss me?" He was feeling playful, obviously. I was trying not to be.

"No." I picked up a rag and swiped violently at the counter tops. "Were you gone?"

"You know I was gone," he grinned and growled at the same time. He spun me around and hugged me as tight as he could without crushing me. "I missed you," he whispered in my ear.

I took a deep breath and hugged him back. "I did miss you. I tried not to, but I couldn't help myself."

He held me at an arm's length then, still grinning. "It's 'cause I'm just so damned irresistible," he teased, then planted a kiss on my forehead.

"Wow," I laughed and pulled away, turning back to my dishes in the sink. "You're certainly quite full of yourself."

"'Tis the season."

"To be jolly, not conceited."

"Oh!" He mocked me. "Is *that* where I've got it wrong, then? I always get that mixed up."

"It's a very good thing I didn't buy you a hat for Christmas, because I doubt it would fit on that inflated head of yours."

And then he chuckled, that lovely infectious laugh of his. I couldn't help it; I laughed with him.

"C'mon then. Y'done here?"

"Yes," I said as I stacked the last dish in the washer. "Let's go home."

"Right, luv." He offered his arm, and I slipped my arm inside his.

As we passed the guests still enjoying themselves, I wished them all a wonderful holiday, and we headed to the cottage. We stopped short so he could admire the new room number plaque on our front door.

"What a nice gesture, luv." He kissed me on the cheek.

Inside we were met by sounds of Christmas music from our stereo, a bottle of champagne, two glasses on the coffee table, and our tree, fully lit and sparkly, with additional gifts nestled beneath. How did he *do* that, I wondered for the millionth time at the very least.

"Merry Christmas, Babe." He planted me on the sofa and poured champagne for both of us. He turned on the television and slipped a DVD into the player – instant fireplace without the heat that would have been so oppressive in the topics. The sound of crackling fire emitted from the speakers.

"I love it!" We clinked our glasses and sipped. It was a lovely Korbel Natural, so crisp and dry it nearly evaporated on my tongue. "Oh, this is such a lovely way to end a difficult day. And," I smiled and nodded to him, "a fantastic surprise to have you home." I lifted my glass in his direction and he responded similarly.

"It's nice to be… home, as you say."

I realized then that this wasn't his only home, but that I should enjoy whatever time we had together. I held his gaze with my own as I sipped. His brown eyes were twinkly and still managed to engage mine. Suddenly I was possessed by a seven-year-old (or thereabouts) child and jumped up.

"You have gifts to open!"

"I do?" He still teased, knowing full well there were packages beneath the tree for him. "It just so happens you have gifts to open as well!"

We sat like little kids on the floor, but with our champagne within reach.

"You first," I exclaimed and handed him his packages. He loved the little ornaments I'd given him and promptly hung each one on the tree in carefully chosen places of honor. The personalized mug

200

delighted him, but it was the book of music that seemed to touch him the most. He flipped through the pages briefly and then set it beside him to study later.

He presented me with three packages. The first touched me deeply. Tearing open the paper I saw a faded blue sports jersey inside, but it wasn't just any jersey. This one was well worn and soft, and had the name Davy Jones emblazoned upon it with the number eleven.

"I thought it might be comfortable to sleep in," he said with a quiet grin. I rubbed it against my face, sighing at the well-worn and washed softness.

"Thank you! I love it!"

He handed me another package. Inside was a bubble-wrap encased ceramic frame with a poem inside, one I'd never seen before.

"This," he scooted around next to me in order to point it out, "is a poem that my mother left for us when she passed. It's been important to my family ever since. My girls hold fast to the sentiment even now, although they've changed it to 'he' instead. But I just wanted you to have a copy and to know that you are always in my thoughts and forever in my heart."

Love Still Abides
She has passed on beyond the range of sight
Into the glory of the morning light
Out of the reach of sorrow and despair
Safe in the shelter of the Father's care
Weep not for her, say not she is dead
She has gone on a few short steps ahead
Faith looks beyond this time of grief and pain
Love still abides, and we shall meet again.

By the time I had read the final line, I could barely see through the tears in my eyes. I looked up at him, and he smiled through his own wet eyes and chucked me on the chin. "It's lovely," I choked the words out. "Really. I will treasure this always."

My mind took a side-trip just then, and I wondered if he was getting ready to say goodbye. My hands began to sweat, my heart pounded, and I didn't hear his next words.

201

"What?" He had placed another very small package in my lap while my mind had wandered.

"This is another frame, but I think you'll be surprised..." his words dropped away as I tore the paper off. The frame on this item was eye-catching. It was metal scroll work with little bits of colored glass, much like sea-glass, scattered amongst the smaller scrolls. But it was the photo inside that made me catch my breath and hold it for several beats. It was a black and white photo, and I blinked through more tears to clear my eyes so I could be sure I was not imagining anything. There were three individuals in the extraordinary photo. My mother stood on the left dressed in a loose-fitting cotton dress, the straps of her swimsuit showing at the neckline. Her arm was around Davy in the center, who was dressed in baggy shorts and a pale shirt, and me on the right, Davy's arm around my shoulders.

"Oh my god!" I stroked the photo with my index finger, especially over my mother's face. She was so beautiful. I jerked my head to look at Davy. "How did you get this?"

He canted his head. "It was with my photos, which my daughters had found. I slipped it out; they won't miss it."

I covered my mouth with my hand and stared at this loveliest of gifts. The tears fell unchecked, splashing on my hand as it held this treasure. "I cannot even begin to thank you," I whispered. "You have no idea. There are very few photos of us together, but especially this day? I didn't even remember anyone taking our photo." I wiped my face but wouldn't let go of the frame.

"Well, it was your lucky day, because there were *always* photographers around me," he joked to lighten the atmosphere, and it worked.

"I'd noticed that," I chuckled through my tears. Chester chose that moment to wiggle in between us and purr for attention.

"Chester, what did you get for Christmas, buddy?" Davy picked him up and pretended to listen to the feline complaints. He looked shocked. "He says 'nothing' – how can that be?"

I chuckled. "He got a new catnip mouse and a piece of fresh tuna, so he's lying!"

"Are you trying to get sympathy, big guy?" He frowned at the cat and kissed his forehead.

Mraoow. Caught in the act.

We'd polished off the bottle of Korbel and reached for a nice red wine, a fruity but dry Argentinian Malbec. Wow, Uncle Wally sure knew how to stock the varieties!

Lifting our glasses in a toast to each other again, we continued to enjoy the peace of the season. I'd set the two frames on the coffee table and couldn't help but gaze at them both now and then. Davy, his arm across the back of the sofa, squeezed my shoulder affectionately. "It's quite nice to see you happy," he spoke softly near my ear.

"I *am* happy," I said as I turned to look into his face.

"Good. Hold onto that feeling. Bottle some of it up in your memory so that you can call upon it when you need."

I grinned and nodded in agreement. I certainly would give it my best efforts. Our eyes locked and he slowly leaned to me, pressing his soft lips on mine. Every muscle relaxed and I sort of melted against his embrace. His tongue was sweet and warm and exploring ever so gently. Reluctantly, we drew away from each other, gazing deeply into each others eyes. I reached up and stroked his cheek with the back of my hand. I saw such sadness in his beautiful eyes, the normal twinkle a bit lacking in sparkle. I turned my hand to caress his cheek with my palm. His sudden sadness rendered me speechless.

He reached up and held my palm to his cheek, turning his lips just once to kiss the inside of my hand. There was no trademark smile on his face though. He pulled me close, and we settled against the back cushions of the sofa, sipping our wine and listening to the music. The fireplace scene on the DVD ended, and he hit the "play" button to start it again.

FIFTY-TWO

Love Still Abides

I awoke the next morning and rolled over to be greeted by the bejeweled framed photo of my mom, Davy, and me. I couldn't help but smile, and then it turned into a grin as I stretched, ready to begin the day. Still, Davy's sadness of the night before haunted me as I showered quickly and dressed in my standard attire, this time white shorts and a tank top in pale pink along with pink flowered flip-flops.

I made a pot of coffee and pulled out some croissants I'd saved from Kalei's Christmas brunch the day before. I popped them into the oven to crisp them up and set two plates onto the dinette table. It was then I noticed the envelope with my name on it, in Davy's handwriting. He'd written "Macca" and drawn his trademark 60s flower next to it. Inside was one small sheet of paper that held the words:

Always remember, love still abides,
Davy

"NO!" But I knew in my heart he was gone. The little hints and the big hints from the night before came crashing in on me and I crumpled into the chair, put my head on the table, and cried my eyes out.

I hid inside my cottage – *my* cottage, no longer *our* cottage – the entire day. Lani checked on me once, as did Bennie, but I assured them I just wasn't feeling well. They kept me plied with enough food to sustain me, despite the fact that I had no appetite.

Once again, I was totally alone in this huge world. I'd survived the death of my parents and the rest of my family and the evil attempt on my life at the hands of Sikes. I knew I would survive this too, but I didn't have to enjoy it or even accept it just yet. I mourned Davy, but eventually went about my days, trying to build a life, much like that shop that keeps popping up all over, Build-A-Bear. I wondered, though if there were a place I could go to get my broken heart replaced.

204

FIFTY-THREE

We Had Seasons in the Sun
(Whaddya Know, Wrong Group Again)

Springtime blossomed like none I had ever seen in California. The fragrances of the floral awakenings on the island were enough to make one drunk with happiness.

I continued to improve our little inn, which was now properly titled and signed as Hale Mele, or the House of Song. Hale Mele was fully booked for many months.

Summer came, along with another late season hurricane, but I was learning how to cope. Dr. Josh, the beloved veterinarian, had asked me to dinner a few times, but I had not yet been ready. He seemed to understand, and I hoped I hadn't hurt his feelings.

Autumn fell upon us quite gradually with no deciduous leaves in our vicinity to signify it, but the bookings were solid, and Dr. Josh joined us for Thanksgiving dinner.

And then, once again, the Christmas season was peeking around the corner. It had been nearly a year since I'd found Davy's note of farewell.

I felt that loss again, as I helped Bennie roll the trees in, first to the reception area, then the smaller one to my own cottage. I dragged the modest, crumbling box from the hall closet and pulled out the lights and ornaments, hanging Uncle Wally's 'stang right in the center. I surrounded that with Davy's guitar, tambourine, and maracas. Winston fluttered to my shoulder and nudged my ear.

Miss Davy, miss him, miss Davy.

"Me too, big guy, me too." I skritched his head and continued to place the ornaments on the tree, the grey parrot on my shoulder bobbing his head in encouragement. Chester watched from beneath the tree, silently reproachful of my decorating shortcomings. I hadn't the heart to leave Davy's knotted garland in the box so I carefully tucked it into the branches from top to bottom.

Daydream believer and a homecoming queeeeeen.

"What? *Now* you get it right?" I chuckled at the sweet knucklehead bird.

I spent Christmas Eve in my cottage with Davy's fireplace DVD running when I wasn't watching actual television. Chester and Winston kept me company. I'd moved Winston's cage in and decided it was the three of us against... the season. Drinking a bottle of Korbel Natural, just as I'd done with Davy the year before, I sprawled on the sofa and watched *National Lampoon's Christmas Vacation*. Chevy Chase could always make me laugh.

"*Hallelujah,*" I suddenly thought I heard him quoting my favorite line from the movie. And then it was real, for I felt his breath on my ear, "*Holy shit! Where's the Tylenol?*"

I jumped up and hugged him so hard! "Davy! You're home!" He was chuckling as he hugged me back.

"Merry Christmas, luv!"

"Oh, Merry Christmas!" And I hugged him some more.

"Bless us every one," he quoted in a high pitched Tiny Tim voice. I kissed his cheek and hugged him harder. I wanted to hold onto him forever.

"But... where have you been all this time?" I peered into his eyes, trying to see the answer.

"I've had many things that I needed to tend to. And the stronger you get, the more settled your life becomes, the less you will see of me. But I'll never go away. I'm here. For as long as you want me. And remember... we have a code word. All you have to do is say it or think it and I'll be here." He cupped my face in his hands. "Okay?"

I could only grin and nod as the tears flowed down my face.

"I'll always be watching over you because I have to be sure, you know," and then he switched into his Artful Dodger Cockney and quoted, "that y'don't let yer petticoats go dangling in the mud, my dahhhlin'."

Epilogue

We were quickly working our way through the early months of winter, but it was a winter unlike most of the rest of the country was experiencing. The seasons in Hawaii barely registered change. There was the occasional day when I wore long pants, but those were few and far between. And while Davy wasn't there quite as often as I'd gotten used to before, he still seemed to shimmer into the picture just when I needed him most.

On one such day I was standing at the computer in the reception area working on the bookkeeping when Sam appeared leading a beautiful German Shepherd dog by a nylon rope.

"Oh, what a gorgeous dog, Sam." I came around the desk to stoop beside it and offer my hand for sniffing. "Is it yours?"

"No, Miss Macca. I found her digging in the trash out back. She has no tags, and none of us recognize her from the area."

"Oh dear," I exclaimed as the dog accepted my hand and gave it a few licks. Her warm tongue lapped at my fingers and wrist, and I gave her a pet on the side of her face with my dry hand. "Where do you live, sweetheart?" I asked her, holding her lovely head between my hands. She simply scooted closer to me and laid her large head down on my leg as I squatted next to her.

"I cannot take her home, Miss Macca. No pets allowed." Sam handed his end of the rope to me. They both looked so sad.

Never one to turn away an animal in need, I stood and led the dog to my cottage, calling over my shoulder, "No problem. I'll take care of her and try to find her owners too."

Once inside, the dog sat obediently while I got a bowl of water and rescued Chester's bowls to a higher level. The feline jumped to the top of the bookcase and voiced his displeasure.

"I expect you to be more hospitable, Mr. Chester."

All I got was a hiss in response.

Setting the larger bowl on the floor in the kitchen, I gave a short whistle, and the dog hesitantly came over to lap at the cool water. I ruffled her fur and opened the refrigerator. Inside was a bowl of leftover brown rice. "I don't have any dog food yet, but perhaps you'd like some of this?"

I fluffed up the grains and set the container next to her on the floor. She sniffed once and then wolfed it down in three bites.

Davy shimmered into the room and stood peering at the dog with a puzzled look. He walked around to one side of her, then the other, and then stooped down to her level. She licked his face. "Suzie!" He collapsed next to her, saying the name over and over again. "Where have you been, my luv?"

"Wait... what?"

Davy and the dog both shimmered out of the room, and I stood there with my mouth hanging open in shock and disbelief.

"No, no no no no no, you come back here! Both of you!"

But I was to find out that their story would have to wait for another time...

ABOUT THE AUTHOR

Jerri Keele resides with her husband, two dogs, and three cats in Salem, Oregon. She has been a fan of Davy Jones since the age of nine, in 1966, when he first hit the scene as a Monkee. Since his sudden passing in 2012, she has worked tirelessly toward fundraising to help care for the herd of retired racehorses he left behind. The horses are under the watchful eye of his four daughters – Talia, Sarah, Jessica, and Annabel – who created the charity The Davy Jones Equine Memorial Foundation (DJEMF).

43806109R00122